AIN'T QUITE WHAT I THOUGHT!

I0668463

A Novel By
Mirika Mayo Cornelius

Author of Secret,
Colored Lily: Poppa Took My Innocence,
& Paton

AIN'T QUITE WHAT I THOUGHT!

ISBN 0-97085174-X

An Akirim Press Publishing

ACKNOWLEDGEMENTS

I first and always thank God for giving of his Son, Jesus, to save me and I acknowledge and confess that without Him, I have and am nothing.

Thanking God always for my son whom I love dearly and forever with overflowing love, and so much love goes to my husband, parents, siblings, and many relatives, friends and fans who have always supported my projects. Thank you, and may God bless you all.

Enjoy.

AIN'T QUITE WHAT I THOUGHT!

I met someone. This someone was sitting in a tub full of water, butt bald naked holding onto a straw with his juicy lips. That straw came from a paper cup he held in his left hand as he sipped down some juice. It was pathetic on my end, I know, to admire a man in his ache, but he was sexy - juice, straw, cup and all!

It was just my second month at work at the rehab center after transferring from another site, and I'd just finished learning the proper procedure for washing those who have been unfortunate enough to lose that ability themselves, either temporarily or permanently. The reason it took so long for me to get to the washing procedure is because under some type of new management, it was decided that everyone had to pass a series of tests in their first thirty days as if we all didn't know how to put soap on a clean rag and scrub a body down. Already being highly experienced, the testing was a review.

It was rumored that all the new tests and rules came about because of under trained employees' mistakes leading to patient injuries. By taking the tests, if a lawsuit came up, there would be some type of proof of training, thus, more back up for the employer. Before those tests were completed, I was just assisting. Not only did I re-learn to wash the patients, but also how to remain professional and courteous at all times. Normally, there would be nice, little old ladies or simple acting, freaky old men to take care of, so remaining professional and courteous wasn't hard at all with them. As a matter of fact, it was rather easy. When it came down to Sir Sexy, however, all my wits left me as I entered room ninety-eight's bathroom.

The man in room ninety-eight, he was oh so fine. Attempting to wash him couldn't have been harder. I wouldn't have called myself desperate because I wasn't. Instead, I preferred to call myself just extra single and heterosexual with a bunch of pride. There was a big difference between that and desperation. If I was a married woman, I think that the succulence of that man wading in that tub would have made me break every last one of my 'til death do you part vows. Thus, I was glad to be single at the sight of him.

Obviously, Sir Sexy must have been in some sort of bad accident to land in rehab as his medical chart echoed. His body was nice and ripped in all the right places which meant he body builds or God really built his body well from birth. He was nice, double packed, and mocha baby! There was nothing like a dark-skinned brownie with the nuts. Not one flaw on his body. If you slapped that joker on the back, you wouldn't leave a mark. He was that kind of dark. Sweet. Sure, I was supposed to be working, not gawking. Technically, I was, but most people already knew that one must be thorough in my line of work, therefore, I did my part and inspected every single detail of this wounded wonder of a man.

As I dipped the rag in the water-filled tub, I peeped over at him for a closer, more intimate glimpse, but his eyes were closed. That simply meant that I couldn't really see how he looked. Everyone knew that unless you see a man's eyes, well, there was really no point. He could have big old bug eyes, or worse yet, old crack head eyes. You know, pupils that were always big with blink-less eyelids. They could be staring right at the sun, and the eyes would continue dilating. Or wait! He could have those, you know, down low eyes. Yeah, the ones that look right on past all the foxy ladies to the man in the back with the sack. That wouldn't be good for me. Yeah, those eyes were what I had to see. I was even hoping that a big, strapping, well-built man walked into the bathroom behind me so I could inspect how this tub ridden gentleman would look at him, but it never happened. Test one on the down low failed.

As I stood there slightly tense, not wanting to get caught drooling, he still hadn't opened his eyes to even look at me at this point. Was he asleep? It was strange he didn't budge because I even had my hand dipped down in the water, moving it around rather aggressively. I thought, *man, is he that sick?* From what I read on the chart, he was only hit by a car, but I didn't read anything about him being deaf or him having a brain injury from the incident. Therefore, I decided to speak to get his attention now that I was finished captivating myself with his motionless water aerobics.

"Hi," I said, trying disgustingly hard to keep my eyes focused on getting this rag drenched in suds so it would appear as if I was on top of things at my job and not on top of him in my imagination. "I can wash you some more if you aren't quite ready to get out or..."

"Girl!" he exclaimed as his head popped up, and his eyes opened. There they were, and thank God they didn't look like the eyes of a beetle. "Crap!" he continued to yelp.

Dang, was I that tore up looking? Immediately, I inspected myself and didn't notice that my nose was where my right breast was supposed to be, so I felt that I still looked a bit cute. However, before I could check myself out anymore, his little paper cup of juice was tilting, getting ready to spill on his...you know...stuff.

"Watch that!" I dropped the soap and reached across his body in an attempt to catch it, but instead of him letting me do that, he leaned over so fast that the cup and the palms of his hands landed over...you know...that stuff I was talking about in the sentence above this one. I watched, with my mouth stretched from wisdom tooth to wisdom tooth, as the juice began to circle around him with the water. That juice should've been me, I thought, just'a slithering all over his body like a sidewinder snake in the desert sands or a shark in the bloody waters.

Shaking his head in disbelief, he asked, "Where's Nurse Betty at? And pull the curtain or something," he continued, stiffening up his face. "Can't you see I was napping?"

"With a paper cup of juice in your hand?" I asked, but he ignored my logic.

" I thought you would've been Nurse Betty because she's

normally the one... never mind." He started laughing, yet still holding on to his attitude. "Close the curtain!"

He lifted one of his hands, flinging water on me in the process, and yanked that thick hospital shower curtain in between us. I had to lean back fast or I probably would've toppled over in the tub with him. What rudeness.

"Nurse Betty's not here," I responded quickly while wiping some of the water from my face after his shut the shower curtain episode. "I'm working her shift from now on. She's retired." Actually, she was dead, having retired just last night. While I spoke, I was hoping he didn't have anything indirectly transferable because he flung all that water on me. If he did have something not too clean, I hoped it died on its way toward the open areas on my face.

As I finished wiping my face and neck with a towel, I left the room, grabbed his file and double checked that this joker didn't put any strange type of new disease on me. I read nothing lethal that couldn't be cured with a pill or two such as occasional migraines and abdominal pain, therefore, I slapped that file back where I got it from and went back into the bathroom.

Hesitantly, I leaned back towards the curtain, sticking my long neck around it. There he was, leaned over his privates like it actually takes his whole chocolate, wet body to cover his jive and two turkeys. Not nearly. Men always exaggerate. Any other time, men love to toss it around, but when men are sick, shut in or in pain, they hang it down and act shy.

"Well, aren't you gonna lean back?" I asked. "You have juice circling your anal area, and that's not too clean." Orange juice anus.

"Man...please, just close the curtain," he complained.

I didn't move. "I don't see a man around here anywhere, so unless you show me a man then stop calling me *man*, man."

"Get from around the curtain, girl! Matter fact," He lifted his hand high and waved it fast. "Go get me Nurse Betty. She ain't retired. She was just here yesterday."

See. I was already tired of him, so I snatched the curtain

all the way back. Then he started staring at me like I was the one crazy. At that point, I tried to ignore him, but felt the urge to respond to his glare down just to let him know who was in control.

"Mister, I am trying to clean you up or help you out of the tub, either one. Nurse Betty is retired I said. Yesterday, she left." It wasn't my job to tell her patients that she passed away. That was for administration. On top of that, I really didn't want to talk about Nurse Betty's death at all. It was heartbreaking enough. I heard that she was hit by a car, and then some rumor started to the tune of her walking out purposely in front of that car that hit her. Suicide. Now, if it was true, I didn't know. She had no family and was only sixty years old. I did doubt the whole suicide thing, though. She wasn't the type. Nurse Betty was what I called a strong and fierce woman. The one woman that was always teaching and preaching, making you want to be better when you didn't even want to be. You know when you want to cuss somebody out from head to their crusty toes, she was the one that reminded you that a silent tongue was the wisest and that the best thing to do was shut the heck up. That was her. Nurse Betty was always trying to steer someone on the right course just like someone her age should, I guessed.

"I don't need to be cleaned. I'm telling you I'm fine." He began to laugh through his words while shaking his head from side to side, and I noticed them. His teeth had absolutely no black spots, grills, or crusty yellows - just white. They were so straight that they appeared filed, even better looking than mine!

He continued, "Go get me somebody older. Real old! Older than Nurse Betty, and shut this curtain!" he shouted again, this time, trying to pull the curtain away from me, so I yanked it right back.

"You shame?" I asked him with a big huge grin and extremely high pitched tone. This fine black man wasn't ashamed! Couldn't be. Not of a young, defenseless woman like me.

"Give me the rag," he said, staring me up and down, in a more relaxed but yet still more like he could reach up and knock the hell out of me and pour some heaven in kinda way. "I already washed myself," he grumbled. "Just need help in and out is all, out of precaution."

"In and out of what?" My mind was slightly frivolous and naughty that day. Besides, he set himself up for that one, and I knew he liked my flirtatious jabs regardless of how he acted.

"The tub!" He shook his head like he was in overwhelming agony from my sexual insinuations, but that wasn't the case. He was enjoying it, and I could tell he was holding in giggles, trying to keep it solid. Since I felt I succeeded in breaking the ice, I covered my eyes from his nudity, then properly introduced myself, sticking out my hand out for him to shake.

"My name is Jeena. I'm not peeking either." That was a lie. I was all over him through the small crack between my two fingers. Good Great God, I thought, I love you, Lord, I do, and that's why I have to stay focused on what is in front of me out of pure admiration for Your work. "I don't wanna stare at you if that's what you're thinking. I clock in and clock out for work only, not *that* type of pleasure. I enjoy helping people - the right way." My hand was still stuck straight out to shake his though it got ignored, so I let the shower curtain fall shut.

"Thank you, Jeena. Andre'," he introduced himself though I'd gathered that much from the chart. "Make a man lose what nerves he got over situations like this," he quietly complained.

"Lose what? What was that?" I teased behaving as if I didn't hear what he said.

"Nothing," he complained.

"Do you still need help out of the tub?" I was just curious.

"I'll call when I'm ready. Ain't that what this button is for?"

"Didn't you already push it? That's why I came in here."

"Well, I must have pushed it by mistake. I can get out on my own anyway. Just stay there in case is all."

Liar. At those words, I sat down on the toilet and kicked the bathroom door shut. I shouldn't have been in there like that, but what in the world was it gonna hurt? Good old patient care! I

11

could've taken a break right there for fifteen minutes easy. After sitting for a moment, I looked around and then started to talk again because of his overt stall tactic.

"Andre', let me help you out of the tub. Then, I will leave you alone." I was aching to see that body standing up all dripping wet. Just seeing it would have kept my man-less behind together for at least another six months. "I can't have you fall, no matter what. It will be my head on the platter if you slip with me in here, so..."

There was a silence. Dead silence. The water wasn't even moving. He was ignoring me.

"Would you hand me some clothes and my towel," he finally replied.

"Whatcha wanna wear?" I asked, remaining seated on the toilet. I shouldn't even get up, I thought to myself. Really, I should've taken all his clothes out of the drawers and tossed them. That would have left him with the old, open back hospital gown with a great view.

"Man..." he grunted, then let out a big, "*Whew!*"

See, right when he said that, I knew he was about to lose his mind. He was tired of me for sure, but I didn't care. What man didn't love a flirt? I was loving every second of it, even though I was riding the border line of getting fired. There was just something about a man when you get him frustrated to the brink. It was cute, especially when he's helpless and sexy.

"Huh, whatcha wanna wear?" I taunted again, knowing exactly what I was doing. I even started tapping my sneakers on the side of the tub.

The water splashed, and I assumed it was his hands beating the water. It didn't phase me. I kept right on tapping.

"Just some pants, Jeena. But you know what, I can deal with my towel right now though, if you could grab that for me please, Ms. Jeena?"

Hallelujah! As fast as my ass tended to be this morning, I yanked the towel off of the side of the sink and slid it around the shower curtain, and this time, I didn't peek.

After he snatched the towel, I sat down on the toilet waiting on him to step out of the shower himself or ask me to grab him by the waist. Then, a thought hit me. I looked down. Why was I on the toilet? That wasn't sexy at all. I twisted around, stared at the back part of the toilet and imagined myself taking a dump. That wasn't how I wanted him to get a better look at me, so I quickly stood up and leaned my nice, curvy body against the wall, not too stiff but not too desperate and loose either. The last thing I wanted to do was position myself as a stripper on a pole, so I practiced really fast. I sucked in my stomach, pooched it out a little, and then right on my second breath, there was a knock on the bathroom door. My breath got lost somewhere in between.

Immediately, I hunched over like a troll, grabbed some toilet tissue that was next to the sink and began to rip the paper off of it just so it would appear that I was up to some good while behind closed doors. That's when Andre' pulled the shower curtain back, and all his everything in my dreams was put on display. I dropped the toilet tissue. That mug hit the floor with my bottom jaw as he completed wrapping the towel on his waist, slowly.

The knock at the door didn't bother him at all, and as far as me making him uneasy, that wasn't the case. The shy, mean patient named Andre' that was talking junk to me earlier stood there wrapping his body at the waist like he was getting off at me seeing him naked, wet and ripe. I swore my soul left my body because I couldn't move one step toward that door until I soaked up all that...

"Baby, are you in here?"

Fantasy over. The voice of the medusa on the other side of the door was about to turn my behind into stone. It was a female! His female! She called him baby, so if anything, let that voice be his young sounding momma, I hoped.

Suddenly, I felt like I was in front and dead center of the fiery furnace, and about to be tossed in like the those three boys in the Bible. Never could remember their names, but it was my mom's favorite story.

I glanced back at Andre', who was smirking at me which totally put me on edge. He didn't even flinch at the sound of the woman on the other side of the door like things were all good! In the meantime, I felt so guilty, like I was sitting in the tub with Andre' about to get my groove on! Rushing, I picked the toilet tissue back up, reached for the handle of the door and swung it open. There she stood, not looking like she could be his mother either, so with the toilet paper in hand, I spoke. Actually, I stuttered, "H-Hi."

As the word that sounded like two words came out of my mouth, the doorknob banged against the wall. It wasn't a normal hit either. It slammed against the wall and then bounced back off, forcing me to jump and catch it from the ricochet. Could I have even looked any guiltier that that? Hell no. To top it all off, what looked to be his wife or girlfriend was glaring at me like *this chick has issues*. If she only knew that I did have issues, and they had to do with me wanting something that wasn't mine. That something was standing in the tub behind me totally skin laced with no man made, out of China products attached. All naturally made in heaven and looking quite tasty.

The thought of him not being single made me furious! I mean really, all I ever had was mediocre type men. Not saying that they were ugly or close to it, but I never really had my fantasy man in hand, body and soul. Dang! Andre' just happened to look the part, the whole part, of what my fantasy man needed to look like. Tall, jet dark and fine.

"Umm," the woman at the door hummed as she began examining me from my waist on up to my forehead. While I assumed she was cussing me out in silence, I glanced down at her left hand sharply, and yes, my worst fear, married. A big, nice, disgusting rock was laid back on her finger. This wasn't just his girl or jump off, but his wife. His flipping, freaking wife!

"Is my husband in here?" she asked.

See. It was the first thing out of her mouth. *Huszz-band*. She stressed the whole entire word, and she didn't have to ask if he was in here because I knew full well that she could easily see

14

that stallion behind me half naked. All she wanted to say was huszz-band, and yeah, I got the picture.

"Andre', baby?" she called as her voice traveled around me, stopped at my ear, called me *sucker*, and then continued on the flight back to Andre'. "Excuse me, please. May I come in?" she asked, trying to peep around me.

I slid speedily over to the other side of the doorway instead of continuing to guard the bathroom door like security. Get it together, Jeena, I thought to myself. You've seen a naked man before, maybe not that equipped, but still, so breathe...

"Sure, I'm sorry. Jeena," I stated, extending a greeting the best way I knew how in the situation I placed myself into. "Jeena Delilah Ray. Nice to meet you." It was obvious what I was going to say next. "You must be his wife." That way, it sounded as if we spoke about her at least.

"Yes, I am. Tina." She reached out and shook my five fingers. Her palm never reached mine. Just the fingers. I wasn't going to let that bother me either. After my thoughts about her man, she didn't have to shake at all. Truthfully, she should've body slammed me and backslapped me with full force.

I left the room thinking, she can help his sexy body out of that tub. I'm outta here. As I exited the bathroom, I noticed the toilet tissue in my hand, then thought, no wonder she barely shook my hand. Toilet damn tissue! Yep, I looked like I just got finished wiping his nice, round, orange juice ass.

Capital City

Two weekends after that fateful day at work, my girl and I ended up at the most happening place in the city.

"Girl, he was fine!" Yeah, I was talking about that *same* man in the hospital tub named Andre'. My girlfriend and I were

15

playing catch up from not being able to hang out the previous weeks, and where we decided to play catch up was at a place called Capital City. This was the place for the classy and never the trashy. People didn't come in this place with no clothes on or looking like it's winter time in Chicago, but only dressed to the nines!

Mind you that I said Capital City was the 'place' to be. Yeah, no person on this side called Capital City a bar, club or spot, but it was the 'place'. As a matter of fact, even the word restaurant was an understatement. The menu was crazy and quite posh. Let me explain.

There was a five section menu - black with white lettering and the sections were Brazilian, French, African, Jewish, and Italian. I would have to save up for two months just to eat here, but it was well worth the agony of overtime because the food was dead on. Every cook Capital City had, they 'imported' from their birth countries. These cooks were bona fide, and they could prepare the best authentic cuisines. Every single cook was cute, too, from one end of the world to the other. Okay, more than cute, more like handsome as the heavens! Capitol City had female cooks representing, too, but I wasn't checking them out like that.

As far as the pricing, a plate of food with dessert and a drink would run a sad soul that wasn't prepared for it two hundred dollars or more. Oh yeah, there were no prices on the menu, so you'd better had done some research before busting up in here and ordering anything with a wallet weighing only sixty dollars and no credit cards. I asked around before my first time dining. Then, I called ahead and asked what was the cheapest thing on the menu...anonymously... just to remain under the hundred dollar mark. Smart.

"And how fine was he, Jeena?" Parri asked in reference to Andre'. "He must be a looker if he was broken down in hospital tub and still turning eyelashes his way."

"Super fine. I mean, for real. I saw an outline of every muscle in his body, and he wasn't just fine from the neck down

16

either."

"Oh, then he has a face that you would want to look up in every day?"

"Yes, Parri, and what a face it was. Make me some cute kids."

Parri and I were the only ones of my very small group of friends who were able to go to Capital City tonight. Everyone else had bigger bills to pay and children to raise. Parri and I, we were still looking to breed, and not breed with any old thing, but with someone special or there would be no breeding to occur. The concept was marriage first, save baby money and then out comes the baby or babies, but the hardest thing of all those was marriage.

"So, did you get his number, or did he seem interested? The reason I'm asking is because I know you asked for it," she asked me while taking a sip of ice water. It looked like something was floating around between her ice, but I didn't mention it. She would've probably made a scene in here, like faked a vomit to score a free meal to go. Parri was good for a great show out in public.

"No, no number," I responded, while I glanced around the dimly lit Brazilian section of the place, "But a wife. He did give me his wife." I twisted my lips at the thought. "I was embarrassed, too. Highly embarrassed, but, girl, if I saw him again, I would hit that so hard, knock that sucka clean out the..."

"Get out of here, Jeena! You wouldn't!"

"Yeah, you're right. I wouldn't because I ain't nobody's side booty or late night secret phone call so he can get off. I'll leave that for the desperate, immoral chick." I was lying. I could only *hope* I wouldn't jump all over him if I saw him again like that desperate, immoral chick I just talked about. Temptation was a killer! "But, no, it wasn't like he threw his wife in my face and shut me down. She walked in. Before that though, I thought he wasn't that interested because he was insistent on me getting the heck out of the bathroom so that he could be alone. He wanted an 'old nurse' to help him out, not that he needed much help. His request out of the tub was more precautionary. Can you believe that? He wanted an old nurse? Anyway, I was wrong though, about him not wanting to hook up with me even a little bit because homey let me see him in all his glory with a smile plastered on his face. Maybe he was just playing around, but my vagina wasn't because it hit the floor and started crawling back to the tub where he was showcasing his gems. She didn't get lucky though."

"Well, that was fortunate for you the wife took that fine hunk of glory down a notch. You don't need that the other lady stigma on you even if he was willing, playing or not."

"Tell me about it," I agreed, then stuck my breasts out like a Barbie doll. "The husband's ho...Jeena D. Ray. Can't get a home out of him, just a bad reputation and a screwed up conscience with an eventual bad memory. Not a fair trade. The wife, she gets the house, car, money, parties, children, family, and doesn't have to be a whore while she enjoys a fabulous rep." I sunk my chest back down to normal size. "I ain't no man's licky lady."

"Yeah, and then God'll get ya'."

"Probably. And in ways I'd never guess," I responded while still casing the place. "You know something, whoever owns this place has either got to be rich or got a really good loan from the bank. As a matter of fact, let me meet him, if it is a guy. I could settle being married to a pot belly and some dollar bills," I clowned. "Eating here every night, the owner has to be big and round."

"Tell me about it."

"Are you ready to be seated?" the hostess asked.

"Yes, we are," we responded simultaneously. I forgot to mention, instead of waiting at the front like at an all you can eat restaurant, Capital City had high tables where you stand and sip any desired free drink until they personalize your selection of the world experience. It was now our turn.

"Are you feeling Italian tonight or maybe Brazilian?"

"Actually, tonight," I glanced over at Parri, "I think we want a good bit of Africa." At that, we giggled because by that we meant men and not necessarily food. Black, tasty chocolate men that we would be able to stare upon from our seats through a magnificent tinted glass while they sautéed our meals was our desire. Unfortunately, to keep the hormones down, Capital City allowed the customers to see the cooks through a special glass, but the chefs couldn't see us. I assumed it was to allow them to concentrate on their work. That meant the owner quickly figured out that the chefs were peepin', too. A couple burnt meals must have given the owner a huge clue in the distractions.

As we followed behind the hostess for the evening, she introduced us to not only the African retreat filled with the scents and fragrances of just plain erotica, but also to about twenty occupied tables of beautiful women between the ages of what appeared to be twenty-five to seventy-two!

"Looks like we aren't the only ones thirsting for a single, masculine male," I stated as I gripped my elegant purse, the only expensive one that I paid for and owned from an online celebrity auction. It was going to be a long night of competition. The ladies were all beautiful, and by the looks of it, many of them were rich, too. The latter wasn't a characteristic that I possessed at all, but I was working on it.

There were the valley type girls over in the corner seated right up on the see through glass where the cooks were located. Yeah, white girls came to the African section, too. They knew good dark meat when they saw it! I knew why they were sitting in that particular area of Africa, too. Prime choice. You see, when a chef would come out, and they would come out every once in a while, that table where the valley girls were seated was more than likely the table that the chefs would see first coming out and last going back into the kitchen. Unlucky me, I'd never gotten here early enough to request that spot, and then I didn't know if I would. Those ladies were pretty demanding of attention and not afraid to let it all hang out. Me on the other hand, I was bold-ish, but not hang my stuff out bold at all!

Now on our side, or should I say, the side where the hostess was having us seated, there were the all naturals of all races for the most part. When I say all naturals, I didn't mean solely hair. These girls didn't have to do much but wake up in the morning and be fixed. No hair weave, no fake nails, no obvious I-have-just-left-the-gym superwomen and no plastic surgery like the some of the valleys. The naturals were born pretty from the womb. It was a guarantee that one of them, a naturally pretty woman, was walking away with my male stud tonight, but I crossed my fingers that it would be my naturally beautiful behind this time. What man wants a girl who goes to bed one way and wakes up another? At least, that's what my male cousins used to say, and I listened. They lied obviously because all their wives wear nice weaves and fake cleaves, sliding their wigs across my kitchen table when they visit from time to time talking about *I need a break*!

Now, me and Parri were as natural as we could get. I had my fake lashes on, and, Parri, she had her toes glittering. She normally crossed her legs higher than Mount Whitney when she flirted, therefore, she had to get them done. She was always one to say, show off what you got, and one thing she knew that she had was legs and toes. She wasn't so certain about everything else. *My man better like legs and toes, because I don't have much breasts, and my butt ain't big* was her slogan, but she was comfortable with that. Love, she said, loves everything about *you*, not everything everybody else has and does. When you elevate to that, that's when one respects love and understands it.

As for myself, I always thought I was an overall lady. My eyes being the best feature on me, thus, the fake eyelashes, just to make my eyes appear darker and deeper at night. Overall, I was great. Everything evened out perfectly. To myself, I was a perfect, not conceited, but still a confident ten. The problem was that I didn't know what I was to the fellas. I would've said a possible high seven, but to the man that ever hooked up with me, I wanted *him* to see me as the ultimate ten. Hopefully, that would've been how I saw him also, both inside and out.

By the time the food was served, I was starving, not because the service was on stall, but because I didn't eat at all before I got here. The food at Capital City was not only expensive but filling. On top of that, there was no carry-out, so leftover food went to waste! Every recipe secret was kept in house. No picking it apart at home. From my very first time coming, I'd learned never to enter Capital City on a partially empty stomach. The sucker better be in a starved state. Besides that, the dress that I had on was close to being too tight, so I had to leave some stomach growth room.

"Anyway, she raised her hand to slap me. Can you believe that?" Parri explained as she shoved her fork into her mouth while discussing some old lady at her job. She worked at this weight loss company, and some of the world's sanity goes out of the window when they enter those doors. Apparently, the woman had come in and disagreed with Parri about the amount of chocolate bars needed in her diet. A chocolate debate over weight.

"I mean, Jeena, it ain't my fault she was gaining weight. That woman just about slapped the hell outta me. Shoot, I had to duck!" she laughed, flinging her fork as if it was the woman's slapping hand.

"Duck? You should have let her make contact, Parri," I responded matter of factly with a mouth full of food.

"And why?"

I swallowed. "So you could've knocked her behind out! Always hit second or third, girl. That's the law of the land. Get your aggression out. Hit back and then back away. Never duck, never do that unless you think you're gonna lose. Take the lick and then bust her up. Get out of jail free pass. Self defense."

"No, Jeena. I can't be messing up my hands on a hooker's face. I'm too delicate for that fighting drama." Suddenly, she quieted and her neck popped back as if she was a goose in a pond. I knew from past experiences that my girl was getting ready to start acting a fool about something.

"What, Parri?" I asked, waving my hand from side to side

in an attempt to break her stare at who knows what. "Girl, don't start that talking about people tonight. You're gonna cause me to have indigestion." Sometimes, I'd laughed so hard at her in the past that I nearly choked up on what I was attempting to get down my throat. She was good for picking somebody, wherever we went, to start throwing slap jokes on.

"No, no, Jee Jee," she said, waving her fingers at me. "You can digest this one. Look at that golden watch on your wrist."

I did. What on earth she was talking about, I didn't know, but it couldn't have been located on my timepiece. "What's on my watch?" I asked, following my second hand around the face.

"Now, check out number nine, and then look up through your periphery."

I followed her up and did as she asked. From my watch, I slid my eyes over to number nine and tilted them up a tad. When my eyes reached the stopping point, I almost missed what my eyes were supposed to see because they incidentally caught a horny, bald man with a beard that reached the bottom of his chest. Almost like the beards in those Bruce Lee kung-fu movies that my dad used to watch when I was growing up, except this was a black man. Maybe not black. No, well, maybe still.

He was dark-skinned, though, of more of an Indian tone. His beard was shaped as sharp as a pencil lead point, and boy was he macking! The female across from him was smiling from ear lobe to ear lobe. I would've been cheesing, too, if homeboy was spending two hundred dollars for my plate of food. All my pearlies would have been like bam! Grill for life!

Then, I messed around and saw what Parri was really wanting me to plant my eyes on. Sexy. And you know sometimes how sexy might make you jerk? Well, I jerked, but not just because he was hot. It was way more than that.

My eyes fell right back inside my plate of food, desperately trying not to glance up at Parri because I knew she was waiting on a sly bounce back remark from me about the man that had her fixated. This time, and only this time, I wasn't going to be able to give her any type of remark at all. I swear, I was so caught off guard that I could've regurgitated what little food I already ate back onto my plate while landing some of the trickles of the vomited entre' over on Parri.

It was homeboy, homeboy from the hospital. Andre'. Married, yet still fine, Andre'. His clothes fell on him like they enjoyed being wrapped around his body. His wife was so lucky. I thought about Parri, and decided not to say a word about who he was based on our earlier conversation about being a married man's licky lady. Instead of responding to Parri, I shoved food in my mouth because my attraction to this married man just reached its peak, and I felt freaking sex struck.

"Jeena!" she exclaimed, wanting me to respond to Sir Sexy over to my nine. I was forced to respond just to get her off my back.

"He is fine, isn't he? Wonder what he's doing here and who he's with?" I added that *who he's with* line with the intention of diverting all conversation to the marriage of which Parri was clueless about to make her get off of his swag. I was sure his wife was here somewhere, hidden in the crevices and cracks. Really, I didn't want her to be though, and yep, that was some hypocritical mess I was thinking but true. I nearly felt like I could be comfortable as the other woman – his other woman – and be fine with it! My attraction to him was just that deep!

Gawking at me like I was losing my mind, she stated, "What do you mean, why is he here, who he's with, and what's up with that stuck up sounding *he is fine, isn't he*? Girl, he looks like he's running this half of the joint. That's what he's doing here! Gotta be. He's just standing there in the corner like he's casing the place. Oops...I was right. One of the hostesses just asked a question, one of those tell me what to do questions, and he told her. Dog, I'm good! I can pick the platinum!" She wiggled around in her seat with excitement at her new discovery. Too bad the platinum she found was on his wife's left hand and ring finger.

As for me, I plummeted at the thought of him managing this place with me in it. Honestly, I was embarrassed about everything that happened at work, but just seeing this man again made my insides flip. If Parri knew that was him, I would be dead meat tonight, put totally on the spot if I were to tell her how my whole attraction just went into overtime for this man. She would put him off limits immediately, and I honestly didn't know if that was what I wanted *completely*. Not yet.

I can handle this, I thought, to myself. Just don't see me, I kept repeating over and over to myself like a sociopath in the depths of my mind. I was even beginning to move my lips with the tune going over and over in my head. This was the last temptation that I needed today, atop of Parri's mouth. If he didn't see me, I knew I could manage remaining seated and silent until this hell bent night ended.

.   "Girl, and," she leaned over inconspicuously, continuing from the corner of her lip, "He doesn't have on a ring." Her eyes were glowing like two big pearls.

Say what? My heart knocked on my chest like it had five fingers and knuckles and my chest had a knob. She had to have been lying. No ring? At that point, I pretended like I was looking at her, but really, I was hopefully staring out of the window behind her wishing that I was there, blissfully standing on the sidewalk in the peace of God instead of in Capital City about to drop my butt directly into Hades on the devil's horn which would hurt like hell.

I wasn't good at temptation, and unfortunately, I desired the deluxe package of a man right now. Sin of selfishness, I supposed, but that's how I was at the moment. Not saying that I needed a man, but just wanted him, therefore, not good at temptation, especially tonight. It didn't help the situation that I had been single for so long, probably making that black man at my nine look even better than he did naked in that hospital bathtub.

Back to the ring, though. The problem that I was now having was what I didn't know about, and that was the status of him and his wife due to the missing ring. This brotha probably couldn't wear his ring at work because just the thought of him being in an awesome, committed relationship would have probably dropped customers by fifty percent. Did he and his wife split up? At that point, I caught Parri giving me the evil eye, more than likely because I was being too quiet. Therefore, I had to make it seem like she was taking his sexy too far and, in other words, lie.

"Parri, don't be so needy, girl. Stop gawking. Let that man look at you and you not help him do it by guiding his eyes this way. Stop fishing so hard."

I picked my fork up and started to chomp hard again, with my head twisted the opposite way of Andre', the highly captivating. I wasn't about to tell her who he was. All hell would break loose inside me because I wanted him - bad! It wasn't like I wanted a married man. It was more like I wanted Andre' who happened to be married - if that made any sense. The one thing I needed was for loud mouth Parri not to draw any heat over my way and maybe this whole mess would flee without me completely closing the chapter on a maybe later.

"What?" Parri let her fork plunk down on her plate, and to me, it was the loudest thud that you could ever hear. In reality, it wasn't, but because of the position that I was in, which was full paranoia, that fork hitting the plate was louder than a dang atomic bomb. I just knew he was gonna look over here towards us and come swagging. I was nervous. You know how you can get so nervous that it's hard to be cute and swallow food? That was the point at which I was. Nervous enough to choke. Parri wasn't ugly, and the last time I checked, she could get a man to turn his attention to her in four seconds flat because of her confidence, including a looker like Andre'.

See, Parri, she was the type that could play with any man, married or not, and not get caught up. Yeah, did you guess? She was an expert tease, but not a ho. A true game player. Not me. I tended to get caught up, and that was something I learned from past experiences.

"Pick your fork up. Eat." I shrugged my shoulders as to behave as if nothing was up.

"Since when don't you drool? Talking about *pick up my fork and eat*. Girl, are you crazy? I'll eat him before I eat this food

25

off of this plate." She picks up her fork. "That's for sure."

Little did she know, I would've eaten him, too. I would have licked every drop of chocolate off of his naturally cut body and made him my three day fast. As I was sitting there, still chewing on that same piece of meat, over and over again, I figured out what I was going to do if something popped off. Nothing. Not one thing. Let nature take its course and dodge the darts. Yep. That sounded good to me. I could handle it. Bad thing was, I knew that nonexistent ring on Andre's finger was going to be my excuse to give in to my hormones.

<u>Maybe...Or Maybe Not.</u>

"Here he comes."

What! There went that four seconds. In an instant, I needed strength. I knew Parri was going to get his attention with her come and get it attitude. A great, big wind left my lungs, and I couldn't get it back. Where was a non-prescribed inhaler when I needed one? Parri, she was tugging on her bra and pushing her chest out to make her breasts just about protrude from her shirt. There she went with that push up bra again. A shame.

"What do you mean *here he comes*?" I asked, holding my fork and knife in the palms of my hands like I could reach over and slice her top lip off of her face. "Did you call him over here when I wasn't looking or something? You're all getting prepped up and mess and you don't even know anything about him!" I exclaimed in the most extremely silent voice I had.

"Sit up straight, honey," she sang, cutting me off before I could say anything else, "Because it's got to be either you or me. And no, I didn't call him. He was walking this way, so it's my job to guide the landing." Then she whispered, "And I won't hate if he picks you. You just better not leave him alone with me because if you snooze, I take. Give him back later." Then, she waved her fingers at me. "Put that knife down and the fork. You ain't stabbin' nobody tonight. Well," she continued, darting her eyes quickly my way, "Not me anyway."

"Thanks," I responded sarcastically. I dropped the utensils, snatched up my napkin and tapped my mouth on both sides. I was so hungry when I got in there, I probably had that caked up white stuff slimed all on the corners of my mouth. Couldn't have that, so wipe I did.

My stomach was in knots. I hated admitting to myself that I was really still attracted to this man even after I met his wife. I even forgot his last name. All I knew was Andre'. I didn't even think that I was going to see him again after he discharged. My attraction to him was so bad that day I met him in the hospital, I went home that night and wrote a poem. I wrote poetry, and the poem I wrote was called The Chocolate Bar. Sad, right? The dumb thing was that I didn't have any real reason to like him. It wasn't love. He was just fine, and who knows where that awful attraction came from, but it wasn't just a *he's fine* attraction. It was animalistic!

Still yet, I wondered why he wasn't wearing his wedding ring tonight? When I finally got a chance to look closely at his hand before he left the hospital, that huge gold thing was shining on his finger. But then again, as far as tonight went, that ring not on his finger meant to me he was single and shopping - wife or not. At least that's what seventy percent of my body was saying, drowning out the other do-gooder thirty percent.

"How are things, ladies?" There was that deep, crisp voice. "May I have one of the chefs personally prepare a dessert which appeals to your tastes tonight?"

He even had an accent that night! Very different from the hospital sound. Whew! A man of many talents. Instead of being my normal loud self, I ignored the new news of his accent and kept my eyes lowered. At that point, it didn't seem as if he recognized me. That was great. However, Parri, oh, you can bet she took full advantage of the opportunity to get with what she believed was her single, hot male.

I sat back. Parri slid her legs from underneath the table, lifted her right one and crossed it over her left. Then, she started to wiggle those feet and giggle. Hey, she paid for those toes, right? Better work 'em! Parri would do the same thing each and every time she met a man for the first time on purpose.

"May I have a piece of that and a piece of that?" She pointed to two spots on his body, and then, placed her finger on her lip. The tease, so close to being a tool. If I didn't know her like I did, I would have hung her picture up next to a sign that was labeled Ho Walk of Fame. Truth was, she had only had official sex, to my knowledge, with only two men - her ex and her dream frat brother who played her from side to side.

Andre' then folded his arms, wiped his go-tee, cocked a side smile, and then asked, "What might those pieces be?"

I wanted to gag right then and there and thus and thorn. It didn't take all of that, but that's Parri for you. I was more the undercover flirt for the most part. I always wanted my desired guy to know I wanted him, but never needed to spell it out like Parri with the point and define. It took away the exhilaration of the moment. Flirting, to me, was supposed to be an insinuation, an art form. Never a direct verbal stab and jab. Flirting always left room for a way out. Without that way out, it wasn't flirting, but a major decision with follow through intended.

Parri answered him, "Your lips and your..."

"Parri!" I had to intercept that pass.

Andre', being smoother than what I remember in that tub, didn't bother to respond to Parri with words, but a smile. Then, he lifted Parri's hand by her fingertips and kissed her hand. Parri relished in that moment but not I, being that I really didn't think he recognized me. Should I have even wanted him to notice me? Either way, it wasn't going to concern me, at least I wasn't going to let it. It was stupid anyway. Who would try and look good for a married man but an over aged and over done hooker, right? Right after I thought those words, I pictured myself over aged and over done getting closer and closer to hooker form with one heel on the street corner. I had to snap out of it.

"Goodnight, ladies." He placed her hand lightly back in her lap. Parri remained locked in on his goodies, but then quickly, he glanced at me. I almost missed it, catching the edge of the glance. Immediately, I darted my eyes away from his, and then that was when it hit me - he noticed that I was the lady that made him drop the orange juice in the tub.

Andre' walked away without saying a word my way. Not one single word. Instead, he walked some distance behind Parri at an empty table and stopped. Parri...well, she was talking, just talking away. I didn't hear her words because I wasn't listening. She was talking about Andre' I guessed while I stared right through her to the man himself who was looking directly in my face from behind her flapping jaws.

At first, I attempted to ignore the image of his body, but couldn't help but get stagnated. He was standing behind the table gazing at me, not hard though, but very soft, like he wanted to start our conversation over where we left off in the bathroom during his towel wrap. There was no question that his eyes were telling me to come on over, and I honestly had no idea why. He hated my guts from what I remembered, but hey, guess things changed or either I looked damn good tonight!

As he stood there in his blue silk shirt that draped his body like a jungle warrior, my vision bled right through the fabrics in his shirt to his rippled pack. I was getting the show that no other ladies here tonight were getting. His pecks shook and startled my gaze. Dang, I couldn't breathe. The very salivating glands in my mouth were working overtime, and my pulse had gradually worked itself up to let's say...one hundred times per minute. I needed oxygen. Then, as I looked into his eyes, nothing but midnight, he coerced me into following the trail his eyes were making all over my precious, lonely, over worked and underpaid body. Finally, he released me from his simple seduction and continued on with business as usual. He definitely knew who I was, and I'd gotten caught the hell up. Damn.

What was that, five hours? My appetite left me

somewhere between his pecks and my loss of breath. I needed a drink. Did he divorce his wife in these last two weeks?

"Stupid!"

"Huh?" My daze was over.

"What are you staring at?" She turned around to look behind her faster than her brain sometimes thought, but thank God, he'd already walked off. "You haven't heard a word I've been saying."

Playing it off, I stated confidently, "Yes, I have."

She just stared back at me. "Prove it."

"An..." Oops. I almost sent his name coasting to her eardrums. "The manager of this joint. You were just talking about him." It wasn't exactly a wild guess. More like evident. Shoot, if she only knew that while she was merely talking about him, I was actually hooking up with him absent all the words, kisses on the hand and toes wiggling.

"Did you just see him? I mean, Jeena, you act like he didn't phase you. On top of that, he just dissed me."

Brake.

"What do you mean he just dissed you? Parri, please, the man kissed your crusty hand."

"Oh, shut up, Jee-Jee. You know that was a diss. Not answering me and placing my hand where it belongs? It was like he was telling me to act like a lady and stop pointing at his goods. Most guys like that kinda stuff, you know," she continued, chomping on a piece of celery.

"Maybe he's a gentleman." Or married, I thought, taking a big swig of my drink.

"Maybe *you're* just acting like something is wrong with you. You act like you aren't interested in these masculine species up in here that are waiting on us hand and foot. Girl, I got to snag one tonight so I can get a free meal or something next week. Nothing long term, just as short as I can make it last until my check comes in!" she laughed.

She just didn't know. I already had a taste from afar and had gotten addicted just that fast. I even forgot his wife for a second. I needed to step off. A ho ain't what I aspired to be.

By the end of the night, I was ready to use the restroom, not throw powder and make-up on, but seriously urinate. I held it though. I'd been holding this sack of fluid in my bladder for one full hour, and it was beginning to pain my insides. Reason number one for holding my urine...you got it... I was terrified to move from my seat. If you needed another reason, it was because Andre' was standing in a position where if I had to go to the restroom, I would've had to prance by him like a fawn. Holding this much urine in your system would prevent that type of promenade. It would have been more like a fleeting gallop.

Even worse, it seemed like Andre' was behaving as if he didn't know why he staggered in that position. Many women passed by him. I saw them all, but they didn't phase him one bit. Andre' was waiting on me. He didn't tell me this, but I just knew out of shear instinct.

I was afraid. See, it was all fun and games when I was in control of the situation. I knew how far to let it go, especially after the wife intro. The game had to stop. Now, the roles had been reversed, and instantly, it felt like I was the one in the tub and he was asking to scrub *me* down. Bad thing was, if I sat here any longer, he would be scrubbing the piss from my legs.

"Parri, I'm going to the bathroom, girl. I've been holding this for a long time, but I can't hold it anymore," I told her, trying to behave as normally as I could.

"Go ahead. I get a better view this way."

She didn't have to tell me twice. Andre' may have been standing in the same spot at the bathroom, but he was tied up at the moment with a woman who looked as if she was complimenting him on the meal she just swallowed down.

I made my move, and boy, was I walking fast, upright with only a slight promenade. As I approached him, I stared directly into his eyes, and while he was speaking with this overly thankful lady, his eyes followed me, but he didn't stop speaking. It was hot, a hot magnetic field as I passed him. He smelled so damn good! It was as if I was rubbing against his bare skin, and we wanted to connect but that didn't happen. Instead, I connected with that toilet.

<u>Relief.</u>

Alone finally. The restroom seemed ten million miles away from Capital City, as if they were completely disconnected from one another. The mirror was my home away from home, and for that moment in time, I wasn't a skank.

As I stood there washing my hands in front of an elegant outstretch of mirror, I wanted to believe I was a better person. Could it be that I truly wasn't? Was I actually contemplating being with someone's husband? The truth of the matter was yes.

I turned away from the mirror and stared down at my toes. What would I call myself if I wasn't inside my own body? What would I call myself if it wasn't me in this web outside of reality? In reality, I would call someone like me a HOOK-ER. Better yet, a shit-grown skank. I turned to face the mirror once more and my thoughts continued.

But then again, what if he really was divorcing his wife? I mean, his ring wasn't on, and he seemed to be on my g-string - hard - which was a big difference from our first encounter. What if things really did go downhill and fast in his marriage, and maybe the slope was worse than it appeared when wifey called him baby at the bathroom door? Being called baby didn't mean love at all.

Justifying the situation was what I was doing, treading down HOOK-ER territory fast. The fact was that I needed to be a woman. My make-up and hair were flawless as I prompted myself continuously to be a freaking woman and ask him. Just let it out, are you still married, Andre'?

I hit the counter with the palm of my hand, not too hard,

but hard enough to release tension. Love wasn't this. Love wasn't first sight. Any idiot knew that. Besides that, he didn't give me anything to love about him except the way that he looked, and all that meant was that it was my own choice. It was my choice to find out the truth, and then do what I would do with that truth, good or bad or nothing. That's what I'd always learned grown folks do, right? They make choices and live with the consequences. Whatever I ended up with, I hoped the consequences came out in my favor. Go with the flow. Destiny, I thought, and play the odds. That was my decision, and I hoped it didn't bite me in my butt.

Exiting the restroom, I didn't even get two steps out before I felt his hand tap my waist, and I swear I almost had that man's baby right there on the dog-on restaurant floor. Choice made. Now, when he touched me, I didn't turn around right away nor did I speak. Trying to be smooth, I sucked that self induced baby that I was getting ready to birth back up my vagina and did my thing. He was suave, and because of what I happened to know about him, I had a feeling he didn't want to be noticed touching me, especially at his workplace and *especially* if he was still married! I hoped he wasn't a real mutt because that would mean that I spoke dog. Arf.

"Jeena," he whispered.

My eyes floated up and toward Parri who was sitting there with her back to me. Good. That's when I took the opportunity to slowly turn around, without seeming too anxious, and come face to face with him.

"Hi." I didn't try to fake it. Yes, I know exactly who you are, Andre', I thought to myself, with your fine-ine self. My waist had already melted into butter as it still felt the residue of sensation that his fingers left on my body.

"I thought you didn't recognize me," he spoke.

I didn't even respond to that dumb ass comment. Not because I was playing hard to get or anything, but dang, this man took my breath away, and he knew it. I couldn't help but breathe him all in. Not notice him? Please. Finally, I recuperated from my stupor and said something.

"Weren't you too busy entertaining my girlfriend over there?" I asked flicking my finger Parri's way. "Besides that, I figured you knew not who I was nor cared. I did embarrass you alot in the hospital, so I figured that being outgoing wasn't exactly your specialty." My eyes remained fixated on him. The noise from the restaurant wasn't gaining any precedence over this pointless, yet pointed, conversation. What I would call the sinful, life degrading chemistry between us told more than what our words could speak which made the conversation even more meaningless, but still, I didn't run away from it as I should have. I was stuck, flat out captivated with Andre', and there was Lucifer - sitting on the sideline grinning. I wished I could've tossed him into the bottomless pit myself, but I didn't think Jesus would have trusted me to that task as any idiot could have noticed the reason why.

"I apologize to you, Jeena. I just wasn't prepared to see a woman so beautiful in the hospital while I was..." He looked away at someone calling his...Dickson! That was his last name!

"Pardon me, Mr. Dickson, we need you in the back," a waitress requested, then glanced at me, "if you aren't too busy. Excuse me, ma'am," she directed her pardon toward me. It kind of shook me how proper it was. I wanted so desperately to say, *hey, did you notice that I look nothing like his wife, Tina, and it's obvious that I am flirting?* but I kept all that drama on the inside of my mouth.

"No, I'm not that tied up. I'll be there." He immediately looked back at me. "I'd like to apologize in a better atmosphere." He slid me his business card as the waitress moseyed off.

"Aren't you married?" I asked, as I grasped at the card extremely lightly, just barely touching it.

He stopped and stared at me, business card still in between his fingertips and all. He wasn't going to release it, and I didn't dare pull it, therefore, I moved my hand back. My married question must have stunned him because it obviously put him in second guess mode! Then suddenly, he let the card go. I mean, this dude literally let it drop without a flinch while still looking me in my face. As I watched it drift to the floor, I caught it in a frenzy before it hit the ground, held it in the palm of my hands, and then lastly thought, dang, how desperate! All twenty of the cool points that I'd earned in my whole life went straight down the drain. I pictured how I must have appeared to him while I was still bent over and thought *geez*. Whatever the case, no matter how I looked, I still had to raise back up and face the fact of my anxious, frantic act while feeling embarrassed like a mug.

Though I felt like walking like a troll back to my seat, gawking at Parri and handing her his card so *she* can call him in the morning, I did the complete opposite. I sucked it up along with my gut while pulling myself straight up into what I thought was an attractive pose. All Andre' did was slightly smile while he got back to answering my aren't you married question.

"Yes."

Oh hell. I thought that fetus just dropped back down to the edge of my vagina. I felt like I had to lay a brick out of my butt from my nerves wilding out! Not lady like, but damn, I felt like a slut. Thus, brick laying was legal for times like these. I mean, I knew he was married, but I didn't expect an affirmative response at all. A lying no would have allowed at least half of my guilt to pass.

While I stood there in my unseen panic, he left me upright with his business card hanging in between my fingertips. He didn't even try to hide it - it being the marriage factor. I didn't even get a chance to respond. The future was all left up to me, and unfortunately, he knew it.

At My Condominium the Same Night...

With my shoes off and hair pulled all the way up in a

ponytail, I sat on the edge of my tub running water. When I got home from Capital City, I dumped bubble bath all in my tub, and the bubbles were coming up in full force. I didn't even monitor how much bubble bath I poured in, but it had to be over half of the bottle.

I sunk in. The water crept up around me, and I continued to sink until the water reached my neck. I couldn't swim, so I knew better than to try that television bull like dip my head down in the water and come back up. It would have been just my luck to have gotten stuck down there, and no one would find my rusted up body for three days. That's not how I wanted to go out, so I didn't play with the notion. Plus my hair and water without a wash didn't mix.

My cell phone was on the bathroom rug right next to me. Andre' Dickson. That was exactly what his card stated as it dangled above the water in my bathtub from my two fingers. Then, I dunked it. It didn't matter because I already had the dumb thing memorized - the work number and cell number. 555-2626 was the cell. How easy was that? It was almost as if it was specially made for the purpose of being memorized. It should have read 555-6666 for Satan. That way, it would have been a case of clear cut evil instead of an evil that you want to give the benefit of a doubt.

When I pulled the card back up out of the water, it was so drenched that it was about to rip at the touch. Therefore, I went ahead and ripped it. I tore it all the way to the edge and then pieced it back together. Why I was doing this, I didn't know, but one thing I did figure out was that I wasn't gonna call him. At least my mind was leaning more toward that conclusion, but curiosity made me wonder what would happen if I called? Would a woman pick up his cell, and if so, what then? In the midst of my thoughts on calling him, my own cell phone rang. I reached out and answered...speaker.

"Hello?"

No answer.

"Hello?" I repeated, hanging my neck over the tub and

speaking a tad bit louder. What was the point in speaker phone if the companies didn't make them loud like a speaker?

"Hey, gal."

It was Parri.

"Hey!" I responded as if I hadn't just left from hanging out with her.

And Tanya. That was my other girlfriend, the one with the children...of the corn. Those jokers were bad behinds. Tanya had the neat idea of naming them after their fathers. Now, I'd never thought that there was anything wrong with naming a child after the daddy, but if your baby's daddy is a hellyun, do anything in your power to stop that cycle, including the name. Other than that, she was great people.

"Hey, ladies. What's up?" I spoke again and then lounged myself back in my island of water, kind of glad they called me. That must have been God's way of getting me out of temptation. It had to be. Mom always used to tell me over and over that my life was gonna be filled with things that I could try, but all things I shouldn't really try because all things wouldn't be good for me. That would be where I would have to tell the difference. That was where I consistently messed up because I didn't realize that the truth was in my face - constantly - but I always took the lie. Bad habit, I guess, and bad habits die super slowly.

"Open the door," they both spoke at the same exact time.

Huh? I lifted my body up out of the warm and cozy bubble bath that I made for myself and propped my elbows up on the side of the tub.

"Open what door?" I asked confused. Please don't say my front door, please don't say my front door, I repetitiously thought.

"Your front door."

The moment I feared.

"We wanna come in," they continued.

"What! Parri...Tanya...what are you two doing at my front door?"

"Girl, the party ain't over. We went and got two movies, some popcorn and sodas. Tanya needed a night out, too, so I decided this would be an all nighter."

"Tanya, who got your little demons tonight, the angel of darkness or the angel of light?" I giggled and sunk myself back in my warm water as I gazed at the ripped business card. Now all I needed was to erase the numbers from my memory and never go back to Capital City. Ever.

"Alright, Jeena," she said slightly offended. "They might be little bad butts, but they're mine. Every one of them. My mom has them, and she ain't no angel of the night, dark or whatever you said. They wanted to spend the night with her this evening."

"Stop yacking! Come on, Jeena! I'm ready to sit down! Open your door!" Parri yelled.

"Bye." I hung the phone up. I never should have answered it in the first place. I was getting too old for this. Twenty nine and counting. I couldn't even come to my home and chill out without having homegirl one and two show up at the front door at nearly twelve o'clock at night. They must've had the mindset that we were still in college. I loved them, but dog! Anyway, they were my girls.

College. I thought back to those days as I rose up out of the tub with all the nice, comfortable sheets of water droplets dripping from my skin. I would generally soak at least twice a week in a tub full of water with bubbles, and the reason being is because I thought that I deserved it. Plus, it kept my muscles massaged for free due to the fact that I couldn't afford a masseur on my salary. Well, maybe I would have been able to afford one, except I would've had to cut back on other things like Capital City, cable and most importantly, clothes along with having to beg from my mom again. I wasn't gonna do it.

As I wrapped my towel around myself, making a strong knot, I continued to reminisce about our college days. Talk about sleepovers. We were sisters every night, practically lived with each other and just collected our mail out of different boxes. All we did was scope the guys until we figured out that we had to graduate. Then, the homies went on the back burner for all except one of us. That was where Tanya got her head start in raising a family. She tried to keep up with the fellas along with graduate, so the fellas stayed up with her as well...in her womb.

When I got to the front door, I swung it open, and as fast as I'd done that, I'd already turned my back to it.

"Girl, is that any way to welcome your girls?" Parri asked while they stormed in like they paid rent. Parri, with her whole Capital City attire tossed, went home and changed into some black jeans and a top. Tanya, well, she was always in jeans which were her second love. Her first love was her children. Her last love was herself.

I stared straight ahead, pretending that Parri's question went right over my head. Guilt kept me staring directly in front of myself like the night of the living freaking dead. I couldn't stop thinking of him. Therefore, I had to play that one off really good because with the both of them around me, they would have been able to read me, figure me out, and place bets on how things would turn out. Yeah, I definitely had to keep a no daydreaming low profile.

"Hey, chick-a-dee. You can't leave me out of the party just because I have kids because I won't let you," Tanya babbled.

As I plopped my moist self on the couch, I stared at the black box in a complete daze. Then, I spoke, "What did you bring to watch? We've already seen every movie in my place so..."

"Shaft!"

"Shaft?" I sat up. Why me, Father? I simply stared at the ceiling hoping to see God's head pop through it at any second and answer me. A sista' was tired, my mind was working overtime tonight, and it really would have liked a temporary shut down and fast. The more I could sleep, the more out of trouble I could get in. However, I couldn't be a party pooper. My day of supreme loneliness would come, and they would have to stay up all night with me, hopefully later than sooner.

In a hurry, I pepped myself up and kept the party going.

"Yeah, Jeena, Shaft," Tanya repeated to my dread.

"Or..." Parri interrupted. She then reached in her purse and yanked out a B movie that we never heard of before. "My Record Box."

"Parri," I asked while pointing into the palm of her hand where the movie rested, "what...is that?" This girl loved some B movies! By B I meant bad, the nowhere seen movies.

"See, it's this good movie," she began, and immediately I interrupted.

"Have you seen it before?"

"No, but..."

"Well, how do you know it's good?" I asked calmly knowing that I was going to set her temper off in a second.

"Just listen! Goodness. You don't always have to *see* a movie to know it's good, Jeena. Stop being so negative acting." Parri then turned her attention to Tanya. "This is exactly how she was acting at Capital City - like she was too good."

Too good? Ha! If she only knew what was really going on with me at CC. She's the one that bought the thumbs down flick to watch on television, and somehow that made me too good to watch the dump movie. See, this was what happens when she was attempting to sell a product on someone. She would put that old weight loss clinic selling technique into action, and this wasn't the weight clinic where she worked. We didn't need a pitch nor good ole psychological tricks that invite the guilt trip in, but hurrah! She was gonna give us either one or both anyway.

She scooted herself up on the couch, all the way to the edge, held her arms way out and held the DVD from the tips of her fingers like she was holding a lose weight, skinny protein bar.

"It really is good," she continued as if she knew why we were giving her the uhm-hmm look. "It's about this record collector who became a killer and started putting pieces of dead bodies in his collection boxes instead of the records."

What the heck? "Huh?" I expressed in a thoroughly disgusted way. It sounded, as we would say back in the day, wack! Yet, it did have a plot.

"It's a horror, girl! Independent film by somebody

unknown, but it doesn't mean that it isn't good and that the film maker won't be extremely famous someday. Remember, fame doesn't always mean you have game! Just a name. Half of the time with that famous name, flop movies come with it. Get a good story telling director with no name, you got yourself a winner and..."

"Just hurry up, stop talking. I'm ready," Tanya said as she sat up straight with eyes bulged out of her head as she tripped Parri up in mid Record Box rundown.

Tanya, by the way, was always ready. She never had any pure fun anymore, so I always felt kinda bad for not making enough time for her. Four children - back to back to back. I truly mean one, two, three and four. Deondre, Navichia, Clinozia, and Pinkitoe - or his real name, Donovan. They chose Pinkitoe as his nickname because he would more than likely be just as short or shorter than his daddy. Tanya was one step away from an oompa-loompa herself. She had to wear six inch heels to reach my shoulders, and my own height stretched to nothing but five feet eight inches.

"Good!" Parri dove off the couch, but I stopped her just in time. She broke my DVD player the last time she placed her hands near it. Not tonight.

"Girl!" I snatched the DVD. "No hands on my electronics. You know better than that crap, Parri."

"Oh yeah, my bad," she smirked. "I still gotta pay you back for that one, don't I?" she reminded herself with her fingernail on the tips of her front two teeth.

Did she have to pay me back? Heck yeah she did! She owed me that and then some. At first, I thought she was just a hater trying to break my junk up for no reason, but it wound up with her just being clumsy. Put it like this, Parri had already broken my door knob, my golden bracelet that I let her borrow on a bum date and my refrigerator handle. How do you break a damn refrigerator handle? I left it up to Parri to explain that craziness but still didn't find out how she did it because no matter what she told me, it made no sense anyway. That was when the hater thought popped up in my mind. The broken up stuff in my humble abode stopped eventually though, thus, saving her reputation with me, but she still can't touch anything but a rug and a chair.

"Oh," I responded while pushing the DVD in the player, "you're gonna pay me alright. I didn't forget. Just let you slide for a while is all."   We put the movie in, and it was lights out.

By the end of the movie, the record collector had cut up his loving wife and mailed pieces of her body all around the world. From a finger to a toe to a rib. She was cross cultural by the time he finished. All the boxes were stamped 'Incoming Bones', and when the postal workers asked was there anything perishable, liquid, fragile or hazardous in the boxes, the record collector would reply none of the above, just dead. Then he would laugh hysterically which would then throw the postal workers off. Finally, when the cops tracked him down, the killer husband managed to find a way to chop his own head off and mail it to the station with a note attached which read - *Now you can see why I did what I did...I lost my head.* The stupidest movie on earth to date.

"Parri, who wrote this movie? You can't mail your own head because how are you gonna tape up the box?" I explained, but she ignored me.

"Ha, ha! That was funny!" She was rolling in laughter, not at what I asked, but at the movie.

"Parri, girl, that was dumb," I smirked while pushing the open button on the DVD player. I watched it slide out.

"Did you see how mad he got at her? She slept around on the wrong man!" Tanya exclaimed.

"More like psycho!"

I went numb. In one glimpse, I saw myself all cut up in that box. That's all it took. I could just see it. Me, myself and I being pulled apart and shoved in boxes on a count of sleeping with someone's man. I sat back, oozing into my couch. Ex-nay on the...

Andre'...Or At Least I Thought.

"Hello? Andre'?" I spoke but got no answer. So much for the ex-nay on the Andre'. I decided to call him at work just to make him aware of the whole fact of us meeting was not a grand idea, and besides that, I wasn't 'bout it - 'bout it. I was too old for that drama, right? Anyway, he had his own office line, so it was safer to call than his cell. It was Sunday. Sunday night. I had to do the right thing on Sunday at least.

Capital City opened at six and closed at ten on Sundays. They didn't serve alcohol on Sundays, but nice jazz sounded all around the place or either a succulent instrumental. Dinners were half off across the board and the menus were cut down size, serving more normal food, and they fed the poor as they walked by. Now, don't get it wrong, half off was still high at this joint. It was a giving establishment, however. To whom much was given, much was required. The owner, I supposed, lived by that motto and also made the exception to be open to feed the poor for the most part on today.

As I sat on the phone, at first, there was that annoying scratchy sound on the other end. I couldn't even hear the person on the opposite end that well either. Then, I just assumed the connection was bad for some unknown reason, so I would wait a bit more until whatever was going on other there settled down. Though I didn't know Andre' like a book, it did sound a little like him in the background speaking somewhere away from the receiver. He had an accent and all, but who didn't in this place. His, of course, was fake. It was all fake and work related.

All of a sudden, I heard more shuffling with the telephone, and when the movement stopped, I straightened up at my kitchen table and listened out for the voice.

"I apologize for the wait. Hello, Capital City."

A male's voice. I was waiting on a name, but one never came, so I spoke again.

"Is this An...well, may I speak with Andre' if he is available?" I stammered over my words, but finally got them to work out in a sentence. I didn't want to sound all stupid, but it seemed like I *was* a tad bit stupid and desperate so far. Why not seal the deal?

"Speaking," he replied.

I held the phone far away from my ear and shook that sucker until I thought the thing would break. Slowly and carefully, I stared into the screen on the cell phone until I forcefully pulled it back to my ear. "Hi. I decided to call you at work."

"Why not on my cell?"

Did he know who I was? Seriously?

I placed my hand behind my neck, fiddling with my hair, and gently rubbed it down to the ends. He dropped the accent. This was stressing me out. He even sounded just as sexy on the telephone, accent or not. I unraveled. Badly. My whole game sunk. It went out the door. Oh Sabbath day, oh Sabbath day!

I continued, "You didn't tell me I had to call your..."

He interrupts, "I didn't say the opposite either. Do me a favor."

I paused. "What?"

"Hit my cell."

Jumping back as if my phone had licked me in my ear, I listened as the phone went silent. This joker hung up on me, so I took the assumed position to call his cell. Fiddling with my cell phone at first, I then dialed. It rang. I hung up.

"Crap, crap, crap!" I yelled, slamming my cell phone on the place mat and shaking my head in my hands. Caller- dog on-ID! On his cell, Jeena? I'd gotten so caught up in *thinking* that I really *did* forget to think! Now, this joker had *my* number. I didn't want him to have my number at all! Slick bastard.

I stared at my cell phone like it had the plague. Please don't let that call had gone through, I prayed to myself, but guess what? My cell rang back. He got my number. I picked it up so my voice mail wouldn't get it, but didn't say a word. Gotta change that voice mail message because it was far too corny, like I'm interviewing for a job.

"Jeena," he called because I still hadn't uttered a word though the phone was plastered against my ear. This time, there was no sound in the background on his end whatsoever. His accent this time slightly southern, you know, dirty sexy. Not a twang, but more a southern slide without the country home on the range sound to it.

Finally, I answered him since he didn't decide to hang up while in waiting. "Yes," I groaned, "My cell..." I tossed my hands up in the air at my loss of words and excuses. "Lost connection or something." I lied. "I got it back now." I let out a deep breath. Whatever. I lost control. Dude got my number.

"Listen, Jeena, I meant to ask you, what made you come in there and mess with me like that?"

I laughed, my guard already down. "I didn't realize what I was getting myself into when I walked in the restroom to see you all ..."

"No, no. I'm not talking about that. I'm talkin' 'bout the last time I saw you."

"In Capital City?" I asked.

"Yeah, there."

On that note, I moved on over to the bedroom, away from the kitchen. I had to get comfortable for this conversation and lie down. Alright, I thought to myself as I skipped to the bedroom, all this is, is chatting. No harm done.

"I didn't know that I *did* anything to you," I responded in a shy yet flirtatious tone as if I was oblivious to the fact that homeboy was hitched. Straighten up, Jeena, I reminded myself with a hit to my leg. "I won't be meeting you, though, Andre'. That's the reason that I called." I had to get it out before my attraction led me down the wrong road. "I don't want you to get the wrong impression of me."

"There is no wrong impression. You were beautiful at

work as it was, and then you walked in Capital City and looked even better, Miss Ray."

The joker just ignored what I said.

"You know my full name? I don't remember telling you that."

After I said this, there was a silence, a dead silence, for like about five seconds, and that's long in talk time! Then, Andre' spoke.

"You told my wife."

Man, what did he say that for? My whole throat collapsed, and there was nothing left to say at that point. I remembered. She came in the room, and I said Jeena Delilah Ray. All of what I said that day suddenly replayed in my mind, and I literally wanted to hang up the telephone. Just slam it shut. Bam! But then curiosity kicked in for just a second because he literally remembered me, full name and all.

"Where is your wife?" I asked.

"She's at home."

"Well," I sang while I got right up from that get ready for a long conversation position on my bed because it was time to reality check and shorten it. "I won't be meeting you as I stated before, and I don't make it a point to do the meat for a dog thing." That should lay him off my cell despite the number he took from that God forbidden caller ID. I hated that crap. Caller ID. That crap has gotten plenty people caught up such as dumb asses like me.

Once again, there was a silence on the phone, but this one was one that I created. I got him, and this situation in the bag. Go ahead and hang up, I thought and waited. He wasn't gonna be gnawing on this neck bone. Ha! The clock on my wall just ticked away as I waited to be called a female dog, ugly, stank and the usual diss names, and then, suddenly...

More Words.

"What makes beautiful women believe that we men want you to come off something other than conversation?"

My heart sank over this extended chat he was giving me. Sure, I could have hung up the phone, but I chose to say more, hoping to put the nail in the coffin on this chatter and light the sucker on fire. Ashes to ashes, dust to dust.

"Every woman is beautiful when a man wants more than conversation. A dog wasn't built to have that much intellect, so I wouldn't expect you to know that much known fact."

"Ohhhh!" he rang out a laugh. "I feel you on that one. I deserved that one, Jee, but I'm not your dog, baby."

Jee? Jee! He already cut my name in half, giving me a little nickname! And baby? Who?

He continued, "I only wanted to show you the real me when I saw you in the restaurant. It wasn't fair how I acted in the hospital or the rehab center. Whatever you wanna call it. I did find out that Nurse Betty died, too. That was messed up. I'm sorry, Jeena. I didn't even know. When you said she was gone, I thought...but I didn't know that you lost a co-worker and I was..."

Alright, Andre', I thought while rolling my eyes at him playing that sympathetic card. "That's okay. I didn't *know* her know her, but yeah, she was good at what she did. They didn't tell most of the patients. Anyway, Andre', I'm sure..."

"Come on down to the place today. We won't be busy. We close up early. I'll stay late. I won't have anything to do since Tina's leaving tonight, and I know nothing will happen because I saw the way you respected her when she came through. I wouldn't do that to you."

There he went again, cutting me off. And where was his wife going?

"Man, Andre', thing is, I don't hook up with married men, and I don't want you to get that impression. If it's just dinner, then that's just it. Dinner."

47

"See you down here, Jeena. Got anything you want to eat? The chefs are gonna be gone, so I want to have it already done. Just wanna chill is all."

I waved my hand in the air and swatted my eyes up with it.

"Whatever tastes good," I replied with the deepest breath left inside me. What was I getting myself into? Just dinner, Jeena. Just food...

<u>And Not Him.</u>

I ended up at Capital City one hour and forty-five minutes after they closed. Andre' was still inside. The only reason I knew that tid bit of information was that there was still one car in the lot in one of the spots labeled management. That had to have been him. I was hoping that he would have left which is why I chose not to call, but then the devilish side of me that I hated wanted him to be there.

As I sat in my small, decrepit Saturn that I'd wrecked two years ago, I looked at myself in the mirror. I'd gotten dressed up. Well, not too dressed up, but too much for a married man that I didn't plan on hooking up with - on purpose. Who was I fooling? I shouldn't have been in the parking lot at all, but I didn't see my foot on the gas and car moving in reverse now did I?

My make-up was flawless. Shoot, it made me look ten times better than ever! It took me thirty minutes to do it versus the five to ten it normally took. I believed that it was more nerves than anything that kept me in the bathroom mirror that long rubbing it on, having to ensure there were no smudges and spots all on my face. Even worse, my neck a totally different shade. For the most part, I didn't wear foundation, but I put on a little tonight along with the powder and eye shadow. Gray eye shadow. I loved midnight eyes at night. That part was habit, not just him.

My heels weren't so high, about three inches, and they strapped up my ankle, tying at the back. There was a sale at the mall, so I had to grab them. It would have been a sin against humanity if I didn't. Tonight was my first time wearing them. They matched perfectly with the outfit that I was about to strut. My outfit showed off my waist and complimented my face. I loved this color on my skin. Pink. The top portion of my outfit stopped at my navel, left a tiny lace gap, and then continued down to the floor. Not hoochie, but extremely figure complimenting.

"What else were you gonna dress like, huh, Jeena?" I spoke aloud to myself in the car, angrily. "This is Capital City. What do you want to look ugly for anyway? There is nothing at all wrong with looking good. Shoot! Get that man excited for what he can't have! Maybe he'll love his wife more." I exited the vehicle after my *feel better about it* pep talk and bumped the car door with my butt to make it shut. It's what I had to do to make the door close completely. A van tore my car up on the side. Surprisingly, I didn't break anything in the accident, just ended up very sore. The wreck was my fault, so I didn't attempt to fix my car in a legit and get a receipt type of way. Instead, I had some mechanic students do what they could to it with what they had. My insurance sky rocketed, and left me broke for a while. At the same time, I was too independent to request help from my family.

By the time I reached the heavy glass door, my gut was bubbly, and my heart felt like it was underneath the heel of my shoe. It was pounding so hard that it started to hurt. What the hell? I stopped cold in my tracks, deciding that I wasn't gonna do it. I hadn't had enough practice being in front of male strippers and keeping my hands off, let alone someone that looked like a super nice ride. While barely being able to see through the tinted glass that made up the windows at Capital City, I attempted to turn around without Andre' noticing that I was there, but then guess who appeared at the door? Ex-nay the Andre'!

"Don't turn around," he stated, and I froze. I must've been desperate for sure because everything about this man was brand new to me! Hell, I felt like an inmate just set free! I was in denial. *We* were in denial because nothing but sex was coming next, and I felt that hell was about to raise any minute. I just stood there, crooked in my stance, frozen solid like an iced over organ incapable of making a sound or performing any function whatsoever.

"Come on in." He had to try and get my attention again because I was dumbfounded at the sight of him...us...about to be locked up in there together. Did I mention alone?

As he held the door open, I shook from my frozen stance and waltzed inside, feeling his eyes follow my hair down to my shoulders, and wherever else his eyes went. My cell phone began to vibrate, shaking up against my ribs and my arm as I held my clutch between the two. Nervously, I panicked for no reason, thus, didn't answer it. Calm down, Jeena. Calm down right now, I preached to my brain.

"What's wrong?"

I didn't notice that I'd stopped dead center of the huge red circular design on the polished marble floor, and Andre' was standing directly behind me waiting on me to move. I was blocking his way.   "I'm sorry. Excuse me. My cell phone," I glanced down at my purse that I was, at that point, squeezing the life from. "It vibrated. Kind of startled me."

That's when he placed his hands around my waist, and moved to the side of me.

"It's just dinner, Jeena."

And he can cut that accent out, too! First it's southern and then it's foreign. Come on now!

"Okay..." I decided to loosen up. "If it's just dinner, you can stop with the succulent accent."

"You like that?" he asked with a light grin as he walked to the table where he had our meal prepared.

"It's alright, but fake," I taunted.

"Fake, huh? My pops is from Barbados and my mom from California, born in Georgia. Can't be too fake. I can switch it on and off. I can sound like this, too," he stated, changing back to the southern.

"I thought it sounded too good." I smiled, attempting not to allow my embarrassment to show through. So much for thinking that he was trying to impress me. He wasn't. It was something he was born with, but what did I even care? Bump his married ass. "So, what do you have for us to eat tonight, Andre'?"

"I had the chefs make us some down home food. You know that good stuff momma used to make."

Maybe his momma because I didn't know how to rate my momma's cooking. Poor momma, she couldn't cook a lick, but we ate it because it was out of love! Her spaghetti tasted like lasagna and her chicken like turkey. It was good though, but you had to look at what you were eating literally or you would think it was something else. I still love myself some of my momma though.

He continued talking while he reached from behind me to uncover my plate. As I sat down in the chair that he so kindly let out for me, I thought to myself, Mrs. wife Tina has herself a gentleman. Then, I checked him out as he came around the table, still talking about the food. I already saw what it was - some collard greens, macaroni and cheese, and not fried, but grilled chicken with a side roll which made for pretty good eating.

Despite the big fact that he wasn't my man, I still caught a nice, elaborate glance at his get up. He was wearing a nice, silk shirt with brown slacks. Once again, just like the other night, his shirt danced on his ripples. I darted my eyes away again with slight hopes that my eyeballs would fall out and roll across the table to see Andre's reaction to them rolling. Bet this dinner would be over then, I thought. *Eye* better get my cheatin' ass back to my wife would be more like it.

"The only things I didn't get are the drinks. What would you like?" he asked me while he rubbed his hands together like he was the one who cooked the meal.

"What sounds good?"

"How about some...do you want some..." he contemplated.

Not alcohol. Anything but alcohol!

"Water!" I blurted out after thinking about it for those three seconds he was fumbling over his words. Afterward, he stared at me strangely, but I cared less. The last thing I needed to gulp down was some alcohol. Water purges your system, and that's what I needed, something that would purge me. Make me clean. Make me whole. Make me sane!

"Be back." He marched off.

As I sat there, stiff as an ironing board, I watched through the windows as people walked by. There I was. Then, I began to second guess the windows. Could they see me if they got close enough? I could see them. I mean, I went to eat at Capital City many times, and I never was able to see inside, but tonight, I was paranoid to the extreme. I was meeting a married man for dinner in his freaking restaurant, and there wasn't a curtain hanging that could hide me!

I gazed back at the restaurant's entrance. Jeena, it would be so easy if you just got yourself up from here and left, I thought to myself. Do you even know if you can handle this? Before I could finish planning my next move, Andre' was walking back with the drinks. My throat was numb.

"Thank you," I paused, "Andre'." Uh oh, I choked. I didn't know why I choked up and paused, but I did, and he noticed. I knew he noticed based off of the slight and nearly invisible grin he tried to hide.

As I tried to take my glass of water from his hand, my fingers stroked his, and he held onto the glass.

"It's alright. Like I said before, just dinner."

I took a deep breath and breathed out slowly and inconspicuously through my nose. I didn't want him to notice more than what he already had about my hesitations. Hesitations were the thing that let the other party know that they were in control, so I damn sure couldn't be the hesitator tonight. I had to get myself together and fast.

"This looks nice, Andre'. Very nice. So, how long have you been working here? I never saw you before, and I come here often enough to recall faces." Especially a face that looked like his, have mercy.

"I moved. Me and Tina. I transferred from the only other Capital City there is, but I've been living here for a good while now. Working with Capital City for about two years." He sat down.

"Where's that? I mean, the only other Capital City?"

"Chicago."

"Chicago?"

"Yeah, got sick of the snow and cold. Needed to get down here to Miami where it's hot."

"Chicago." I didn't know what else to say. My dumb behind sounded like a broken record on a dusty record player. Finally, I just shut up.

"Are you from here?" he asked.

"Yes...kind of. Orlando," I responded dryly while taking a sip of my water. "I grew up there since I was one year old, but born elsewhere, in Jacksonville."

I finally lifted my fork and began to eat. My first stop was the collard greens. That was my thing. I loved them probably since my momma's womb, and I'll probably be buried with 'em when I die. Even though I liked mine hot and spicy, these mild ones would do.

"Where exactly were you born?" I asked.

He began to eat on his macaroni. ""I was born in South Carolina. Columbia."

"Why did you leave?"

"Momma was visiting family when she gave birth. After she finished with pushing me out, I guess we left. Haven't been back since."

"Funny."

"True."

"Is your wife from Miami?" Just thought I would toss that wife question on over in there next to his chicken. Make him choke on a bone.

"No, near Chicago. It's a city about an hour away from there, but," he paused while staring me down. "Why are we talking about other people?"

Man, what the hell? Don't do that dumb stare B.S. I quit chewing because Andre' started staring in my mouth. It felt funny. Somebody staring at you while you eat that you barely know, yet dig. Was this how he felt when I was gawking at him in the tub? Immediately, there I was having a blanket of paranoia engulf me, so I freaked out. Grabbing my napkin, I wiped my lips to make sure there was nothing on them, and ran my tongue over the fronts of my teeth to be sure nothing was sticking there. He kept staring, so I finally asked.

"Why are you looking at me, Andre'? And we aren't talking about other people. We're talking about your wife."

"You have a beautiful face."

Oh hell no. Make-up, baby, just make-up. Got acne all on this forehead here, honey. Don't try that slick shit.

"Not like the face your wife has." That's right, Jeena, keep bringing up the wife, I told myself in order to get out of this situation with feet flat on the floor and legs closed.

"She's beautiful as well," he started again, beginning to take a bite of the chicken he handled in his hand. "Are you as beautiful as she is inside and out?"

What type of insanity was that? Was he now comparing me to his wife? I didn't know his wife! She should have been kicking my you know what up and down this side of the earth about now, but hallelujah she wasn't.

"What do you mean? I don't even know your wife." Gulp went the water down my throat. I wasn't going to get on his wife in a bad way. Not me. No way. And I wasn't gonna play into this fake man made competition that he wanted me to fall into. Andre' was slick but not that slick. He would have to wake up early in the morning to shade my eyes.

"I mean, do you have a sense of self?" he asked, and nonchalantly at that!

"Say what? Are you taking a stab at insulting me?"

"I'm never going to insult you. That's not my plan, Jeena. My plan is learning a little more about the person sharing a dinner with me tonight. That's all."

"Andre', I have plenty sense of self. How about you?"

"Yeah," he responded, wiping his mouth with the golden colored napkin, then tossing it down on the table. As he leaned back, his shirt melted into his chest, and my vagina grew a heartbeat for one quick second. I squeezed it tight though, and shut it down. Suffocated. "I know myself really well, Jeena, and I'm not about denying myself what I want. I also know that you don't want to eat this food because you've barely touched it, besides the collard greens. Tell me what you want. Tell me why you really came to see me."

Like hell I will, I thought. My sense of self will keep my mouth shut because as much as I wanted him right now, I just couldn't handle this situation. He began to stare the clothes off my back, and my vagina resurrected. That was it.

"I'm gone." I got up from the table, grabbed some mints, popped them in my mouth and headed for the door. Fast. I figured, hey, these mints will hold me as hungry as I was. Keep my sugar up so I won't pass out from all this stress.

On my way to the exiting destination called the damn door, I heard the sound of Andre's footsteps behind me. It was all I could do to keep that man out of my mind! Everything that I imagined from the images I retrieved from my memory of him slam dunk ass naked began to quickly feel like real life. I even began to see myself on top of him in that darn tub with my own clothes off, us both dripping wet! My hormones just wouldn't stop. The more I tried to stop them, the less I wanted to. It was becoming too much, and that door was one million miles away.

People on the street were walking back and forth, some waiting on cabs, some across the street at the hotels, and others just enjoying the night. I saw all of this as I peered through the glass windows and reached for the handle on the door. Suddenly, his hand landed firmly on top of mine. The more I pulled, the more he held. Terror began to rip through my skin, and my heart began to flutter at the same time. The damn door wasn't going to come open. I wanted to choose right, but he chose for me, and I let him.

Andre's arm...his hand...his fingertips gently glided across my belly button, and my stomach tightened. He wasn't even tugging on me to keep me with him, but it still felt as if he was. I'd never been held in place before with a touch as soft and simple as that, but there I was, stuck in my stance. I slowly began to breathe again, his hand still barely around my waist but enough for me to feel the heat from his palm. I didn't turn around. The hand that he had placed on my hand while I held the knob to the door, he slid off slowly, bringing my hand away from the knob with his. Then, I felt as he caressed his whole body closer to mine and whispered in my ear.

"Don't go, Jeena."

His voice almost made my ear lobe jitter, and that mug was never supposed to move! Just the tone of Andre's voice made me want to comfort him, shoot, and myself, too, for that matter! All this stress! Isn't it healthier to release and roll with it?

"Jeena," he stated softly to me again. His breath on my neck made my toes curl and a freaking chill drip down my spine. I almost jerked. "Jeena," he repeated once more, and then, he grazed his lips across my shoulder near my dress' strap. It fell off of my shoulder. As I reached to push it back up, his lips kiss my fingertips all the way down to my wrist and moving up my arm.

"Will you stay?" he asked quietly, leaning his head down as I turned to face him. He was trying to look into my eyes. He was taller than me, so he had to lean over a bit.

Even though the fact was that I heard his question, I wasn't going to answer. I knew what he wanted, and I also knew what I wanted. We matched. Like bees to flowers, I felt I needed to feed off of him. Like everything I needed, he was my source. He read my mind, so without my answer to his question, he continued to lean over, attempting to kiss my lips. I looked to my left, through the window. People everywhere.

"Don't worry about them. They can't see us."

"Andre'," I spoke, but then he interrupted with my name.

"Jeena."

That was it. His lips met mine, and my eyes went shut. Our first kiss. My first kiss...

To A Married Man...

And I couldn't stop. I needed to stop, but his body told me keep going. My body was already his. For just one night, I desired that he be mine. It would be over after tonight, I thought. Just tonight. I could change my number tomorrow, and make like a ghost and disappear. He would never find me in a casual setting again.

As I raised his shirt off of his body, it landed on the floor and my hands landed on his bare skin. He unstrapped me from my dress, and it fell next to his shirt. There I was - single and sexy in my bra, string and heels. Sure, I was guilty having planned for this *just in case his eyes saw me* moment, but oh well. Momma always said wear your best underwear just in case of emergencies. This was an emergency.

My fingers slid up his made for Friday night and Saturday morning chest from his stomach, and I swear I almost began salivating and foaming from the mouth like a dag on rabid puppy. His hands never reached my butt, but they cradled me at the waist right above my curve. Just feeling his hands against me and the scent of his body made me want to climax. He smelled so good.

Our favorite table in Capital City became the one in the very center. He raised me up atop my resting place, and that's where I...or we ... made love. And the food...what food? He filled my appetite. I couldn't blame him for any of what happened because I knew what was inside of me. I wanted him just as much. I couldn't help it. I just couldn't shake it, and that's why I made love to him in Capital City, enjoying every moment.

"Father!"

The altar was empty. It was just me on the floor in front of the pulpit. Tears streamed down my face, and the more I cried, the more folks murmured, *"What did she say? She don't have to tell all of that out loud, now does she? She done turned into a ...I can't even say the word! Used to be a good chile...uhm uhm uhm. Done backslid all the way on this one here! I know her mom and sister, yes I do, but was this one here ever saved? Well!"*

"Oh, Lord, please forgive me, Jesus! I slept with him, and I didn't even try hard enough not to do it, Jesus. Please, Lord, what do I have to do?" The more I kept trying to get further up the pulpit, the harder it was for me to move.

"Child, child, get up now," Some lady came up to me pleading, but I knocked her over. She hit the floor so hard that ropes fell from the roof of the church, gripped and carried her away. I continued to scream and yell all my sins, telling everybody, not just God.

"Lord, I even met his wife, Jesus! I don't want to go to the hottest part of hell! I wanna be saved right now, Jesus! Jesus!" I was screaming so loud that my throat lost all sound. Everyone around me had their hands covering their ears, but it was only I who couldn't hear myself screaming anymore.

That's when I began to scratch at the carpet. I knew that only the preachers were supposed to be on the pulpit, but while the deacons were pulling my legs toward the pews, I was pulling with all the might in my arms to reach the top of that pulpit so that I could drown in the baptismal pool, all the while carving claw marks into the floor. Then, a gust of wind blew that opened the doors of the church, and while we were yanking and pulling, the red dress that I had on flew up over my head and exposed all my

58

stuff to the whole congregation. That's when the deacons dropped my legs to the floor, turned and shut their eyes. Then, I made a break for it.

"Father!"

I dove into the pool, but couldn't swim, thus, started to drown! In the background, I heard a roar of applause, and hallelujahs rang out until I heard what sounded like glass of the windows shattering.

"Girl, wake up!" It was my sister. My sister was pulling me up from the bottom of the pool. She was literally breathing under the water, and it wasn't affecting her. Her face was full of wrinkles and her hair was matted together. The more she spoke and tried to lift me out to catch my breath, the more I sank.

"Father," I woke up chanting in my bed. It was a dream.

"I'm your sister, nut, not your father! Wake up!"

I grabbed my face and jumped up out of bed. She wet me up! I couldn't believe her, pouring water on my face.

"Faith! Faith, what did you wet me up for?" I started pulling at my hair. "Look at what you did. Can't you see I'm black! Man, Faith, you can't go wetting my hair like that. I was drowning! You almost killed me!" I yelled frantically with my breath dragging through the air. Whew, it stank. It was time to brush both my hair and my teeth.

"Get up, Jeena. You're crying in your sleep, and it wasn't me trying to kill you. That's for sure. In here sounding like a girl who lost her daddy or something," she said, tilting her eyes above her glasses while she cut those same eyes sharply at me. "Father! Father! Yeah, don't look at me like that because that's how you sounded."

"What do you want, Faith?" I was too tired for nonsense today.

Faith. My sister. She was my younger sister at that. I could never be too mean to her, but then again, at times like these, I really wanted to knock her in the nose. Faith was only three years younger than me but a century older in other ways than physical. Bad thing was that she was nosey as a mug! If you didn't keep her out of your business, like a undercover cop in a drug ring, she would blow up your spot. No lie.

Other than that, my sister was gorgeous. Outside of those reading glasses that she loved to have hanging off of her nose, you could tell she was a part of the family line. Wasn't an ugly soul in our family. Not to brag, but it was true. Faith didn't date much, but then again, no man could date her. She knew men too well as far as what she thought they wanted, and to seal the deal, she was absolutely in love with Jesus. Because of her love for God, she just didn't have time nor did she want time for a relationship since her last boyfriend back in eleventh grade! Faith had that never put the Bible down love for the Lord, and it showed, damn near seeped from her skin.

See, most folk, when they think of wisdom and spiritually gifted people, they think of people in long dresses and no make-up with bucked teeth and a shiny hat. Not Faith. She was regular dressing, regular talking, and maybe a little bit doofy when she went out of the house in public. It didn't matter at all how she looked, however, because I must admit, she had a couple gifts, and they all had to come from God because she just knows stuff! Just stuff! Stuff for no reason stuff, and it was always right!

As for me, well, I got stuck with nothing but a wack brain and some study guides that, without those, I didn't even understand the Word of God. I never understood why I just didn't get it. Easier commands like don't do this and that, sure, I got it. When it came down to the deeper stuff, like parables and prophecies, I'd just as soon fall asleep because it took my brain just that much work to comprehend what Faith could write a full essay about!

"What are you *really* in here hollering about, Jee?" she asked suspiciously. "Seems like..."

Shut-up, Faith. I tuned her out, flopped back on the dry side of my bed and flung the covers back over my head. Blah, blah, blah was all I heard, and Faith's voice in my room didn't take precedence over the blah. As I thought back to my dream, I was butt naked in church when my dress flew up. Cold butt naked.

No panties naked. Glad it was just a dream. Where did the ropes come from? And was that Sister Grate that I pushed down?

"Ouch!" I yelled, after getting pinched on my thigh from nosey nosed Faith.

"Don't ignore me, Jee."

"I wasn't hollering about anything! I was having a bad dream."

"Father! Father! Father! And kicking your legs around like somebody was attacking you."

Quite the opposite. If she only knew that it was the deacons yanking on me from behind while my butt cheeks were giving a show. I closed my eyes and yawned, but in the middle of my yawn, my insides yanked me up from up underneath my sheets to a sitting position on my bed.

Oh crap. I nervously thought, what if I blurted out more than what I should have while she was listening? What if I said something about my malformed mischief in Capital City last Sunday? What if my dumb ass unconscious told the truth about my consciousness?

"What else was I saying?" I asked curiously and more frightened than I'd been before Faith hit me with that water upside my sleeping head. I hoped that I didn't say Andre'. As a matter of fact, I prayed I didn't say Andre'. The last thing I needed was Faith snooping in my business over some guy I just met and slept with across the tabletop.

She turned to walk into my bathroom while responding to my question. "Oh, you didn't say much, nothing more than calling on God. I mean, that's the only one you or I ever called Father. We never in our lives called daddy father unless we were acting silly, so..."

"You sure?"

She peeked around the bathroom wall. "Why?" Then she cracked a smile, the kind of grin that made me want to slap her. "You think you said something that I wasn't supposed to hear, huh, sis?"

"I don't *think* I said anything." I laid back down attempting to dismiss all anxiety from my appearance on the non wet side of my pillow. "I just wanted to know. You know, how you can forget some of the stuff you dream about."

She knew something was up. I had to shut up and right then or I would unconsciously let the cat out of the bag. Faith was crafty. She smelled plots and solved mysteries as if she was a detective on a spy reality show.

Letting out a sigh Faith then stated slowly, slyly, sarcastically and in a not so quiet whisper, "It's funny how we always forget dreams but never nightmares. Seems like we would remember the good stuff in a good way and not the bad stuff in an unforgettable way. So which one, a forgettable dream or a memorable nightmare. Jeena, or both?" Then she smiled from ear to ear.

I swear I just saw the devil's musty, hot ass just enter into her body. If I would have responded to that, I would have allowed anyone to nickname me dumb and crazy, so I didn't fall into that trap. Faith was trying to pry by opening up conversation, but she wasn't about to get me to discuss anything else about it. Instead, I got up off of my bed, dropped into my house shoes and went to cook and clean...

Up My Life.

I polished to a spit shine the glass dining room table, the coffee table and the sofa table. The whole time I was polishing, I saw me and Andre', and I imagined us disappearing along with the dust I was cleaning up. What continued to help remind me of our little escapade was the statue I had of two brazen bodies intertwined in the art of love making that was sitting on the coffee table. That was exactly why I walked over to that thing and tossed in the garbage. Every time I looked up, there it was. It was like a hard pimple. No matter what I did, it was there reminding me of the dirtiest spot in my life when I looked in the mirror.

Shoot, I was burning my grits! I shot over to my stove and yanked them off of the burner. Dag on! Finally, Faith came out. She'd been back in my bedroom picking out one of my pocketbooks that she adored. See, I rocked the best pocketbooks - on sale pocketbooks - and Faith wouldn't even pay for that with the sale price, thus she borrowed mine. I should have never in my life gave that girl the key to my condo.

"Aren't you going to church?"

"No." I said that, but it was a lie. I was going to go but it actually felt like I just went. Dream Church Nightmare starring Jeena Delilah 'The Home Wrecker' Ray. It had been a week, one full week from Capital City Sunday to this Sunday, and no, I wasn't over the center table sex. Not even close. Church was my only option. I had to go. My soul needed it. Thus, I rushed into an outfit, got my hair together and left right behind Faith to get some Word in me.

On the end of the pew I sat. Everyone looked nice in their reds and yellows. All the colors of the rainbow showed up for church this morning except for me. I was wearing black. Jet black. Nightmare black. Shadow black. Hell fire and ash black. If I farted, there would be smoke kind of black. The whole congregation walked by as I sat there on the back row looking like the dead. I swore I stunk like a three day old rotting body. Thank God it wasn't resurrection Sunday. Somebody should have brought me an urn to dump me over inside of it.

I'd been sitting in this same spot since ten thirty, and it had already turned eleven o'clock. So there I was, glued to the back pew, but not Faith. Noooo! She waltzed all the way up to the front of the church with her Bible in one hand and a pen in the other along with *my* purse. As I stared around at the flock, many people had Bible covers. Not Faith. She believed that the Good Book shouldn't be covered. It was a better witness that way.

Wide open so the world could see where the good news came from. I bought her one once, a Bible cover, and she used it for a make-up bag. One eyeliner pencil in the whole Bible case, along with blush and lip gloss, and I just knew I saw her one Sunday taking notes and starring scriptures with that black eyeliner. I guessed a pencil was a pencil.

Even though my jet black attire, to me, represented death, the sermon wasn't burying me when it started. It was good, representing life. I felt relieved at the sermon because it was so nice, easy and loving, letting me know the goodness of God and His mercy. I felt horrible about my decision last Sunday, and I would be Satan's hunch back if I didn't feel any type of guilt. The problem was that another part of me, the evil side that liked Andre', was still feeling for him more than what should have been allowed. I was in need of a healing because this guilt wasn't blasting away the memories of how good Andre' felt. I should have run up the aisle like in my dream, tearing at the altar, but didn't.

That was when it happened. I began to notice them. They were holding hands, talking to their little ones, and praying together. I noticed the couples, the married ones. They were everywhere, and then there was me, the humping harlot. I had no one.

Slowly, my attention to the nice sermon went to a somber slump because I managed to make myself feel like Lucifer. I sunk - sunk all the way down in my seat desiring to evaporate.

"Praise the Lord! Praise the Lord, everyone, for He is worthy to be praised! He woke you up this morning, even when you didn't have to see the sun shine. God is truly a good God!" the pastor shouted into the microphone to the Amens of the crowd.

All the happiness made me feel light headed. God did wake me up this morning, and He had been good to me, in spite of my own actions. That made me feel even worse. I felt like crying, but I couldn't do it because I thought of all the times the pastor would say how people cried of joy and praise, but all my tears were of guilt and feeling something that I shouldn't feel for a married man. Did Andre' even have children? Did I break up a happy home?

That's when I left. I got right up and left church. I just couldn't sit inside the walls of the house of God and know that inside of me there was something there that I didn't want there anymore, yet still enjoying the feeling at the same time. As I left, my eyes caught the top of the doorway: Thou shalt love the LORD your God...and not someone else's husband. I hustled to my car. The latter portion of that doorway signage was my imagination, but that's truly how I saw it at that time.

Driving down the street, I passed every car I could while making my moves in the furthest left lane. I wasn't looking for a police officer, and I certainly didn't care if one was looking for me. All I was concerned about was getting away from my mind, but I couldn't run away from it. Recalling last Sunday at Capital City with Andre' and the things I heard at church became like a rehearsed speech in my head. I was confused. Mom taught me a long time ago about a double minded man being unstable in all his ways. She got it from the Bible, and it was one of those sayings that she used to repeat that I couldn't find if I cracked the Bible one thousand times. Last Sunday was the beginning of that double minded lesson for myself as I'd just figured out what it meant truly. I was double minded, thus unstable and thirsting for a husband who was not mine. I didn't want Andre' but then again, I couldn't resist the thought of him.

I stopped at the light when I exited the freeway on my way to Bayside where Parri worked, but when I passed by her job, nothing. There was no sight of her car anywhere on the road where it normally was, but the shop was open. I parked anyway and got out.

As I jogged past the tattoo kiosk wearing no shoes, I peered inside the new and improved weight buster store to find no trace of Parri despite my desperation for discussion about what exactly happened to me. Truth was, all morning, I wanted to call him. Shoot as a matter of fact, all week I just wanted to talk to him. I didn't shake it off the way that I thought I could. It felt like he was *my* man last week, and it spilled over into all my todays. I couldn't have been falling in love with a married man because those feelings that I had weren't supposed to last that long. It just wasn't supposed to go like this. One night stands were just that, stand and stay away.

I ran back to my car, got in, and sped like a wild maniac to Parri's house. Calling her from my cell was an option to find out where she was, but I was too afraid to turn it on today. I felt like a huge cloud was about to form, and I was at the...

End Of My Life Line.

"What's wrong with you, Jeena?"

I dropped my keys on her table after I busted through her door nearly in tears but trying hard not to let it show. She met me at her front door because I was beeping my horn like a mad crack head in her yard.

"Nothing. How you doing?" Yeah, I lied. Everything was wrong with me.

"I'm trying to be cool until you walked in," Parri responded a bit confused looking, "with your eyes all swollen. Hopefully, you have an allergy or something and not sick, girl, because you know it's around that season. People coming in my job sneezing and blowing and stuff." She shut the door and then plopped down on her floor in front of a bowl of soup. "I don't feel good too myself, but anyway... "

"I think so. It's probably just allergies." Yeah, I had an allergy alright. Andre'. And it was getting worse by the hour. I squeezed my cell phone in the palm of my hand wishing it would break, but this was the only line I had for my civilized survival.

I needed to vent and get this deed off of my chest, but I

didn't know how. I just kept staring a Parri while she sucked up her soup in her own peaceful, delight of a life while I contemplated the big reveal. After my table top rendezvous with Andre', my feelings for him got so deep because he...it...felt so good! Just being with him, a man like him, was too much to just forget. The worst thing was that Andre' hadn't called my phone once since our encounter, and it pained me not to call him. That would have made me weak, and I certainly didn't want to come off like weak and in a little more than lust for the man.

Andre', he didn't say much after we had sex. He only kissed me, and dumb, head-over-heals me kissed him right back and with so much passion that we almost did it again! Then, he watched me from the door as I walked myself back to the car in the middle of the night. Before I left though, he made me feel like it wasn't a one night thing, though he never said it. It was the way he held me close before I left and whispered to me how beautiful I smelled and looked while he laced me back into my dress. I knew deep inside that it wasn't over, that he really wanted to know me better. Because of that, I felt I couldn't reject it. I wanted to know him, too, but I just didn't know how to get to that point the right way, if there was such a thing as the right way after doing it the wrong way.

With my head down, I spoke. "I slept with someone last weekend, Parri." That, more than likely, wasn't the best way to enter your homegirl's house on a Sunday afternoon when she was trying to get her eat on. "Parri?" I asked, but got no response. What the hell? Dammit! She was choking! I jumped down from my chair and slammed her in the back. Shit! I busted her back again as hard as I could with the palm of my hand, but nothing happened except her arms flaring around.

"Parri! Cough, girl, cough out loud!" Nothing came out. Lord, Jesus, I didn't mean to half kill her! "Parri!" I called while grabbing her around her stomach about to thrust it, but then, a noise comes and that means air. I fell back in relief while Parri started to catch all her lost breath.

"Oh, Lord Jesus, I almost died!" she said, scrambling her

words together while soup poured from her lips.

Jumping back in front of her, I grabbed her by the throat. "Are you okay?"

She yanked back. "Jeena, don't grab my damn throat!"

"Oh, I'm sorry, Parri!" I responded, grabbing the hair up in a ball atop my head with my hands, completely stressed out. "I didn't mean it, girl, dog, just trying..." I stammered, but then she cut me off midway.

"To kill me!" she yelled as she got up from the floor and scooted on the couch. "Father, forgive me for every last one of my sins. Whew, I coulda' died...should have gone to church this morning, been praying and praising," Parri continued, fanning herself. Then, when she completely caught her breath and terminated the could have would have chants about death and the afterlife, she just sat there and stared at me blankly. At first I thought she was in shock about what I told her about me and Andre', but then I realized that I was in the middle of her shag rug on her hardwood floor with my knee stuck in her soup. I didn't realize it until I felt a warmth crawling up my thigh.

"Dang it!" As I lifted my knee, drip, drip, drip was all I heard hitting the bowl.

"You had sex?"

Okay, maybe it wasn't the soup that had her staring in disbelief. Parri made my sexual encounter sound like the plague! I mean you should have heard her. *You had se-ex*? Like it had two syllables or something. Se-ex instead of sex. She just dragged the word all out into an annoyance. To make matters even worse, she continued.

"You slept with who?" she asked in disbelief.

I stood up and ran into her kitchen to get a dish towel to start cleaning my black, souped-up suit. Yeah, I heard her question, but ignored it.

"Jeena!" she blasted from her non-choking vocal chords.

Immediately, I stopped wiping and peeled my eyes upward.

"Huh?" I answered. Why was the first question the who

factor? Why not ask something like how was it or where?

"Who, Jeena, dang, stop stalling?" she repeated.

She wasn't moving, but only sat there with a you better tell me look on her face. I mean, you would have thought that the noodles getting caught in her throat would have spiraled her into an I don't care about your sex life type of mood, but it failed to do so. As she sat and I stood over in the kitchen with the dish towel, the clock next to the television made a click noise. How did I hear the clock so well? It was just that quiet up in that mug! I placed the damp towel on the oven handle and walked back over to the couch right beside her, knowing I needed to change the subject. As of right then, regret for saying a word about my liaison crept in, but I had to move forward with the story because there was no turning back.

"I couldn't stay in church this morning, Parri," I stated hoping that she would know just how bad I felt about it before I got in too deep with my story. Unfortunately, Parri didn't flinch, so I figured that I might as well just splt It out. "It was a man I just met, Parri. Hadn't known him but for that long," I stated with a snap of my fingers representing just how little I knew about the man. I felt the tears coming, and I glanced down at my cell phone which was from whence some of my troubles started.

"What happened, Jeena?" Parri stared to get more concerned than what I thought she was originally after seeing me tear up. "Girl, you don't look okay." She leaned over to comfort me, but the only thing was, how could she? It was my body, my emotions, and they were just too powerful to comfort.

"Nothing happened that I didn't let happen, Parri. It's just..." I paused. I couldn't tell her the whole entire scoop, so I said something else, veering more toward her being more on my side about the situation. If I told Parri the truth and nothing but the whole truth, she would slug me because she didn't get down like that. Parri left married men alone. Therefore, I played halfway innocent. "I'm scared."

"Jeena, was it a mistake or something?" she asked. "What is it? It seems like there is more to it because you're so damn hurt. Who was it? Do I know him? How long did you really know this guy? He gave you a disease or something, girl?"

I pulled back from Parri's hand that had started to pet me up on my back. "No, no you don't know him at all." Lie! Lie! Lie! I pictured myself banging my head up against a stone. "His name is Andre'. I met him a couple of weeks ago, and he seems...seemed so nice when we met, and he was interested in me and...no disease. We used a condom."

Before I could even finish spilling my heartbroken guts, Parri hopped up out of the couch trying to get crunk, for lack of better words, which was synonymous to the way that she looked. I mean, she was bobbing and weaving like she was getting ready to throw down.

"Oh, what? He dissed you or something after getting in between your legs? Oh we can handle that, now can't we? I don't know who the hell he thinks he is, but homey got the wrong one, baby, because ..."

"Noooo!" I held my head in the palms of my hands like I was getting ready to go crazy. He's married, Parri. He's married! I wanted to scream it at the top of my lungs, but I was only emotionally challenged, not crazy. "I just don't know if I can handle it if he doesn't call me. I feel..." Okay, here went the big one. "Used." I didn't feel used. I felt like a waste bucket.

"Is that why you are gripping your cell, girl? He'll call." She lifted my head and pushed my chin up. "Whether it was good or bad, he will call." Then, she put a grin on her face which was normal when she was trying to cheer someone up. "Because the one thing a man will call for is sex. Call you four, five times an hour! Then, you'll find out where his head is at and tell his ass off for not calling you sooner. If it was a one night stand, Jeena, maybe you should call him if you think you want to get to know him more. Gotta watch that just meet and then sleep with me garbage, Jeena. For now, give me the cell phone and stop crying before I have to find him and beat his..."

70

Ass.

Yep. I was a complete donkey butt. I told her everything. Well, almost everything. I was in love and couldn't admit it, with a total stranger. Parri calmed me down that day as usual and sent me on home to call Andre' myself, and not necessarily wait for him to call me. Luckily, she didn't know who on earth he was nor that he was the same exact man that slobbed her hand down at dinner in Capital City. As a matter of fact, she made me feel so good about calling him and him calling me, I left her place in a great mood, even in my soiled suit. When I got in my car, however, I remembered everything that I'd left out about me and Andre' which made her advice a bit slanted and in my favor.

To Parri, because of all my twisting of the story, she advised me that it could end up a healthy relationship that got off on a speedy start which was a mistake, and that mistake was the reason behind my fear and insanity, causing me to run out of church. She just didn't know how wrong she was.

It had been three weeks since I spoke to Parri at her house about me and Andre'. She was out of town and wouldn't be back for a good strong minute. That left me with Tanya and Faith. No good. They wouldn't understand. Good thing was, for all three weeks, Parri was right, Andre' called. We laughed, joked, whispered, and made love on the telephone even. At a certain time of the night, we got off of the telephone, and I would always dream about him. Me... being in his wife's place. How it was more than just a fling because he told me that he cared deeply for me, even that he loved me. We had more sex, too, and my goodness did we have sex a lot! We met after work, and our bodies meeting was like a full fledged meal. Where his wife was, I didn't know, but at one point, I was happy to take her place. It was obvious I had fallen for him and was content with just being all fantasy because he had fallen for me, too.

I began to look at myself differently in the mirror, too, and that look was nowhere near as I did about a month ago. With someone else's man looking at me, I had to look damn good! My shit was together to get that kind of attention from Andre's fine ass. I must be much better than his wife in the bed, too. Gotta be. Andre' was an excellent ego booster. All my morals went out the window, and I became his mistress. He told me that he needed someone like me in his life, but as far as his wife, he didn't discuss her much at all which led me to believe that she was the last person on his mind. That made me the first person he thought about. Their marriage was virtually over. If it wasn't, then why was he with me? I was feeling better and better about us with every minute that floated by, convincing myself that it was going to be the right thing eventually.

"And who is this? Who?"

What? Who the hell was in my place answering my phone, I thought to myself as I leaped from the shower and ran out of my bathroom butt naked, cold and dripping wet. It was Faith - in my bedroom and answering my cell phone! Oh hell no!

"Faith!" I stood there shivering and naked to the bare skin. There she stood, too, in front of me, smiling from ear to ear fully clothed and amused. I'd put up with too much little sister drama in my life, and I probably needed to cut her from my blood line for like a good month.

"It's Dre'." She leaned over and pressed mute. "Do you want me to tell him that you're busy standing up in front of your sister butt naked over his telephone call, or do you want me to tell him that you're busy and you'll call back?"

I couldn't answer. If I grabbed for the telephone, she would know beyond a shadow of a doubt that I was into him, he was my man, and would definitely want to meet him. If I acted as if I was only stunned I heard someone talking in my bedroom, well, that would be more natural.

"Don't scare me like that. I'll call him back." Then I started frontin'. "Got me jumping out of the tub soaking wet

72

'cause you didn't think to announce yourself up in here. And you can leave the key on the counter," I argued. "That's so you can't come barging in here like that anymore."

Unmute. She started talking on my cell once again, and I got back in the shower praying that she didn't continue to talk endlessly. Didn't really know who I was praying to either because God, more than likely, wasn't listening, and if He was, He was probably shaking His head like *don't come asking Me for anything until you do what I ask. I don't play that!* At least Andre' didn't give his full name to Faith on the phone. Smart.

I must have stayed in the bathroom for about one hour after busting out of there naked and still didn't hear the front door slam which would have alerted me to Faith leaving. The point was to force her exit by my absence, but clearly, Faith was too comfortable and nosey. I was able to get dressed in my bathroom because my closet is on the other side of my bathroom with ironing board and all. By the next hour, my hair and nails were touched, body clean, and clothes on with creases in the pants, so I stepped out. There Faith was to no surprise. She was sitting on my bed reading a magazine, and flipped backwards facing me was an article that read, *Ten Reasons Why Married Men Cheat, But Won't Divorce.* I froze.

"Whatcha reading?" I asked, lackadaisically. Dammit, if she doesn't flip the page I am gonna break damn her neck, I thought.

"This recipe about how to bake a carrot cake."

"Does it look good?" Breathe, Jeena, dammit.

"He said to call him before seven tonight."

"Cool."

"You didn't tell me you had a boyfriend."

I went to stuff my pajamas in the drawer. Think, Jeena, think.

"Now, why would you say that he is my boyfriend? Just because a guy called me?" I responded cockily.

"No, because he said to call him *before seven tonight.*"

"So!" I went to rolling my eyes. What on earth? I tried to

think of every possible thing that could have been revealed in that statement *call before seven tonight*, but I couldn't think of anything.

"So just call him then...before seven," she responded ultra calmly with a slight hum to her cracky voice. "I just stopped by to bring back your purse and see how you're doing. Hadn't seen you since that Sunday. You remember? Was everything alright on that Sunday long ago when you left? You know you haven't called a sister or anything for a couple of weeks."

"I thought I told you that I had the runs that day." Yeah, I blamed that run out of church thing on diarrhea.

"No, you didn't tell me anything, but crap happens, huh, sis? For weeks? You should be dehydrated," she hinted at me, crossing her legs at the same time and swinging those God forsaken toes. Corns on every last toe and always got 'em hanging out. Proud of 'em, too.

I didn't answer. Yeah, for weeks. Diarrhea like a mug. That was my alibi.

"I'm leaving something on the bed. It's a good article." Then, she walked out. "And I will leave your stank key, too," she stated raising her eyebrows and winking as well. "Love you, sis." That's when I knew that she knew something...something horrid... and just wasn't going to say.

As soon as that front door shut, I flew on top of my bed to get my hands on that article she so happened to leave wide ass open. The magazine was left on the article I dreaded. The one about the married man and his freaking infidelities. I wanted to throw up. I lifted it off of my bed and tossed it in the garbage. Who cared? Men have different reasons, and Andre' seemed different. My problem was, what did she know?

She knew something. Her smart ass. Faith was too smart for her own good. I then stared back at the waste basket that sat in the corner by my bathroom. The tip of the magazine was showing from the top of the heap, so I went over and slid it back out. As I found a seat on my bed, my thumbing through it began. Dieting, black hair care, books, and then, men and...

Why?

"Hello?" I called him right after retrieving that great for nothing article in the trash.

"Hey, baby, what's up?" He sounded like he was in the perfect mood. It was time for me to spoil that completely.

"Nothing. Just calling you back. Did you need anything?"

"Naw, baby, but who was that?"

"What...I mean, who?" I was nervous.

"The *what* that picked up your phone. I almost messed up. She sounds a little like my dancer."

Oh, dag. I forgot to mention. He started calling me dancer, and you can only imagine why. No explanation needed.

"My sister," I moaned.

"Why so short? What's up, Jee?"

"Andre'..." I started, but he cut me off.

"I didn't tell her anything about us, Jeena, so don't worry. I even told her a shortened version of my name. For all she knows, Dre' is all there is to it."

And it was now my turn.

"Why do you sleep with me, Andre'?"

"Say what?"

"Why do you sleep with me?"

"Why do you sleep with *me*?" he asked in return.

I wasn't about to answer that ignorance. No way. I knew why I slept with you, big poppa. Trust! Fine as hell, and you're good at it, I thought.

"Come on, Andre', I'm serious. I asked first."

As I waited for his answer, my eyes scanned the article running into one of the reasons why married men like to lounge atop other women. Immediate gratification. Then another reason, mid life crisis. He ain't old yet, I thought. Number three, thrill.

"'Cause I love you, baby."

Say what? I held the article up high while reading all the subheadings about why some married men do what they do, and not one of them said...*cause he love you, baby*! And what the hell kinda way to tell a woman that you love her? *Cause I love you, baby*. That junk didn't even sound real! Honestly, it sounded like he said it with a shrug. Then, there came a knock on my door.

Wait a minute, why was I trippin'? My sister's mind is playing tricks on me. I didn't have to wonder about Andre'. He had always been straight up with me, so I had no reason to believe he would lie nor mislead me. What did Faith know anyway? She didn't even know his full name, much less who he was to me!

"Andre', I gotta call you back." There went that knock at the door again, so I hung up in his face. Didn't really mean to hang up on him in such a rude way, but I knew that it probably came off that way. Thing is, every time someone was around, I got paranoid when Andre' was on the phone, thinking someone would find out about us. That would make me do stupid stuff like hang up on him out of fear of being busted.

"Who is it?" I completely turned the cell phone power off. Didn't need any surprises. Mom might have decided to pop up at my door mat or something. She was good for that kinda thing, just stopping on in from way across the USA to go shopping with me or just go out somewhere. See momma, she had money, and daddy, he had more. Together, they had super money, so they could fly wherever whenever.

"What's up, Jeena!" I heard that big mouth buster from the other side of the door. It was Stay Black. I opened the door, leaned back and crossed my arms at the sight of him. Poor thing.

"What?" I asked, in a sighing manner. He just stood there with his arms out to his sides and a big grin spread across his face. Stay Black. His last name used to be Johnson, and he was light-skinned. He was the kind of light-skinned with only enough black in his blood to bring a slight tint, but one would think by his name he was dark chocolate. And yes, his name was legally changed! He called himself The Black Story, the real black story of how the white man tried to bleach out black, but hands down and fists up, it still rocks on in the genes, the blood and the thump of the heart. That was only the beginning of his madness. He wasn't a racist, just tired of folks asking him what race he was so he took the one that he felt suited him.

"What you mean, what? Come here, baby, and give Stay Black a sista hug." He stretched his arms even more and grabbed for me. In spite of my leaning back, he still didn't catch the hint, and pulled me in on him anyway. And what in the world is a sista hug? That didn't even make any sense.

As he was hugging me with my arms held out to my sides not wanting to touch him at all, the word that came to mind was *aggravating*. And when I say aggravating, I mean really irritating, and you better believe I was stiff as hell when he gave me that hug, too! You know how somebody can just make your skin crawl when you are around them? Well, Stay Black was just that. Not only that, but he swore up and down he was fine along with his all the way blackness. Granted, yes he was what he was, and that was black, but homeboy acted like his momma wasn't white at all.

"Ummm, ummm, sista sista," he called out and then let me go. "Can I come into your abode, sweet cakes, and holler at you for a spell?"

"No," I quickly retorted. Hell no. Ain't no way in hell. Matter fact, Jesus gotta come and whisper *let him in* inside my ear for me invite homey inside.

"No?"

"No," I repeated.

"What? You got something to hide from a strong, sexy brother, Jeena?" he sang, crossing his arms. "Why won't you let a brother in, Jeena? What ya' hiding in there, girl?"

"What do you want, Stay Black? I'm in the middle of cleaning up," I responded not amused by his antics.

"I got some flowers for you."

"For me? Man, Stay Black, you *work* at the flower shop, so stop with the gifts that you probably snatched."

"Naw, sweet sista. They're in my ride, but they ain't from me.
Had your address on it, recognized it, so I decided to deliver them on the way to my crib. Lemme go get 'em." He turns away on one foot and then twists his old pin head back around my way. "That way, you can fill me in on this brother. See how I can cock block a player."

Flowers? I felt the bubbles start to boil in my stomach. He didn't! No, Andre', please say that you didn't! Immediately, I hit the cell power back to on and waited. It seemed like it was taking an eternity, so I started shaking the mess out of it until I saw that ten second hello that pops up when turning it on. Stupid greeting. I didn't need to be greeted every time I turned on the dog-on cell phone, shoot! As soon as that cleared up, two voice mails ready and waiting. I knew who was on the other end of the recording. Had to be Andre'. I was just getting ready to dial my voice mail, but Stay Black came running up with his dreadlocks bouncing right with him, so I tossed my phone to the other side of the room. It slammed into the wall. Dag, I hope it didn't break. Please don't ring, I prayed.

"Two dozen, and a man don't send a lady two dozen unless he's trying to get with my girl, and I ain't..."

I went tone deaf. Peeking over into the roses, I was terrified to even touch them. I gotta act dumb as hell over this. As I spied the card, I was hoping it read secret admirer, stalker, or from a friend. You know, some crap that wouldn't identify with whom I was sleeping. It would be just my luck, somebody would know Andre' and then bust my spot with a married man. Everyone would find out, and then I would be branded as home wrecker.

"Who is it from?" I could've asked that better. I haven't sounded that fake since Andre's wife busted up in the hospital bathroom.

"I want you to look. I can't open it up. Against delivery policy at the shop. Can't have you telling on me like that, you know. Might have it in for a black man."

While I ignored this strange brother that stood in front of me, I reached for the flowers...all two dozen. They were beautiful. Nothing but red. All of them risen to the occasion, just like him - always risen to the occasion for me. After grabbing the flowers, I bounced up out of my stupor and glared at dread locked flower boy.

"Stay Black, don't trip. I know they have a list and order form and stuff. When you found out it was my address, I know you went back and looked."

"Why look there when I was gonna bring 'em and get the low down from you, anyway?"

This dude lying. He's just trying to set me up. Gotta be. Immediately, I saw myself beating the life out of him with these heavy dozens of roses, knocking him out completely, and hiding him in my freezer until this all blew over, but that would be impossible. I can tell Stay Black has a big mouth, and I was getting paranoid, slowly, but definitely getting there.

"I don't have time to talk, Stay Black." I heard my phone vibrating, and honestly, I had plenty time to talk, just not to him. Truthfully, I needed a therapist. What does it sound like - I'm in love with a married ass man! What the hell would a therapist say? Dumb ass or well why the hell ain't he married to you? All my cool points would evaporate, but my emotions would be the same. Just in love with my dumb ass attached.

"What's that buzzing sound?"

I cut my eyes only a little to see my cell phone bumping up against the wall.

"Can you mind your own business sometimes? That's my phone. Gotta go." Slam. The door crushed his breath right up against it. After locking Black completely out and double checking the locks, I tossed all twenty four of those long stemmed roses on the chair and ran to that phone as fast as I could.

"Hello, hello?" I answered frantically, but it had already

hung up. Pressing for my missed calls, I found it was Andre'. I
redialed. Pick up, pick up, pick up. I started pacing the floor.

"You have reached..."

The dag on answering machine! This mug must've been
leaving me a message.

Holding the phone up in the air, I yelled into the phone,
"I'm trying to call you! Pick up the phone!" I hung up. Breathe! I
called again. This time, I got an answer.

"Andre'."

"Baby, why did you hang up on me? I had..."

"Andre', did you send me some flowers?"

"I love you, Jeena."

Dang. He sounded like he meant it that time. I sunk all
the way down next to the two dozen roses on the chair and
dropped my face inside them. They smelled delicious.

"Andre', why did you send me roses?" I asked, my head
still engulfed in rose petals.

"I just told you why. I love you, Jeena."

See, I was gonna tell him all the reasons why I love him,
but first, I needed to get it through this brother's head that I wasn't
trying to look like the slut that stole somebody's man in the
meantime. I lifted my head out of the flowers.

"Andre', you can't be sending me flowers, and before you
say anything, it's not because I don't like them. It's because that's
a paper trail."

"Paper what?"

"Paper trail. You gotta learn to let me know what you
plan on doing before doing it." I couldn't help but treat our
relationship like something you see on television forensics. With
Faith, Parri, and now Stay Black, between all of them, something
would have spilled over into real public life. That I didn't want.

"How would it be a surprise if I'd told you?"

I don't like surprises, I almost blurted out, but instead I
said, "You could've always just brought them over to my place
personally so that I could give you a succulent thank you. Not
send someone to deliver...named Stay Black." I had to drop the

dime just to see if they actually met. Once someone meets Stay Black, he's quite hard to forget, starting with the name.

"Who?"

Good. They didn't meet.

"Just next time bring them yourself. Forget about what I just said, baby." There was an eerie silence, and I figured that the resistance to his great roses gesture didn't go over well with him. I mean, he did spend all that money on me. Maybe I shouldn't have called him with all this don't do this and don't do that jive. I had to fix this. Give him something he might like in return. I softened my voice. "I wanna give you the keys to my place. You can come in whenever you like. That way, whatever you have to give me, you can give me, whether it be in the middle of the day or in the black of the night."

"You got some keys to give me, baby?" he asked like his you know...stuff...was on the rise. Whew! It worked. I really didn't want him upset with me at all. We had too much a good thing, and though he wasn't honest to his wife, he was honest with me.

"Anytime," I sang. "Now you just have to pick a time to come and get them." I must've really dug him because those keys Faith left behind, were now his, and if I was guessing right, he was going to be at my place tonight.

"I'll be there, Jeena. Love you, girl."

"Love you, too, babe."

We hung up, and I had to go get another comforter set. White. His black body will glow on it. I ran out of my condo after yanking up my things and left for the store knowing good and well he was going to show up tonight - thirsty. Good loving and some keys to the castle? Yeah, Andre' would show up. He told me that his wife was out of town as usual, so that left us together. Was I gonna have a hot Saturday night or what? I didn't even have to worry about Faith busting in anymore, and better yet, she does some missionary work down at the hospital for her healing and deliverance ministry. It's not only good for the souls up there but great for my physical body over here, too!

In my sneakers, jeans and black t-shirt, I jumped in my Saturn and took off with my full night planned out to a tee. After all that money he spent on those roses for me, atop of those petals, we were gonna do the wild thing! How would it feel to make love on a bed of roses with my man? Hell-a-good!

As I pulled up to the lingerie shop, I decided that I wanted to look like a present, you know, something that he could unwrap, and there it was in the window. Exiting my car, I knew I had to have it, so I
took my credit card out of my wallet and tossed my purse in the trunk. Just the plastic is all I needed. Everyone knew me in this store, so I didn't really need identification. Even when I didn't have a man, this was my place of preparation.

Opening the glass doors, all I saw was sale, sale and more sale plastered all over the walls and hanging from the ceiling. This was my lucky day. I had gotten roses from the man I fell in love with, and then I was about to get a good two for one deal in my favorite store. Could it get any better than...oh no. Not again.

"Ouch!" I bumped my head against the corner of the wall next to the dressing room as a result of super panic! I wasn't Catholic, but I had to do something, so I drew the cross on my chest with my finger just to see if it worked. Sweat began to pour from my deodorant protected underarm glands, putting the antiperspirant out of commission at the sight of Tina, Andre's supposed to be out of town wife, buying up lingerie! She was coming out of the dressing room in *my* favorite store! What the hell?

Immediately, I scurried over behind the pajama sets and bent my knees to make myself a tad bit shorter, hiding from her line of view. Oh my gosh! What was she doing here? And she had the same outfit that I wanted to wear tonight in her hands!

As I continued to rip myself apart, staring at her through the clothes, I noticed that she was wearing high heels, toting a purse that was from out of this world and wearing some rich woman sunglasses. How I recognized her, I really didn't until I heard someone say *Tina* out loud as I walked in. Only then did my eyesight steer me into my memory banks.

We even knew common people! The high chipmunk voice that was calling her name so much was, Kyaiki, the assistant manager of this joint. That was not good, not good at all. Suddenly, I didn't want lingerie after all, but only desired to get the heck out of this forsaken give your man what he wants type of store. Leaning all the way down so that big mouth Kyaiki wouldn't spot me, I began to make my move. They were still chatting, so I wouldn't have to be too sneaky. My ears started to cringe when I kept hearing their giggles, and I truly didn't want to get a hold of what they were giggling about. It could only be one thing up in a lingerie store! Making my way to the edge of the rack, the glass door opened at the front of the store and the little ding dong sound rang out loud. Damn!

I hit the floor. Hard! My credit card flew out of my hand, only to land underneath the display counter. As I reached for it, I found out quickly that I was louder than what I thought I was because everyone was looking at me. Everyone, including the man that just walked through the door - Andre'. Thus, in order to avoid more embarrassment, I scooped myself up off of the floor. Andre', who was now watching me get up from off of my butt, walked over to me, as if he didn't even know me at all, grabbed me by the hand to play like he was helping me up even though I was already halfway there.

"What are you doing here, Andre'?" I whispered.

He gave me the eye, and I knew what it meant. Shut up.

"My gosh, Jeena? Jeena, are you okay, honey? What happened? I heard that big thud over here, and I thought, my God, someone must've fallen and broken their neck!"

Shut up, Kyaiki. At the same time Kyaiki started running her mouth, my situation got to the worst stage imaginable. Tina came over, and touched Andre' on his pinky. That's how they ended up before my very eyes, holding hands by the pinky fingers. Somebody should have stabbed me in the chest before their next physical moment of pure passion came up. Oh wait, never mind, too late for the stabbing. She kissed him dead on his lips. I wasn't jealous in the least bit. They were married, but dog, Andre' could have had some mercy on me! Shoot, he kissed her right back! He could've given her a side lip or something to make me feel better.

"Kyaiki, my credit card. It's under the display count..."

"I'll lift it up for you," Andre' stated, butting in while deciding he was going to take this time to play credit card rescuer. Thus, he went and lifted up the display counter just enough for me to grab my card.

"Aren't you the girl from the hospital?"

While I was stooped over, Tina's question sent a chill down my spine. She recognized me, even with those big behind sunglasses on. Why on earth was she wearing them in the store anyway? Crawling under a rock wasn't an option nor was crawling under Andre' while he was holding up the display, so I rose once again to the unpleasant occasion.

"The hospital? Do I know you?" I asked, as if. Of course, I knew her. Tina, I'm having an affair with your husband, I thought. You know, the man standing right next to us that sent me 24 red roses today and told me he loved me. Yeah, the man on your pinky finger. What you are tasting, so am I, I thought while feeling slightly ill at the taste of her in my mouth as well. "Yeah, now I remember. What's your name again?"

"Tina." Her teeth were even perfect, no plaque, tarter, grill, nothing. Those had to have been fake fronts in her mouth, and if they weren't, I've got to do better.

"Yes, good to see you, and this is Andre'!" I gawked at him like I hadn't seen him since the hospital as a fully equipped and well built human male. "Wow! You have come a long way."

Andre' didn't even respond right away. He just lowered the display case, and looked over at Tina. Then, he glanced back at me. "Yeah, I got better really fast thanks to all your help."

He was damn right thanks to all my help.

"Anytime," I shakily stated, quickly looking at the garment that I was planning on sharing with him dangling from Tina's arm.

"You like this, baby?" She held up her choice of lingerie.

"Nice to see you," I gagged. I didn't even wave bye-bye, but ignored Kyaiki and left. Fast. Forget the white sheets and lace. I was gonna toss those roses in the garbage.

Humiliation was what I felt. Like a complete dumb ass for the cause. I couldn't believe I fell on the floor in front of Andre' and his wife! My forehead hit the steering wheel and while I rolled it around on top of it, I stuck the key in and started the ignition. As I started backing up from my parking space, I caught a glimpse of Andre' staring at me through the window. I pressed on the gas harder and drove off. Asshole!

I didn't even know why I was raging mad. Over him and her? Ha! I stopped at the stop sign and looked in the rear view. The signage for my favorite store was still within view. I slumped. Man, who was I fooling? I was still in love with the man, and my feelings were all broken inside. He was all up in my face and sending me roses...and all up in his wife's face buying her lingerie. I was the idiot buying my own! At least she got her stuff paid for!

As I pressed on the gas, my phone vibrated in my pocket. A text message alert. I hated text messages. Who could it be? Everybody knew I hated text messages, I thought as I slid my cell out of my pocket. When I opened it up, I saw that it was Andre', so I pulled over off of the road and read it. Yes, I could have kept driving but why? I sooo didn't have to rush home for anything at all anymore, and on top of that, there was a no texting and driving trend going on to save lives. For that, I was all in.

I'm sorry about that, Jeena. It won't happen again. Are you okay? was what the text read. I wasn't even gonna entertain that text with a reply. What did he mean, was I okay? Did I look okay five minutes ago as you sucked your wife's lips off her face while I watched? Yeah, I was fine. Just what in the world was wrong with him? All he had to do was ignore the life out of me and let me leave the store, but no. He had to put some extra drama into it so that I had to look his wife in the face and save my face all at the same time! Was I alright? Please.

The white sheets were still on sale, so I decided that I was going to go make my purchase anyway regardless of Andre'. Besides, I could have fun on my own, shower myself, and lie back on my own roses in my new sheets while watching my television without the drama of an Andre'. My phone went off again. Another text. I didn't even pick it up. Probably another I'm sorry. Really, I didn't even know what he was sorry for. For being with Tina? That's who he was supposed to be with. I'm the freaking third wheel, and that's why I was rolling out. I was rolling out forever from mistress mayhem. I needed to fall...

Out of Love.

Well, wasn't it lovely? Instead of tossing the love hate roses in the garbage, I plucked the petals just for myself to toss on the sheets. Oh so fabulous. I'd gone into the mall and got the most expensive three-hundred thread white sheets I could find on sale and fitted my bed perfectly. All it needed now was me and the strawberries that I picked up right before I pulled into my parking space at home.

There the cell sat. It was face front on the center of the bed and stared at the twenty nine texts that Andre' sent to my phone attempting to explain what happened. He just didn't realize that there was no need. Why would a man need to explain something to the sidekick? That was me - the sidekick.

Finally, I sat on the bed next to the cell with my legs curled up and my DVD remote ready for the right moment to press play. If I was the sidekick, I was the best sidekick there was, I thought attempting to take a stab at making myself feel more than worthless. At least Andre' could be seen with Tina shopping for lingerie where I would always have to be obsolete.

I was hurt. In the store, on the way to the mall, even

when I was trippin' with the cashier at the grocery store while buying my strawberries, I was having to hold back the tears, fooling myself that everything was okay and that he had to do what he had to do, that he didn't mean most of it when he disregarded me. It wasn't like he ignored me for nothing because due to the situation that was in our faces, I couldn't even recognize him as the man who sent me two dozen roses a couple hours earlier. That hurt though. I felt not worthy to be kissed in public, in front of his friends, nothing…like his wife.

One lonely tear drifted down my cheek, but I wiped it away quickly.

"I don't want to be in love with him," I whispered in my overly decorated and scented bedroom. Everything in my room had something that matched but me. The white sheets had a comforter, the windows had curtains, the floor had polish, the candles had fire, and even the television had a remote. My cell phone even had an operator! I had nothing and no one. Andre' couldn't love me back how I loved him, and why did he have to? Why did I even expect it?

Another text. My cell just vibrated away. This time, I picked it up and stared at it for a good moment before I read it. It was time to start using a house phone. Can't receive texts that way. All men get a land line number from now on, I decided to myself with a head nod, then I opened the newest text.

OPEN YOUR FRONT DOOR, JEENA. IT'S ME. DRE'. PLEASE.

Andre'! At the front door! I tossed my cell phone across the bed and jumped up from my comfortable rose nest. Then, I looked around, planting my eyes on the mirror in front of me, and what I looked like was a crying shame wrapped in a T-shirt. Then, I thought for a second. Why do I care if he's at the front door? This bedroom was off limits. When I got to the door in my little raggedy tee, I stared out of my peep hole.

There he was, fine as ever. He was wearing a white shirt and some blue jeans and was leaning up against the wall awaiting the door to fly open and me to jump inside his arms. Wasn't gonna happen. I did open the door, though.

"Yes?"

He didn't budge his body but only turned his head my way.

"I came to get my key, Jeena."

As I leaned my body on the side of the door, I responded to what I considered a stupid request and reason to come over after what I just went through in the store. "What key, Andre'?"

"The key that you gave to me today, baby."

I didn't give him a key. I *said* I was going to give his ass a key, but I snatched that generosity back in the lingerie store. As we both stood there in silence, I glanced at him again - and again and again. Hell, the key was his. I was playing hard to get, but Andre' was fine tonight. How his wife let him out like that was pure insanity. I couldn't keep my eyes straight. Every time he looked away from me, I undressed him. He must have spotted me checking him out because he started coming towards me, but I wasn't gonna freak out.

"Jeena, I'm sorry."

"Sorry for what, Andre'?" For embarrassing the hell out of me? That's what I wanted to say, but I didn't. I just stood there hoping that my eyes weren't red from those tears that I was fighting back in the bedroom.

"Why are your eyes red, baby?" He placed his hand gently on the side of my face and moved my hair back.

So much for hoping. I wanted to fall over and melt. He knew how much I cared for him.

"I apologize, Jeena. I came all this way to see you. I will do anything. I didn't lie when I told you that I love you. Jeena, she's my wife. You knew about her from the beginning."

Slammed on the brakes! I moved my face from his grimy little paws. "So this is my fault, Dre'?"

"No, that's not what I'm saying," he replied as I watched his eyes drift toward the bottom of my t-shirt. "All I'm trying to say is don't expect me to be perfect in every situation that comes before us."

Well, lah dih dah! Perfection? Man, we are sleeping with each other, and you're hitched! Perfection? Neither one of us has even consulted with Jesus about this one! I started feeling dirty again. I didn't know why I didn't feel this dirty all those other times, but this time, I felt the mud drying up on me, and it was drought hard. Thump me and I would have cracked into a million dirt droppings.

"This," I began, "Is nowhere near perfect, Andre'. Nowhere near it." I didn't move from the door despite noticing him make a sly attempt to get in.

"We can make it that way, Jeena. Let me in."

"No."

His hand reached around my waist, and my hand met his hand there, moving it back until he kissed me. And then I kissed him back. I fell for it again. Andre' got his wish. I let him inside...

And Inside Again.

Good morning, Andre'. He slept in my bed with me for the first time all night long. As I looked over at him, he lie there with his hand across my stomach still asleep. The rose petals I could still feel all in between our bodies, and the morning sun was bouncing off of our skin. Whew, he was sexy. I loved him. All the way around, I knew I did.

Last night, he walked his tongue up my spine and across the back of my neck, and I tasted the flavor of his pack to his chest and on to his smooth lips. It was indescribable. The way he made love to me induced some sort of psychological mishaps inside myself where the entire world would disappear, leaving just us. There had never been a man up until that night to make my skin feel as soft as cotton and my body feel as light as a feather.

The way he picked me up and placed me how he wanted me, and how I just fell into each position with ease was so gratifying. No fumbling allowed. Wherever he felt I needed his touch, he massaged me right in that spot. I swear I almost cried.

There was no rush. He never rushed with me. His pleasure was pleasing me, and I couldn't help but receive everything that he wanted to give. Everything. It was as if I was the baby, and he was my spoon. He fed me, nourished me and put me to sleep in his arms.

His phone. My eyes caught a glimpse of his cell phone blinking. The light continued to go off, and I knew who it had to be. Slowly, I slid from underneath his arm and crept out of my bed because I had to see, maybe even get a number off of that bad boy. A home number. Not that I was going to call, but solely for curiosity's purposes. What I was so curious about, I really didn't know because there was no dime to drop about him having a wife. I already knew long ago, but I really wanted to know was it really his wife on the other end? At one point, I even wished that I *could* pick it up to find out

As I neared the window sill where the cell was sitting, I took a quick glance back at Andre' on the bed. He didn't even know I was up. Good. I picked up the cell and looked at it. There was number - 656-0907. Right away, I put it to memory and placed the phone quietly back down. Then, I thought, if it wasn't his wife, she was a nut. If my husband was out all night, that phone would have been blowing up, or I would've found that car and gone to town on those tires and windshield. But then again, she was supposed to be out of town since last night.

Stepping away from the window, I picked my T-shirt up off of the floor and went into the bathroom for my shower. I needed a long one. Quietly, I shut the door and sat on my toilet seat. 656-0907. I pulled out a tube of lipstick from my bathroom drawer and then yanked off a piece of tissue to write that number down before I forgot it.

"656-0907," I whispered while I wrote. Then, I folded that bad boy up and put it in my sneaker. Who looks in a sneaker for evidence? Not a man with a key to your crib. At that, I got into a nice and steaming hot shower. "656 huh? I wonder who that could be? Could it be wifey?" I sang lightly while the water pounded on me, but wait a minute. I stopped right in the middle of scrubbing my underarms. What if he had another lady third to me? It sounded silly but true. Could he have been with me and someone else this same week other than the natural person, his wife? I stopped. Diseases. Right then and there, I glanced down at my vagina. Ain't no way in hell. I started scrubbing again with the thought eating at me despite the fact that we used a condom.

Honestly, I hated when I allowed my mind to make things run wild and cause more anxiety than what they were worth. I loved Andre', and the only reason he was probably still with his wife was because he didn't know how to get out or something reasonable right? Really though, had I ever asked him? I just assumed he was going to be mine eventually.

I turned the water off because it was making too much racket, and besides that, it was time for me to get out. Exiting the shower, I decided to ask him about a divorce. My breathing became heavy at the notion unfortunately, and I felt nauseated. There was the toilet right beside me, but I wasn't about to let myself go right then and there. Rationally, if I was in love, then, I needed a true answer, and if he truly loved me, then he would own up and let a sister know how he was going to split with his wife. There was only one way for me to find out about our future - ask - and the best time to ask him such a question was while he was in the bed, half asleep and not thinking clearly enough to lie. Yep, that was my best bet, so I skipped my half moistened booty right out of the bathroom and captured a nice view of his body still draped in my white sheets.

As soon as I got more nerve, which took a minute or two, I went over next to the bed. It wasn't the question that scared me, but it was more losing him that did. The mirror was to my right. I stared at myself and again, that same question in my mind - how did I allow myself to fall in love with a married man? My reflection didn't answer. What good was it if it couldn't talk back?

"Andre', baby?" I glanced at him, but he didn't budge. "Andre', wake up, baby, I need to ask you something."

"What's up, baby?" He grumbled and then turned over, but before I got a chance to ask him, he immediately sat up and got out of the bed, walking toward the bathroom. "Hold up a second."

I just stood there wrapped in my towel waiting on him to come back out. He didn't even look at me. Just got up and went to use my bathroom. Could a sister get a good morning up in *my* room? I let it slide. He might have been a semi-grouch in the morning. That was cool. Who wasn't? Thing was, his whole getting up and going to the bathroom went against the plan. I heard the water running. He was waking up when I needed him half asleep for the question.

"Baby, you got some mouthwash? My mouth ain't good."

"Um, yeah...look in the cabinet," I replied sticking my neck out and pointing like he could see me with laser vision through the door. I was going to have to get used to a man going through my stuff, our stuff, in the morning and late at night. If he left his wife, certainly we would have to get a new place or he would have to move here for a while because sleeping in his wife's bed would be out of the question for me, let alone living where she did.

I, then, started to think about that key I promised him just to make him happy with me again. Was I moving entirely too fast being that he didn't even hint that he would leave Tina? Before my thoughts concluded, Andre' walked his naked behind out of my bathroom and all my mind could think about then was...*do it again. Surprise me. Let me pretend I didn't see you come out of my bathroom and just walk out again.* His naked body, when in action and upright and all, was just way too exhilarating. It just demanded my attention. Shoot, I almost forgot what I woke him up to ask him about! Divorce who? Nevermind that, just bring your fine self over here from time to time so I can touch ya, babe! Yea-yuuh!

"What's up, baby?" He walked over and gave me the

sweetest kisses on my lips and neck.

"Andre'?" I turned to face him while we both sat on the bed. Maybe the bed was a bad place. I got up.

"Wait a minute, what's up?" He grabs my wrist and pulls me lightly back in front of him, in between his legs. As I stood there speechless, trying to get what I had to say out of my mouth, he slowly moved his hands to my thighs and caressed them, grazing the hump that separates butt from leg. Thump, thump went the nest. I placed my hands on his shoulders and backed away. Still, he grabbed me by my hands. I wasn't too concerned about that. The hands on the thighs had to go.

After standing there while he stared in my face like I was the sun and he was the earth, I finally spit it out. "Do you plan on being with me?"

"I am with you, Jeena. In every way, I am. You're in my heart, in my spirit. What's wrong, baby?"

Uh oh. He stood up and pulled me in by my waist. I melted.

"Well," I began, turning my eyes away, beginning to feel a bit uneasy. Just breathe, Jeena, I thought as he rubbed the small of my back. I swore I was getting ready to die. "If you love me, Andre', do you even plan on leaving your wife?" Before I gave him a chance to answer, I continued. One...out of fear of the unknown. Two...because I felt I had to explain myself. "I mean, I understand everything about us, but love means being together..."

That's when he kissed me, stopping me cold dead in mid sentence.

"We are together," he confirmed, and then that's when we made love...

Again. But Then...

"You did what?!"

Parri was back home later on that day, and since she
already knew partially what was going on, I figured I would
partially tell her some of the rest. Yeah, it caught her off guard,
but hey, in this situation, feedback, no matter how slanted, was a
must.

"So he can get in! What's so wrong with that? He's my
man, Parri."

"Girl, you done lost your mind! You don't give no man the
key to your place if he ain't paying no rent! He can just trample all
up in your place whenever and however. No, girl, you got to get
off of this phone with me. Love ain't never been that serious for a
key with no rent, and that's for damn sure."

"Parri!" I was in shock with her opinion on the matter.
"He's really good to me."

"And? I'm *good* to you, too, but I don't see you giving me
an all access pass to your refrigerator, running water, lights and
cable."

"And, Parri," I stated indignantly, "We are in love, really."

"Where the ring at?"

"What?"

"Where the ring, Jee, or else I'm getting off the phone?
Love from a man puts the money down on a ring, so where is it?"

"There ain't got to be..."

"Yes, there does. You don't ever give the first big gift,
girl, and you just did when you tossed over the key to your place.
You're giving him everything, and you're getting nothing unless
there is something you haven't told me about."

I got her! See, I didn't buy the first nor give the first
anything. Andre' bought me two dozen roses.

"I didn't buy the first gift. He did. He had two dozen
beautiful, expensive roses delivered to me."

"Oh, Jeena, please! That's a coochie trick, which by the
way, you are giving up for free, too!"

"What?" Unbelievable! "Parri," I dropped the telephone,

shook my wits back into me, and then picked it back up again. "You're crazy. Every man isn't coochie crazy and giving away roses to get something in return."

"A gay man, you mean, isn't coochie crazy. Girl, he sent you those to get some, and I'm not talking about if he loves you or not because he just might, but even if he did, the game still works the same. Get coochie from a lady you love or get it from one you don't love. Men are the kings of emotion production. Roses don't care. They just do as they are told, and that is to create an emotion inside of the recipient by setting the mood for some coochie.."

"And what are the roses actually told to do again, Parri?" This was stupid.

"Gimme some of that...gimme some of that!" she sang, "And then they only make you *feel* loved...when you really ain't!"

"Shut up."

"No, you shut up those legs and that front door when you get that key back," she retorted.

I was sick of this conversation to say the least. Whatever happened to support from you girls? "I gotta go," I blurted out.

"No what you *gotta* do is go get that key back, and I don't care if you're mad at the truth. It's the truth, and the truth doesn't care about what you think either." She managed to get in that shout before I hung up in her face.

I wasn't going to take Andre's key back because I really wanted him to have it. Besides, I could pay my own bills, so giving up my key was my decision. On top of that, I never needed any man nor him for his money even though he had to have a lot of it and probably wouldn't mind letting me take what I wanted. Andre' drove a nice ride, and it was all decked out with the finest interior, nothing but leather with that wood grain finish and all that. I sat in it only once. Didn't ride anywhere though because it was too risky, not for him, but for me. His ride was always polished and clean making me curious about what his wife Tina drove. Her ride couldn't have been as wack and busted up as mine.

Anyway, I had to get dressed and go to the hospital.

Faith caught a cab there today and needed someone to pick her up from her ministry work. After that, I had to take her to pick up her car. She left a message that she would be on the third floor visiting with those who needed the Lord in a mighty way. Maybe I should have been in one of those rooms considering my whole sin soaked relationship with Andre' that, sin or not, felt so good. It felt like destiny had made a mistake, some type of fatal error that had two lovers apart from one another. The design of this type of love I was feeling was decorated with a bunch of holes that needed mending into a relationship that could be not only possible but ...

Public.

Room three zero eight. That's where I had to be for Faith, but I was in a full drag! Boy, did this weekend kill me! Being with Andre' all night took it's toll, and one of those was missing church - again! There was more than one reason why I was loving picking Faith up from the hospital, but the main one was that it gave me a reason not to face the guilty side of my actions in church. Yeah, I understood that everyone sinned, and by no means was I perfect, but I couldn't shake that fact that the love I was making with Andre' was like the longest sin in the whole Bible! Fornication and adultery! Man, it took hours to complete, and even though I was doing it everyday, it took effort many times to push the sin of it all to the back of my mind.

I stopped at the red light on the main street in front of the hospital. What if Jesus was to stop in and rapture the church while I was in the middle of it? I mean, I could have cursed somebody out and robbed a liquor store in a shorter amount of time than it took to be with Andre'! The entire world could potentially come to an end in the middle of me making love, and despite the whole fear of it all, I still couldn't dig myself out of this hole. I really didn't even want to get out of it anyway, except when I got around Faith or someone with God sitting so close to them I could feel His presence. Guilt would overpower me, and I would cave. The sole reason why too much church was no option for me lately, but I knew time was ticking. I couldn't do this forever.

"I gotta stop this," I said to myself, but I couldn't control it. In the back of my mind, I heard my mom's voice telling me, *tend to your own affairs, mind your business and don't want what belongs to somebody else. Keep God first. Let things fall the right way, and don't mess them up with the wrong way, you hear me? Love will come and hate will, too. Choose your blessings or choose your cursings, and when you're done, don't you dare blame God for your choice.* That's how she would summarize the Bible. Never a verse, but many of them in one. If we wanted to know what verse it came from, we had to find it. Faith would always find it first. Me, I would wait on her and look later, if at all. Whatever mom said, that's what I knew. It rarely came from reading it. Mom basically was my Bible growing up, then Faith.

I turned into the parking lot, parked and hopped out, hoping that when I got up to the third floor, Faith was ready to go. She probably went to the early morning service today. The only time she came to the hospital on Sunday is if it was absolutely necessary, and to her, anything made everything necessary when it came to God and people.

As I entered the main hospital building, the smell rushed into my nostrils. Yuck. I hated the smell of the cafeteria food mixing with hospital odor. It was just disgusting. Anyway, I looked around for a couple of minutes hoping to see Faith somewhere around here so that I wouldn't have to ride the elevator up there, but no luck, thus up I went. I entered the next available elevator and rode to the third floor.

"Three zero eight," I sang after exiting the elevator, counting the room numbers up to the room I was to stop inside. I hated to intrude. Outside of the door, I heard Faith in prayer so I stopped just to listen out of respect and for them and our Father.

I might have been living in sin, but still...

"Dear, Father God, we love you, and we also know that you loved us first, in spite of all our wrongs. Thank You for Your Son, Jesus, that gave His life for us before we even knew ourselves. That's the greatest love on earth. Dear Lord, help us where we are weak..."

The longer she prayed, the lower I bowed my head. "Father, forgive me." That's when the tears welled up in my eyes at my history and present state with God. I decided to walk in silently, not to disturb and continue to listen.

"...and forgive us where we fall short. Thank you, Jesus, for presenting us to the Father that we may enter into eternal life in heaven, causing our sins to be remembered no more. Father, now give Your child the wisdom to do what is best in Your sight, Father, to choose blessings over curses, to forgive those who hurt us, and love those who hate us. May she remember that vengeance is Yours, and You will repay. Holy Spirit, guide her into all truth. In Jesus' name we pray, Amen."

"Amen," the voice stated from behind the curtain in agreement with Faith. I felt sort of out of place, but at the same time, wanted to be in place with all of them...those two and Jesus in the midst. At that moment, the feeling of two people in one body felt so real. My insides were in full combat, wanting to do wrong and right at the same time. I called for Faith.

"Faith, it's me." I stumbled inside a little more, pulling back the curtain after the prayer had concluded.

"Hey, sis. Tina, this is my sister, Jeena."

Before I could swallow my spit good down my throat, I began to choke, coughing violently like I had heard the worst news of my life when that saliva went down the wrong pipe.

"Oh, Lord, Jeena, baby, you okay? Let me get you some water. Hold on." As I stood there gasping for a break from coughing, I stared at the woman that lay beneath me. She was bruised all over her face, and her arms were knotted up as if they were one step too close to being broken. Her top lip completely covered her bottom, and her nose was swollen almost double what it looked like it should have been. Worst part was that I knew who she was. It was Andre's wife, and she was black and blue.

"Here, Jeena. Take this," Faith said, handing me the cup of water.

I swallowed all of it in one gulp and then whispered to her, "What happened to her, Faith?" I felt the sweat begin to creep behind my ears because I was getting ready to panic.

"She got attacked by some guys outside her car..." She looked away and then back at Tina. "At least that's what I know, from what she said."

I glanced back at Tina. She was looking at Faith as if she was saying thank you, but didn't want to say it out loud. I couldn't believe it was her! Tina was lying there, appearing as if she didn't know me or at least never met me, and we have run into each other at least twice in the last couple months. That's why I didn't say a word to her. She was ashamed, had to be, so I stepped out and away from the bed.

"I'll wait on you outside, Faith. Finish up, okay?" As I pulled the curtain back together, I caught another glimpse. That's when Tina locked eyes with mine with what was a seriously disturbing look. Maybe it was my own guilt making me see things in an odd and incorrect way, but the look she gave me nearly pierced my soul. Still, she said nothing, and Faith had no idea that I knew her.

My heart sunk because I was with her husband all night. She had to have gotten into the incident last night when she was supposed to be out of town. I yanked my cell out of my back pocket and searched through it like I missed something. Where was Andre'? His wife was up in the hospital half dead! Did he even know that she didn't make it wherever she was headed?

Instead of the elevator, I wanted complete silence. As I scurried down the hallway to the exit sign over the staircase, I peered back over my shoulder to see if there was any sign of Faith coming out of the room. Nothing. The door shut behind me, and I plopped down on the stairs. The phone was ringing.

"Answer, answer, answer, answer!" I repeated over and over again, but then I heard the staircase door open at the same time there was a hello on the other end of the telephone. I hung up!

"Why are you in here?"

I sat terrified with my body twisted all the way around staring her in face as she scoped the staircase out in a disgusted manner as if she was thinking *get off these dirty steps why don't you?*

"It's just sad. I hate hospitals, and the way your life can be almost taken from you in an instant...needed some time...make a phone call to get that scene, that lady out of my head."

She came and sat down beside me. "Girl, stuff happens. That's why we got God, remember?"

"Yeah. That's why we got..." Before I could even finish my sentence, the guilt came, my cell began to vibrate, and then tears started to roll down my cheeks. I glanced down at my phone and saw the letter A, placed the cell face down on the staircase behind me and finished my sentence while weeping on Faith's shoulder, "God." I just cried there for what felt like an eternity while the cell continued to vibrate, and I could sense Faith was totally confused. The cell, I didn't even turn it off. Bump Andre'. My heart began to suddenly feel different. I started feeling for Tina, and less for her, or for that matter, our man. Almost immediately, I started to wonder, did she honestly get jumped or was it something far worse inflicted on her by that someone we both love?

It felt good in my sister's arms, and right then, I wanted her to be my ear, my warrior, and my...

<u>Friend.</u>

Grinding up onions and tomatoes never smelled good to me, but it tasted good when they were all chopped up and cooked together on top of some rice. That's what my grandma used to make all the time. I would suck it down, too, me and my grandpoppa. The aroma would smell up the whole house. Now, cooking it exactly like grandma, I could never do, but eating like her, at that I was a pro!

There was a knock at the door, so I placed my can of tomatoes down and went to see who the knock was. It wasn't Andre' I knew because he had a key. Besides, the number he called me from while I was crying my eyes out on the hospital staircase was his work number. Guess he was there while his wife laid up half dead. Even though I was determined not to allow my feelings to overwhelm me, I knew if I spoke to or even seen Andre', I was liable to explode. If he was the one that nearly killed her and had her sitting in ICU, Andre' wasn't just a lover, but one cold mother fucker that I wanted nothing to do with.

Before I opened the door, I resolved to push the situation to the back of my mind because it did no good to think about it much. I had no one to cry on nor tell the complete truth about Andre' and myself. Fact was, I was alone to live with what I knew, and I knew I couldn't live with it. Not anymore.

"Hi, Stay Black," I greeted him as I opened sesame. Not even waiting for him to say anything back to me, I turned and walked back to the counter top where I left my deluxe, unfinished meal.

"I can come in?" Stay Black asked from what sounded like way back at the front door. I turned around. Yep, that's where he was, so I waved him on in.

"Yeah, I left the door open for you. Come on in." I was way too calm. Normally, I was negative and giving him the hand when he came around. Today wasn't gonna be that day, especially after earlier at the hospital. I needed a fresh conversation. I'd already refused to talk to Andre' by letting the phone ring off the hook after he first called me while I was guilt tripping myself into Faith's arms at the hospital after not being able to get his mangled wife out of my head. What was so bothersome was why didn't I know about it, and why wasn't he the least bit concerned about her and still calling my phone?

The whole situation floored me. The circumstances, I still didn't know, so I had to calm down before even deciding to talk to him because the more minutes and hours went by, the more Tina's so called gang beat down didn't make sense. Andre' at work, wife bruised up in the hospital and he slept with me the night it all obviously went down. No, something didn't make sense.

"This is a first." Stay Black grinned at the notion of me letting him in my home. I didn't even have to look at him to know he was cheesing because I felt all those teeth gleaming over the thought of his feet hitting my bare floor finally.

"What's up, Stay Black?" I tossed the onions over into the pan to let them cook a little with the tomatoes.

"Nothing, I mean, you know, just stopping by to see you like I normally do." He looked around my pad. "And got something abnormal in the process," he continued under his breath.

"Well, you see me. Hope I look the same. Here's a profile for ya'." I turned to the side and struck a pose. "I look the same, right?"

After a long pause and no answer from Stay Black, I started my cooking over again until suddenly...

"No, you don't look the same, and you darn sure ain't acting the same. Jeena, what's wrong with you, posing for me and ...?"

"What do you mean I don't look the same? Same hair, make-up, same everything. Wanna taste?" I held up the steamed tomatoes and onions in a spoon with my hand underneath it.

"No thanks. It makes your breath stink. Can't come in here and get all close up near you with the foul mouth on the first date, now can I?"

"Suit yourself, date man." I tossed it back in the pan.

Truly, I was mixed up and needed someone. Not Parri, not anyone that would scold me. I needed somebody, thus, Stay Black. I didn't know if I would even end up saying anything to Andre' about my knowledge of his mangled wife after giving it some thought. At the same time, I hoped that Andre' wouldn't bust up in here later either with that key I gave him, that by the way, I should have taken back. Unfortunately, I can't just ignore a call for too long now because he can pop up anytime.

"Jeena, why so nice?"

"Stay Black," I interrupted, "Have a seat." I watched him as he backed up as a result my ignoring him, put his hands in the air and found a seat in my living area.

There. Now that he was down, maybe the person that I needed today really was Stay Black as it would make for good company. Good in a sense that we have no ties. Just good ole chill out and talk type company. I went ahead and put my rice on since my baked chicken was almost finished in the oven.

"I didn't know you were a cook, Jeena," he called with his back turned away from me on the sofa, reaching for one of my many magazines. I collected every type of magazine from art to home to money making. My favorite was art. Just the whole design of it was extremely breathtaking. It was somewhat near heavenly. People with that type of creative gift had to have gotten it from God and no where else to make dirt and grime look so good and livable.

"Yeah, I do a little something something on the side, Black. You need to try some." I rolled my neck. "Even if it does corrode your breath, it feels good in the tummy."

"Oh yeah?" he responded, twisting my way.

"Oh and what, you didn't know? Well I guess if you ain't heard, then you wasn't supposed to know!"

"Oh it's like that now?"

"Like that all day, Black."

"Well then, when everything is said and done, a brother will have some if that's an invite, Jee Jee."

"For sho' ya' right!"

It felt good to talk with someone you didn't have to front with, sex with, or even primp for! It was all good, and it even put my mind at ease. Nice. For the first time, Stay Black wasn't a pest, but someone that I called a solid. What was a solid? Someone that was just there, but never a harm. Sometimes a solid could be anything and everything at one time for you, but the one thing a solid wasn't was gone. No, not ever gone, but there to stay. Not a family member, but someone that's there like a sister or brother. More than a best friend. Maybe in between them both, but who knew? A solid was like a tree in the lawn...beautiful in one season, annoying in another season and plain ugly in the other. However, it never left. Ever.

"Hey," I reached in the drawer and pulled out a deck of cards. "Wanna play me in a game of Rummy?"

"Rummy?" he asked with a frown in his voice.

"What's wrong with Rummy?" As I walked back over to the living area, I shuffled the deck in my hands, concentrating on the way the cards fell. The cards in my life weren't falling well at all it seemed, so why not concentrate on something I was more in control of - these cards and Stay Black.

"Nothing." He scooted over on the sofa. "Sit on down here, Jee, so I can show you how it's done."

I stole a seat on the other end of the couch and put a chess board in between us to mock a table. Oh yeah, it was on and poppin'.

With a blank face, I stared at him cold in his eyes, and said, "Prepare for me to mop this dirty floor with your face, Black."

"Oh snap! The jokes are on! We will see! We will see four eyed, Jee Jee."

"Four eyes? I don't wear glasses," I responded.

"You don't now, but you're gonna need 'em after this game, baby girl. Lemme pick up my cards and school you on a little something."

"Pick 'em up if you can grab 'em, playa!"

Stay Black. Tonight, he was my breath of fresh, clean...

Air.

"Why don't you pick up your cell, Jeena?"

I forgot. It had been ringing all day, and now that it was night time, all night. Still, there was no sign of Andre' at my front door. Me and Stay Black had already eaten, and by the way, he tore my tomatoes and rice up. Grandma taught me skills.

Anyway, he managed to beat me in Rummy and was getting ready to call up some folks so that we could play Spades. Unfortunately, Spades wasn't about to happen in my crib. Spades was that game that everyone knew would get your house torn to shreds, and my place wasn't gonna be the pad we played in.

"No reason, Black." I shrugged my shoulders. "Just didn't want to answer, ya know. Peace for a change. As you can tell, it rings off the hook."

"I hear you." He gazed at me for a quick second, and after I noticed that he gave me one of those I want to be more than friends with you glances, I moved on over toward the farthest end of my couch and picked up my DVD remote.

"I have a nice movie in the player. Wanna watch it?"

"What's wrong, Jeena?"

"Nothing, man, I'm telling you that..."

"Jeena." He touched my wrist as I leaned over to grab the other remote control, prompting me to release it. Looking at his hand on my wrist, I pulled back fast. How on earth did he know that something was bothering me? Was it that obvious? Time for Stay Black to go!

Standing up, I attempted to walk towards the door which was about eight or nine paces beyond him. I was doing this to put an end to the night before it got too personal. When I stepped in

105

front of him, he didn't touch me at all, but instead blocked my way by standing in front of me.

"I'm not trying to intrude on you in any way, Jeena, but I know something is wrong. You never *don't* answer your phone, and you've never, ever let me in here, but um," He ran his whole hand through his hair as if he was under some type of anxiety, so I spoke.

"Black, I..."

"I can tell, Jeena. It's alright. It'll be alright. You've had that nervous chatter all night, so stop trying to pretend. You're normally not uneasy. Never seen you with so much on the brain. I'll leave since I see you are trying to put me out for prying, but you need to let it go, Jee. Feel better."

As he was standing there in front of me, I rested my head on his chest, and it just came out again. I wept and did it like a baby. Still, he didn't touch me, but I felt okay with touching him. Therefore, I embraced him as if he was my very own heart. There were so many emotions running through me that I didn't know which was making me cry, but I knew that I had to let it all out and stop lying to myself. Finally, I felt Black's hand caress my back, and then, he took my arms from around him, kissed me on my left cheek, told me everything would be okay, and walked toward my door. At that point though, I didn't want him to leave anymore.

"Black," I called, "don't leave. I'm sorry, but don't leave, not now."

He came to a standstill as soon as I spoke while reaching for the door knob. He didn't turn around, but just stood there with is back facing me. I wanted to literally beg him to stay, and there was no pride to drop, thus, the begging started.

"Please, Black."

His head dropped a little before he spoke, "I want to be here for you, Jeena, but..."

"Help me by staying, Black. I need you right now. I'm sorry for not being able to tell you..."

"No," he quickly responded, "don't apologize for anything."

"I just need you to stay with me tonight." With tears falling down my face, I waited on him to leave his door knobbed position, knowing full well that I didn't deserve him with me. It seemed like my full conscience was coming clean, and I needed Black, not in a sexual way, but a good way. A solid way. He wouldn't judge me. I just felt he wouldn't.

"I messed up, Black." The guilt behind my relationship with Andre' was overwhelming me, especially after seeing his wife in the hospital. I just couldn't take it anymore.

"Don't even talk about it 'cause you don't have to." He lifted his head. "I'll stay. For you, Jeena, I'll stay." Seeming like he really didn't know what to do and a little apprehensive, he put his hands in his pocket and walked back near me.

"Thanks."

The whole night, he stayed with me. At times, he let me lie in his arms, and then, at other moments, we sat up and talked. Into my bedroom, we didn't enter. The sheets from last night were still covered with rose petals because I didn't change anything from when me and Andre' met up together. Besides that fact, Stay Black never asked nor motioned toward the bed. In fact, he looked all too comfortable chillin' just with me. The real me. Nothing faded, fake or laid to the side. I enjoyed him, also. It wasn't until two in the morning that we fell asleep, and at six thirty, we both woke up to my alarm. It was...

Monday.

Who was I kidding? I wasn't about to go in to work today. I was too drained on the inside, and nobody was gonna pry in my personal life to try and dig all of it out after they see my tear puffed eyeballs. Stay Black woke up right beside me.

"Dang, that's a loud alarm clock. Oh hell no!" He jumped

up off the couch like a crackhead going to meet the crack dealer.

"What's up?" I asked, stretching my arms out.

"I gotta roll up outta here. Work starts in an hour and thirty." He kneeled down in front of me. "Are you gonna be okay?"

I nodded. I wasn't going to tell him work wasn't in today's schedule for me. Decided to keep that to myself so that I could have some time alone and ponder over some issues within myself.

"Good." He tapped my knee. "Time to bounce. Love ya', Jee," he stated as he headed out.

"What?" I barely heard it or I thought I heard it wrong even.

"Time to bounce. Love ya'. I'll check on you later."

I leaned back against the couch. "Thanks."

He left. I thought about those last words *love ya', Jee* from the time I got in the shower until the time I heard my front door slam. As I quickly dried myself off, I wrapped my towel around my body and listened really hard from behind my bathroom door. My cell was in the bathroom with me, so I picked it up and looked at all the recent calls. Eighteen calls and some messages Andre' left for me. All of them went unheard and disregarded.

I tightened my towel for the extra assurance that it wouldn't come loose and fall off when I exited the bathroom. I knew it was Andre'. He wasn't calling my name nor was he making too much noise. I should've parked my car in another spot and walked to my pad as a fake out so he would think I wasn't at home. Because I knew it was him, I sucked my breath in, decided to keep a firm grip on the reality of today and yesterday, and left out of the bathroom.

There he was sitting on my bed. Instead of raising my head to greet him, I kept my head low and turned away from him while making my way to the dresser to get my undergarments.

"Getting ready for work, Jee?"

"Yes." I lied. As much as I called out at my job, I was

shocked they didn't fire me already. Probably because on the days they need me to work double, I do just that and double.

"You didn't answer any of my calls. What happened from the other night to this morning?"

"Nothing much, Andre'. Just busy."

"I been looking like a fool calling you, and you just staring at the phone ignoring it. You ain't that busy," he stated with some sort of *I own you* attitude. Clue though, I wasn't his wife, so he could kill all the noise.

"Not mostly, but yesterday," I pulled my panties out of the drawer, turned and glanced at him with a very fake and happy smile, "I just happened to be *very* busy."

"Busy with what, Jeena?"

Busy with what he asked? Ha! "I had to do some things with my sister. We had some stuff to take care of, some things that she had to do." I pulled my work clothes out, pretending like that was where I was headed so he would get the point and get out. I still didn't know whether or not I should tell him I saw his wife yesterday, and on top of that, why he hadn't told me about everything – as if I couldn't already take a good guess why he didn't? But then again, maybe it's on one of the messages that he left on my cell.

Finally, he got up from the bed.

"I'm gonna let you get ready for work," he stated frustrated.

"Okay." Hell yeah! Get out!

I felt his arms come around my waist, and I had to firm up so I wouldn't cave in. He turned me around to face him.

"I love you, Jeena, and whatever it is, let me know. It'll be okay, okay?" He then kissed me on my lips. I kissed him back, and he left.

Hallelujah! I tossed those work clothes back in the closet, and went to my bed, nearly ripping the sheets as I pulled them up from the mattress. The completely dead rose petals, all wrinkled up, fell to the floor, and I sat down on the bare mattress with gobs of sheets in my arms. Peering into my bathroom at my cell, I thought, I needed to listen to all those messages, so that's what I did. The sheets hit the floor, and I tossed that cell up to my ear as soon as I got my hands on it.

"You have ten messages. First message," the voice mail recorder told me in a stale computerized voice. It was Andre' of course. *The other night, you were sexy baby. I like the way you put it down, lady. Love you.* Message two. *Where you at, Jee? Call me, baby.* Message three, four and five were hang ups. As I concluded the messages, none of them were about his wife. No, not one at all. This made no sense. It was like he wasn't even phased. Maybe I should text him, I thought, so I flipped my phone to texting. *Just what in the hell is your wife doing in a sick and shut in hospital* is what I wrote with about five question marks behind it and then an exclamation point.

"Yeah, I'm gonna send this sucker," I said, boosting myself up. "Send this text right now!" I stated again, shaking my head up and down with my hand on the send button, but no matter how hard core I tried to get, I sucked. Couldn't do it. I aborted the message.

As I stared around my room, I wondered what I was gonna do? Then, I looked down at the cell, called my job, coughed my excuse out, literally, for not coming in and tossed my cell to the side.

I had to clean up this mess in my condo. That idea was exceptional being that it would help me lose that thought about all that happened yesterday - from Tina and then Andre'. My night with Stay Black was impeccable, and who knew he was a great shoulder to cry on?

I started at seven thirty sharp cleaning up to forget about every single thing. When I say I cleaned up, I mopped and polished. The dust had started piling up again on my entertainment system and both of my dressers in my bedroom. The living room coffee table was always pretty neat looking, so I didn't have to polish that as much.

The lemon scented furniture polish made love to my nose, doing wonders when mixed with the scent of a nice wicker candle and mopped floors. The air just smelled fresher over all my damn personal dirt, and I even yanked out some new air filters that I purchased two weeks ago, installing them at the vents while I vacuumed that excess dust that set in around the sides. Fresh air it was!

By the time I was finished, it was twelve noon sharp, and by twelve thirty, I was sitting on the stool on my patio that was surrounded by beautiful green grass while I wore my booty shorts and tank top, painting my toe nails and finger nails at the same time. I didn't need any company, just enjoyed life, living and pushing things that made no sense and that I wasn't ready to face away from my mind. Then relaxation reality struck. My cell always rings at the wrong time.

With my neck cocked over to the side and body getting ready to tip over in my chair, I viewed my cell from the patio floor. To my surprise, it wasn't Andre'. It was Stay Black, so I hit the speaker.

"Hello?"

"What's up, girl?" His voice was very upbeat.

"Nothing's up with me, Stay Black, but sounds like everything is up with you." I screwed the cap back on my nail polish and tuned in to the conversation. Speaker off. "What's happening? You sound extremely happy today."

"Naw, I was just, you know, checkin' on you. Making sure..." he paused and then made his voice a bit calmer, "that you felt better. That's all, Jeena. You alright?"

That kinda shook me! Dang! It sounded like Stay Black had true heart for me, so I sat back to take it all in, especially after I had decided to move our relationship from hate him to homey-friend.

"I'm good, Stay Black," I replied as I shut my eyes. Hearing him was so relaxing, and that was a miracle in itself when I recall my past with him. "I'm glad you called. I feel much better."

"Good, I'm glad things are better, but are you not at work? Thought I would have gotten your answering machine..."

Suddenly, everything around me went dead at the next sound that came piercing through my ears. I mean, at first I thought my ears were fooling me like *what the hell*? Furthermore, I wanted to open my eyes but didn't because of who I thought I would see. Actually, it was who I *knew* I would see.

"Thought you were going to work?"

It was, Andre', and he got inside with that damn key my dumb ass let him have. I noticed Stay Black was still on my phone saying *hello, hello,* but I didn't answer because Andre' was standing up at my patio door like he was supposed to be my daddy and I was his daughter sneaking on the phone.

"I gotta call you back, alright?" My finger hit power and my phone shut down in Black's face. Then, I stood up from my nice, contented position and moved over toward Andre' slowly, staring him in his eyes harshly. "No, I didn't go to work today," I stated, scooting around him while giving him a disgraced glance up and down his body. "Are you going to work? Doesn't your shift start at one today?"

He had the audacity to come in *my* place questioning me about my whereabouts and why-nots when he hadn't even filled me in on his recent life yet. What my mind was thinking was something I truly didn't want to believe, but from the time I started cleaning up until now, that bad feeling didn't go away. Was some sort of gang beat down really what happened to his wife because that doesn't make any sense? Where on earth was she hangin' out and why? A gang in his neck of the woods or at the airport? That sounded like nonsense.

I turned around to face him from inside my kitchen while he stood there at my patio door. "Well? You come in my place with questions, so answer mine. Aren't you supposed to be working instead of in here snooping around me?" I had to repeat myself because he was behaving as if blocks of wax had his ears plugged up. Bet half that attitude he had was from hearing a man's voice on the other end of the phone calling for me.

"What's the attitude about, Jeena, baby? Come on, now. I just felt you up all night long the other night, and now you gettin' on me like you don't know me. What's up?"

At that, he walked his sexy body over near me to grab me. I backed up, but he pulled me again tighter. I wasn't going to lie to myself, therefore, I gave up on the resisting because I cared for him deeply. The more I was with him, the more I felt. Only this time, that feeling of love was mixed with some sadistic, unimaginable bull crap that I didn't want to digest nor believe he could do for that matter.

"Andre', I love you, but I don't think we are a good idea anymore. Your wife..."

His hand left my side at the word "wife" which prompted me to glance up at his face. It was frustrated, so I knew what was about to come from those luscious lips next – something not so luscious.

"What about my wife, Jeena? Didn't I tell you that I loved you? Didn't I tell your ass that?"

Say what? I looked at him like he had gone and lost his mind coming off like he was about to do something to me, like *he probably* did to his wife. After his rant, he suddenly quieted down to a more even tone.

"Jeena, I apologize for cursing at you like that, but I wouldn't be over here with you wondering what's up," he whimpered, while he glanced toward the patio where he last caught me on the telephone with Black, "if I didn't love you. Baby," he continued as he reached my for my hands. "I thought you loved me back the same, Jee. Now what's up? You're not acting like your normal self around me."

As he caressed my hands and kissed my cheek down to my neck, I wanted to forget about his wife, and that *your ass* with which he addressed me. Truly, I wished I'd never gone to get Faith from that hospital, but I did. I saw what I saw, and with the way Andre' was acting, something was not right. His first time staying overnight with me was the night his wife was supposedly out of town. She was out of town alright. Sure, I was sleeping with a married man, but I'd never condone beating someone half to death. She looked like the elephant man, I swear she did.

I backed up away from his seduction and pulled my hands away from his grasp. Then, I decided to bring his wife up again but in an innocent way...kinda. "Will your wife find out about us ever?"

"Never."

"How do you know?"

"I do."

"Why don't you want her to?"

"Timing."

"Where is she now?" Bam! I slam dunked that one, and Andre' got as silent as a tack stuck in a fluffy carpet. "I mean, how do you know *for sure* that she isn't watching us, or you for that matter, right now? I don't want people talking trash about me, calling me homewrecker to the world, Andre', because that's what will happen if she catches me and you together. It would be different if you just left her. Like for real, where is she?" Still dead silence.

Umm hmm, say something, I thought, as I backed further away from him and around the other side of the bar as I tapped my fingers on the countertop. I knew full well why Tina didn't know about us at this very moment, and that was because she is sitting up smashed faced on a hospital bed, probably just coming out of brain death as bad as she looked. Not by gang hands either, but by Andre's hands.

While I stood there awaiting his big reveal, he remained like a statue with a plain face. No frown, no grin, no nothing in response to my question. All Andre' did was stare at the design on my floor. Got your lying ass now, I thought. Speak up now, brotha man, I taunted him in my mind.

"Who was that?" he asked, still with his eyes to the floor.

Huh? My high from asking him a pointed question about Tina came right back down, lifting my eyebrows up in total *huh?*-ness.

"Who was who?" I responded, lost and confused as to how we got on some other question and answer game besides mine.

"On the phone. Who was that on the phone you were talking to before you knew I was inside listening?"

"A friend of mine from back in the day." He didn't need to know all of that. For all he knew, it could have been a cousin or uncle. Fact of the matter was that it was none of his business and that was with a point, blank and the period.

He looked up at me from the corner of his eye and calmly put his hands in his pockets. Then, he took a deep breath. As I leaned over on the counter top with my elbows, I started getting the feeling that little Romeo here was getting jealous. It almost made me giggle, but I didn't dare. It was too funny though! A *married* man jealous of who a single woman was talking to on the telephone was pretty hilarious until...

"Jeena," he paused, "you're lying." He removed his right hand from his pocket, reached over and opened my utensils drawer, pulling out a small knife. Shit just got serious. I ended up in an apparent shock because my heart began to race, but my feet went flop because I wasn't running. Stupid but true. I was in a state of disbelief obviously because I wasn't ready to digest fully that the knife was meant for me.

Good for me that instead of my body, he started to carve an apple that was on my counter beside my fruit bowl. My heart's rapid thump started going stead, but as he peeled and carved, he stared directly at me. There was no love in his eyes. Honestly, this mug slowly started looking like a psychopath because he wasn't paying any attention to the damn apple! It was jacked up, but he kept cutting! All the apple peals and core were hitting the countertop, so I knew he had no intention of eating it. Finally, I concluded that knife was for me, thus, the return of the rapid heart rate.

I was beyond scared stiff because I had nowhere to go. Dude had lost his mind, and he also looked like he was about to lose it on me. I scanned the room really quickly, but where I was standing, there was nothing – nothing to grab, nothing to block a stab. Nothing.

Taking a deep breath, I contemplated running to the door,

but that was the dumbest idea since giving him my key. He was standing too close to me, and if he was about to go madman on me, running would get me caught. My best move was to remain on the other side of this counter top. We can run around and around if we had to, but I wasn't turning my back on him. Hell no. I would bite the heck out of this mug like a vampire before I turned by back on him.

While Andre' continued going flipping ape with the apple, I glanced away in an attempt to calm myself and gather thoughts other than death. When I looked back, his eyes were still on me, but in those small seconds I batted my eyes away from his, an idea came - behave like a lost puppy. If I had to do so, even make love to him again, but my only objective was to not die. That was my only choice, especially after seeing Tina's face.

I crept back over to him, making certain that I didn't hesitate with this rabid joker because he might snap. My next move was to become the pitifully in love and hurting female, but really, I was scared as hell he was about to cut me up like that damn record collector movie Parri brought over the other week. That movie was a sign, I declare, it was a sign.

"Lying to you about what, Andre'?" I asked. "After a late night, I just wanted to chill at home, so I called in to work."

"After you told me that you were going to work this morning, Jeena?"

"What about the question I asked you about..." I began, but he cut me off cold.

"This ain't about Tina!" He stopped carving, and I nearly crapped in my lace panties because he wiped blood off his finger. As I stared at that red DNA on my counter, I already knew, I wasn't gonna clean that evidence up. No way. This joker just cut through his skin to the white meat! Top things off, he shoved the knife back in my drawer, blood splatter and all.

"This is about you and me, Jeena. I take our relationship more seriously than what you may think, Jee, and my marriage doesn't weigh in on that." His hand went on the side of my neck and gently rubbed it. If this moe-foe tried to choke me out and if my vampire bite didn't work, I was gonna snatch that knife out of the drawer and take my chances.

"I chose to love you, and I won't ever leave you, not even for my wife. We have nothing to do with my being married or unmarried because you knew what it was from the start. That's why Tina is irrelevant. I love you. I'm just married to her," he paused, "until death. Now, who was that over there on the phone? He got a name, baby Jee?"

I placed my hand on his hand, of course, moving the one that was on the side of my neck by giving it a slow, soft kiss to calm the beast about to manifest out of him. It seemed to work.

Thinking about how fast he could have potentially killed me, I continued to sooth the savage. "I'm afraid of getting hurt," I stumbled, "...my feelings hurt, Andre'. This is different ground for me, so I just don't know about it all. We are getting so deep, and I really want to be your only love, the only one. Not to be shared with anyone else." When I said it, Andre' sort of flinched like a bug stung him in his ear, but then changed the subject again.

"Be honest with me, Jeena. That's all I ask for, baby. You hear me?" With his index and middle fingers, he tilted my chin up. Then, he moved in closer to my face, his lips against my ear lobe. I began to rub his back with my fingertips, trying not to breathe really hard because I knew something could go dead wrong and fast, so I had to play it cool, like normal. I kept thinking about him snapping my neck like Jason on Friday the 13th, but then...

"Who else you sexing, Jeena? I look like your damn fool? Cut the bullshit. I didn't make no deals to share you, baby." He asked, proceeding to kiss the back of my neck up to my hair line. His bloody hand also went back up to my neck and wrapped around it snuggly like a glove. All that tender rubbing I was doing on his back ceased along with my breathing. Then, he kept talking.

"I never lied to you. I told you about my wife, and that means I respect you. I need that same respect, Jeena. Let me know whatever you feel, baby, or whatever you're doing, especially if it's with another man. I'll understand. I want you to believe me though when I say that I love you. You love me?"

Without hesitation, I told this fool yes. As I stared off at the patio where I left my cell, I thought about Stay Black. His behind wasn't ever at my door at the right time. Andre's nibbling on my neck and massaging the small of my back didn't take my mind off of Stay Black like it would have just minutes prior to this mess. Instead, my brain was working overtime while he was lightly squeezing the back of my neck.

"I'm not sexing any other man, Andre'. I'm just afraid."

"Of what, baby?"

Of your ass, I thought.

He loosened his grip on my neck, and I felt the blood from his deep cut crawl slowly down my skin. At that moment, my life was in danger. He knew his hand was cut and bleeding, and he didn't even behave as if he felt it. He knew what he was doing. This was a threat that he planned on putting into action. No, he may not have stated it with his words, but with deed, it was everything a promise was made of.

"When I ran into you two at the store, it made me worry about us and everything, and that's why I didn't call you back or anything because I got to thinking about all that could go wrong and I know you couldn't tell I was stressing when we made love but..." Yeah, I knew I was rambling a mile a minute with my words, but it was more believable that way. I just kept thinking talk, Jeena, talk as much as you can.

"My wife is away. She's away for a while on a trip, Jeena," he interjected. "Don't worry about her. Worry about me, Jee. I'm your man, not her."

That lie he just told about Tina confirmed my worst fears. Andre' had to be the one who busted up her face. The worst of my thoughts were coming to a head. Now, I never claimed to be the smartest woman on the planet, but I did have intelligent conversations with her from time to time. She was telling me to break away from Andre' as soon as possible because something just wasn't right, and substantiating that was his blood on my neck. Who wiped blood on someone but a sociopath?

"When did she leave? Yesterday?" I asked playing it off as if I didn't know.

"No, baby. She left the same day we saw each other in the store. That's why I came over that night. I wanted to be with you."

"Oh," I responded. The floor must have had a five star movie showing because I was fixated on it. I couldn't even look at him. To think he beat Tina down that bad to come and have sex with me? He knew he would beat her down so bad that she would spend time in the hospital aka vacation! What kind of sick shi...?

"Really. I need you in my life, Jeena." His eyes met mine forcefully as he pushed my chin back up to look him square in the face. "Listen, I gotta go, baby. Answer your phone next time I call, and don't worry. Things are cool."

I weakly smiled while he reminded me to not have "*no more brothas that he doesn't know about on the phone*" and then he...

Left.

I just stood there thinking, this nut has the key to my place and a bloody knife in my drawer. Immediately, I plopped down on my sofa and rocked back and forth, watching my reflection in the blank television screen. The whole reflection looked like a scary movie, circling around me at high speed.

"I'm gonna die if I leave this fool," I stated quietly. He already had me talking to myself and picking at my fingernails, ripping them apart. That's what I did when I got nervous. My fingernails would start off hot and sexy but then run into busted and disgusted really fast.

There was a Kleenex hanging from the box on the coffee table, so I wiped my neck. His blood got all over it. I bet Andre' had a criminal record a mile long that included strangulation and attempted murder. Before I'd even thought about that notion fully, I'd already turned on my laptop to do research. But then, I thought about Capital City. No, he had to be clean to run a place like Capital City, but it could be that he never got caught.

Panic struck as I thought about being the unsolved mystery that my mom and dad would have to watch on television because I didn't tell a soul who I was sleeping around with. That fact alone prompted me to go back up to that hospital to get words from Tina's mouth herself, even confess that I was sleeping with her husband if I had to do so. That way, I could get her angry enough to turn him in. He would be arrested, and that would leave me in the clear and safer than ever.

Needing to know more about Tina's situation consumed me like the oxygen I breathed, and I just had to know for a fact for my own emotional stability what happened fist by fist, including how possibly sick her husband actually was. It would be my worst nightmare if I'd messed around and sexed up a psycho.

That was why I got up from my seat and slowly walked back to where I left my cell on the patio. By the time I got to the phone, I'd already spotted a message on it from someone because the big envelope symbol stared back at me from the screen. That was one time I wasn't in a rush to listen to who it was, but I did. As I listened to the message, it wasn't Andre', but Stay Black. Oh yeah, I did hang up on him, so I called him back.

"Hello, Stay Black?"

"Yeah. Jee, you okay? I heard…"

Shut that down quick. "Forget what you heard."

"Forget what I…"

"Yeah. So, yeah, I'm doing okay. Sorry I got off of the phone so fast. I forgot I left my door open, and my cousin strolled his nosey behind on in," I sang nervously which made it obvious that I was lying from both sides of my mouth. Guilt makes folk do that. Dead give away. I slipped up, and he knew it because he wasn't as stupid as I used to call him. Knowing Stay Black though, he was gonna wait on me to tell him.

There was silence at first like he was thinking, *Jeena you think I'm stupid*, but instead of verbalizing it, he said, "You shouldn't leave your door open like that. Anybody can come in on you." His voice was monotone and flat.

All the name calling wasn't necessary. *You shouldn't leave your door open like that* - meaning my legs, and *anybody can come in on you* - meaning orgasm. It truly wasn't funny, that whole sideways slam he just gave me, because my mind is not for all that talk down to Jeena mess just because he heard a man's voice in my place. He was seriously off base, but who was I fooling? He was partly right, and I wasn't going to argue because I knew I deserved that lesson a while ago.

"Well, I'm getting ready to go and..." Stay Black continued, sounding bothered because of the whole excuse I gave him about a guy being over, so I cut him off again.

"Black, sorry for cutting you off again, but I need you to come over."

"Why?"

He had an attitude, but whatever.

"I need you with me on something I have to do. It's important. Will you come?"

"What is it, Jeena?"

"I have something to do, and I need some company while I do it. It'll be okay, Black, and you won't find yourself in jail, prison, none of that. Will you? For me?"

"Jeena," he sighed, sounding like he was in supreme agony. "I can't come right now, but..."

"That's fine!"

"You're just on a cut me off tip today, ain't ya', baby? Can't get a word in," he stated sounding a little less tense.

"Oops. Sorry, but I don't need you to come over now. After work. It will be late, really late but I need you to meet me at my place. I'll ride with you." I glanced at the clock on my counter. Plenty time! "Yeah, just after you get off, come on over, okay?

121

We won't be leaving until late, but I still gotta fill you in on the plan."

"What plan?"

I heard frustration setting in once again.

"Just be here, k?"

"Cool."

"Bye." I hung up and couldn't wait until he showed his face at my doorstep. Until I saw it though, I had some investigating I needed to do. Where did old Andre' live? Now in spite of the fact that I had all that information at work because he was once a patient, I didn't ever think to look it up because I wasn't ever going over there anyway. Stupid it was, I knew that already, but I hadn't been flying on the smart jet in these friendly skies either lately.

Another problem was that I wasn't at my job today, so getting my hands on the information was slim to none in the time that I needed it. Andre' had already halfway cracked up, and I didn't want the full deal before it was too late. All I needed to do was keep things in tact and my reputation clean without a big blow up and that meant somehow getting his wife to have him arrested for beating her ass like I know he did.

Then, my mind began to calculate a plan - the plan that I told Black I had. There was none. I lied. Well there was – kinda. It was that me and Stay Black were going to follow him home when he got off from work to see where he lived, but that would never have worked because Stay Black in all of my business like that was a ton of not happening on a side of trouble. Truth was, I needed Black to come over here with me anyway in case Andre' showed back up. Andre' had to work, but still. If all I could get Black to do was just be here, then that would be my plan. If Andre' came in the door, I would scream, tell Black I don't know him and bam! Knock out punch and arrested. Then, I would find a way to sneak my key back without Black looking, and I would be in the clear.

As I sat there rethinking my plans about Tina, Andre' and Black while twiddling my fingers, a big hell naw popped up. How the devil would I sneak some keys from Andre' after a brawl? On top of that, Black would end up arrested for knocking out Andre' who would be busy telling the cops everything! The absolute last thing I wanted was Black to be in any trouble, so I nixed that plan.

Instead of receiving comfort from my thoughts, I began yanking at my hair until I heard..."Jeena!"

Who the devil? My whole gut sunk in by the loud shout at my door. I was already on edge, the voice sent me diving into another realm of nerves. It sounded like my girl Tanya screaming in some sort of panic, so I ran over and looked out the peephole. Yep, it was her and her hell raisers outside waiting on me to let them inside. After digesting it all, I took a step back and wondered, how did they know I was home from work today? I needed to find a less noticeable parking spot for real!

"Tanya," I began, opening the door while taking on the appearance of confusion although I already figured that her being at the door was going to be nothing but drama. "What's all this noise about?"

"I got to come in, Jeena," she stated, breathing so hard that she looked like a woman in labor. "I need you to hold my kids 'til momma comes to get them." That's when Tanya motioned to her children to enter my domain, and when they came across the threshold, they darted to the fruit on my countertop.

"Wait a minute!" I yelled at them to no avail. I remembered the blood I hadn't cleaned up, so I yelled again. "Get outta my fruit! That's for my bowels, dang it! Sit down!" Finally, they all sat down in the middle of the floor like little gremlins.

When I turned back to face Tanya, her hair was a mess. I mean, it was jacked up, and she never allows her hair to look a nightmare on her street or any other street. Her face was as red as a strawberry fruit roll-up on her light skin, and she looked like she'd just come from a full day at the gym.

"Where are you going, Tanya, that you need to leave your kids with me?" I quickly twisted back to see what those little sneaks were getting ready to uncover and attack, but when I saw things were still good, I turned back to face Tanya.

"Oh, where am I going? I'm getting ready to go to jail, then to prison," she responded calmly as she fidgeted around in her pocket. "The cops on the way already 'cause I done stabbed that fool. Going back to finish this mutha off, too."

"Say what!" I yelped instead of blowing off steam with a quick *what the hell* because of the presence of children, but those same children she was gonna have to get up outta here before I wind up an accomplice to this mess that she'd gotten herself into. I got to call the po-po my dog on self now! It was that or either she was gonna roll off of my porch right now! I loved her, but I honest to God didn't have that much love for her follow her to prison.

"At least I *tried* to stab him. I think I only managed to cut his cheatin' ass, and that's why I had to take my kids out of there so I can go back and finish him like Mortal Kombat."

"You cut him? Tanya," I sang her name as I shut the door behind me, blocking the kids from the conversation. I was in pure shock that Tanya was actually in mid-murder! "He was creepin' on you? Did he hit you or one of your babies? For that I could see a good cut, but you ain't got to kill him, girl, for creepin'! Just call the law and get him out of your place is all, Tina, I mean, Tanya."

Lord, I said Andre's wife name, and it scared me so much that I had to push my piss back up! My kidneys and bladder lost complete focus while talking to Tanya because I'm so stressed out about that blood on my own counter, a psycho married man for a boyfriend that I probably should've stabbed and dumped behind a barn but didn't, and top it all off he had my key! Thank God Tanya was far too left field to catch that Tina fumble, so I continued, "The same way he came, the same way he can and will go. You're lying about cutting him right, Tanya, please say..."

"Does this look like I'm lying?"

This crazy heffa yanked a shank out from her pants' pocket. What kind of prison made stuff was that? I was 'bout to pass out, but thank God for the door I shut because it caught me in my lean. A bloody dog-on shank at my residence! D.N. damn A. evidence of the murder of some dude that I didn't even know! It was time to pray. I had too much criminal activity surrounding me, so I knew good and well how to take a hint. This was God. Tanya had to go for right now, and so did Andre' forever. Forgive me, Father, for cussing in my thoughts again and for all the other days I cuss out loud, including all the evil stuff I have done in the last weeks. I truly am going to do better, especially now, so please take Tanya away from my condo and lead me away from danger because it's coming to get me. Death. I feel it breathing down my naked neck! Amen.

"Girl, you gotta get that thing away from here!" I screamed in the lowest tone I possibly could muster, quickly glancing behind her on both sides to make sure absolutely no one was anywhere in sight watching the shank slinger. "Tanya, you ain't gonna be implicating me in no crime! Put that crap away! You crazy? I don't even want to see you right now because you're putting me in a bad position, T! A really bad position. What if I get questioned over some dumb junk, Tanya? You ever thought about that? I would have to roll over on you, and I'm telling you to your face so there won't be any surprises, I can't take a murder wrap, I'm sorry. I got your back all the time, but this is serious, girl."

She rolled her eyes so heavily that I just knew homegirl had lost it long before she got here. Demon possessed was an understatement. She looked like there was absolutely no turning back unless Jesus Himself took the shank and took the wheel.

"Tanya! Tanya, baby, Jesus Christ, have mercy!"

I turned to the left, and sure enough, that was Tanya's mom limping up here in her green robe and house shoes as she screamed at the top of her lungs for her shank totin' daughter.

"Momma! Momma, I'm sick of him, momma. He put some tramp in my bed, dammit!"

"Tanya!" her mom yelled back in an *I'm warning you* tone.

"Rolling that bitch around on the sheets I bought and that me and my babies cuddle up in when they get scared! The bed I saved my hard earned money on, ma!" Tanya yelled back at her.

That was it. I was officially what we call *'shame,* the shortened version of ashamed. Tanya and her mom were so loud that the blinds across the street at the other condos opened up. Time for the news crew at any minute, I thought, and then I'm going to have to stare directly into the camera as Tanya's kids leave my home, to tell the world that those kids aren't mine waving in the background with apple all on their mouths calling me Auntie Jee and saying cheese!

With Tanya holding that bloody shank in her hand still screaming, her momma, Miss Bell, big Miss Bell, walked up to her and back slapped her dead in the face! My entire chin hit the door mat because the sound of that slap must have ricocheted off Tanya's face to bust me on my jaw! I was so shocked! You know how if your sibling ever did something wrong, everybody got it? Well, there ya go! I knew I had it coming if I said one word to hold off Miss Bell. Tanya, well, she almost fell over, and immediately after the slap, she stared at her mom in disbelief.

"Momma, you don't understand..."

"Don't you ever stab or cut nobody unless they trying to stab you, you hear me? Told your fast ass about acting married anyway. Keep your legs shut, and don't you ever cuss my way again. Them cops gone. I helped your boyfriend to forgive you fast, so ain't no charges pressed. Don't know what he told the cops, but they're gone. Your crazy behind, and Lord, forgive me please because I don't wanna cuss, but she got it coming, Lord. She has it coming."

"Momma, he had a girl in..."

"And!" Her mom placed her hand on her hip and leaned back, sucking in a deep wad of air. "Buy another bed and get married to the next man you meet! Least that way, you might just get to sue somebody! Get paid for your troubles! Can't get a bit of money laid up with a man who isn't even married to you. You don't ever let a man and a woman with no self discipline or respect for their own bodies or others land you in prison. And as a matter of fact, you need to get some self respect, too! Now, where my grandkids? And you need to clean yourself up!" she spoke as loudly to Tanya as she could without making the veins pop out of her throat.

When she asked for her grandkids, I didn't waste any time getting those grandchildren of hers out of my personal vicinity for fear Miss Bell would dive on me. I simply kicked the bottom of my front door and open it came. As soon as the kids saw their grandma, they ran out.

"Grandma!" they all shouted at once.

"Come on, babies." They all crowded around her, hugging her legs and waist. "They're staying with me tonight. Get that man out of your place, child. Be by yourself! It's the best thing, but if you can't keep your legs shut and you need something between them that much, get a husband. Whether you love him or not, least you won't burn. A man is a man. The huge difference between a boyfriend and husband sleeping with you is the word burn. You hear me? Better love yourself enough to keep your tail from it." She dropped her head toward her grandchildren. "Come on, y'all," she continued under her breath. "Talking about he cheated. Shoot! They all cheat! Walk a mile in my shoes, you learn real fast. That's why I ain't touch one since your daddy left this earth, and I was happy to bury him, believe it or not, especially after his girlfriends showed up at the grave! Set me free from his mess!"

"Ma, don't talk about daddy in public. This isn't about him!" Tanya pleaded, but it didn't phase her mom because she continued to ramble.

"I even kept those flowers I bought to put on his grave for myself, too. Never told you that. Went right back and got 'em. Left this girlfriends' flowers right there. My plot's not even next to his anymore. Nope! Surely isn't. I won't be buried anywhere near the man! He tortured me in life, but won't be close enough to him at death for it to happen again, believe you me. Forgive me, Lord, but hell no! Let his girlfriends lie next to his old rotten body when they die. Life been peaceful ever since he hit the grave, too. Sex ain't never been worth the headache of a silly

127

man." Whatever else she said, she said it too quiet for me to hear as she walked away - with all those kids.

"Bye, momma!" All of Tanya's little creations hollered at her as they skipped away..

Without even asking me, Tanya decided to enter my residence, nearly knocking me over in the process. I thought about kicking her back out, but then again, maybe I could soothe the savage, thus, I shut the door.

"You walked in on them, Tanya?" I asked sitting on the armrest of my sofa. Boy, my life was becoming more and more filled with drama the longer that I lived. Maybe I needed to go lie in peace next to Miss Bell's husband in place of all his girlfriends.

"Man, hell yeah, Jee Jee, with my kids! That's why I had to cut him, girl. I had to cut his *ass*!" As she rocked back and forth, I honestly didn't know what to say or do. I didn't want her to cut me, so I wasn't gonna say too much. Might have slipped up and said something too loaded that would get me stabbed up in here with that same *I don't know if he has disease in his blood* shank she cut him with.

"It'll be alright, Tanya. Just drop his butt. There are plenty men out there that won't do you like that."

"I know, but Jee, it's just the principal of the whole thing. And just what the hell kinda of woman is gonna come up in somebody else's bed and have her damn fun. Nasty heifer. I should've cut her ass, too, but I let her go. I should have cut her right in her..."

"Tanya!" That was too much information. "Girl, shut up!" I started to laugh. "You did right. Let her go. He's the one that you should've cut if you were gonna cut, not saying that what you did was right. You want something to drink?"

"Blood."

I got up from my sofa and marched toward the kitchen. Blood to drink. She was losing it. As I approached my refrigerator, I knew that the closest thing I had to blood in it was cranberry juice, besides the real blood that Andre' left drying up on my counter. That cranberry juice was what she was gonna get. Surprise her butt. I iced that baby up and took it to her. I poured myself a glass, also, and that finished the bottle.

"Thank you, girl," she graciously stated, taking the glass straight from my hand. Then she took a swallow, and just as soon as that bitter taste hit her tongue, she glanced up at me. I answered her facial expression.

"You asked for blood, so I gave you the next nastiest thing."

"You tried to be funny."

"A little. So were they in the act...act," I asked her, not willing to spell it all out.

"Just finished. Her smelly behind. I don't smell like that, that's for sure. Coochie stunk just like her. I mean, I wanted to beat her..."

"I know you did, but look at it this way."

"What way? Is there another way to look at this? Where do you want me to go, under the bed to get a better view at how hard they were pounding?"

"She gotta deal with that stank coochie and bad rep when you finish blasting it loud in the streets, and you can tell her business for life and not get sued because it isn't slander. The truth is the truth. Just playing, girl, don't do that - unless you're pushed!" I laughed, attempting to lighten the cheating atmosphere above our heads. "You're gonna get a good man sooner or later for sure." I gulped down my cranberry juice. I was so used to drinking this stuff that the twanginess of it didn't phase me. "He'll be ready to be your king and put it down like you're the queen because your heart was broken, and he'll be ready to fix it."

"Whatever. I'm so sick of men right now."

She stood up from the chair, with her short, tight and white top revealing trickles of blood on it. No doubt that the blood was from the shank she had hidden in her pocket.

"You need to borrow a shirt or something? Yours is quite the bloody mess."

"No, we're getting ready to go. Come on."

Huh? Uh uhh! *We* ain't going anywhere. I wasn't about

to walk around in broad daylight with a stabbess, returning to the crime scene like I was to help her dispose of the body! I had my own ass to wipe shit from and little did she know, my shit was top priority. Dang, I did it again. Lord, please forgive me for cussing in my brain, I prayed. Why not try and get right now, I thought.

"We?" I rose up from my somewhat relaxed position to a more tense one. "Where did you have in mind for *we* to go?"

"I'm going back over there. That's my place, not his. I don't care that he made up some story for the cops to let me off the hook. Truth is, he better have his ass out instead of thinking about saving me from the cops before I cut his ass again."

"What you need me for, then, Tanya? Don't you know the way back to your place?" She lived in the apartment complex about a mile down the road.

"That dude ain't jumping on me without me having my back-up!"

On that note, I looked all around my condo and up underneath the chairs and all. Didn't find her back up, and I hoped she wasn't talking about me. I'd be dogged if I was gonna go to jail as I told her at the door. He wasn't mine, and even if he was, I didn't sign ride or die contracts for no man nor friends. I ride to a point and then get off a the nearest stop sign before the danger – well most of the time. Point was, I got off when stuff got ugly.

"I don't know, Tanya," I responded, even more apprehensive than before.

"Girl, you don't even have to get out of the car. Take your phone in case so you can dial 911 if something pops off and I cut him again for jumpin' at me. If you see me running, start up the car, let me jump in so we can bail." She turned away, heading for the door.

I would have asked her to pass me the shank to make sure her hands didn't reach out cut and someone, but I didn't want my fingerprints on it. Nope! I'd watched too much Forensic Files.

"I don't think I want to go, Tanya."

She turned back and stared straight into my eyes in disbelief at my rejection of her situation. Then, a tear drifted down her face. At that point, I identified. It was the visible manifestation of heartbreak, and all she needed was for someone to give her the courage to get that mess straightened out and fast.

"Please," she begged. "I just want the man out of my apartment. I got my shank this time to protect myself if I have to while making him leave. Please, Jeena."

I had to go. Shank or no shank. She needed my emotional...

Support.

"No the hell I'm not!" a male voice shouted.

"And it's yours, and you better believe I'm gonna get mine. That's why I cut your ass! Carrying your baby, and you're gonna do this to me!"

"You can lose that baby down at the clinic. I can't lose my money for eighteen years." he responded. "I'll give you five hundred dollars right now to end it, but I won't pay you that for no eighteen years every single month!"

"Get out!" I heard something get thrown across the room. That's right. Heard, not seen. I wasn't crazy enough to accessorize a murder with my presence. Despite my hesitation, however, I had to get out of my comfort zone, and go see about Tanya due to the fact that I'd already gotten the mommy memo.

On the way back to her apartment, Tanya told me the reason that she thought she could go insane atop of the fact that there was a woman in her bed. She was two months pregnant and only found out last week. To me, that was a crying shame, not because she was pregnant, but because there was no denying it as his and he just screwed around on her.

131

I think his real name was Anthony. Tony and Tanya was on this gold bracelet she wore, so I just assumed based on Tanya's past serious boyfriends, that she fell in love with this one, too. She did the same with every one of her serious men, purchased a bracelet and engraved names into it. I didn't agree with it. My name and only my name was gonna go on anything that I owned and purchased to wear on my body. Later for that tattoo and engraving mess. Must be my future son or Jesus Who I, by the way, needed a better relationship with ASAP.

All their shouting, I heard from the car. The windows were open with fans sitting on the sills. Tanya never had too much money, but she made due, and if putting fans in the windows was how she did it, then more power to her. I gave her much respect for her hustle with all those kids she fed and clothed, mostly without a man's help. Her only downfall was men though, unfortunately. She just couldn't keep them from in between her sunshine and rain, thus causing her heartache and pain.

Tony, according to her on the way over here, was supposed to be the one that she thought was gonna marry her. Be her soldier. I thought not. He already had four baby mommas and no place to stay, hence, Tanya's apartment. No legit job that I knew of, but he always had so called money in his pocket and would shower her kids with toys. To me, it was more like, stolen goods. Everything was brand new Tanya would say. I would think to myself only two words - professional thief. I wanted to ask her where he worked for all this brand new stuff all the time, but failed to do so. Why? Because of the don't ask don't tell policy of our friendship that kept it crime, criminal and cuss you out free. Tanya had been known to catch an attitude with folk if they ask too many questions that she may not want to answer, so I would always allow her to voluntarily give up the goods in her own time.

"You ain't got to worry about me leaving up outta here, Tanya," he yelled, "Just back up!"

"Get out now!"

The next thing I heard was not good, meaning that I had to make haste to the apartment. Tanya had started screaming.

"I said get off of me!" she belted at the top of her lungs, so I started to run. I had no idea what I was gonna do, but I needed to do it. It sounded like Tanya needed some real help in there.

"This how you treat me after protecting your ass from the police, huh?"

When I got to the front door and pushed it open, to my surprise, it wasn't Tanya that needed saving. He was holding her back so she wouldn't stick a shank to his side as she straddled him on the floor.

"Tanya!" I ran right up behind her and grabbed both of her arms and yanked them as hard as I could yank. That's when...

"Tony, right?" I asked the man getting ready to be stabbed.   "Yeah," he responded, as he slid from underneath old bat head Tanya, leaving me and her to fall backwards onto the floor. Was she nuts? She knew better than to act like she was acting while pregnant! Gathering myself up off of the floor, I watched her as he tried to help her up, but she snatched away from him. Then he threw his arms up in the air as if he was thinking *why did I even try.*

The apartment was a pure wreck. Holes in just about every area I looked at on the walls. Boy, she better not move out anytime soon, I thought. She would definitely have to pay more than the security deposit! They wrecked this place! I honestly couldn't imagine what on earth she was throwing, but then, I glanced at the floor. Oh, that's what it was. The phone, a big cast iron skillet and a broken iron sat unhappily out of place on the rug.

"Get away from me, Tony! I hate your ass!"

"Tanya! Not meaning to be rude to your man, but he ain't worth all this, girl. He obviously thought you weren't worth it, and that's why he did what he did."

"Who are you? You don't know me! You don't know how

things go down in here!" he shouted at me in response to my words. "All you know is what she tells you."

He went there. What *she* tells me is what he said. Clown ass man.

"No, Tony, you're wrong. All I know is what just went down in her bed, and there isn't an excuse in the world for you and another woman having sex in here for any reason at all, no matter if you were cheating with a different woman everyday. That's Tanya's bed. That's the issue I have because that's the issue that I know about. That was foul because you could have gone elsewhere if you're gonna do it with a hoe. Why in another female's bed, to top it off the mother of your child's bed? What else is needed to be known, that I need to know, besides that? It gets no worse, *playa*! Sorry for getting in your business, but this is my friend. You ain't." I said it calmly, but with so much attitude ole Tony probably thought I was screaming. After that, he got the rest of his stuff and left. This is when all my attention went back on Tanya.

"Girl, you're pregnant! You don't go tussling with no man over some girl, especially when you're with child. Get up off the floor, Tanya."

She didn't move. She just sat there motionless, void of any type of reasoning or understanding. It was as if all the life that was trapped inside of her was lost or dying, leaving her hopeless. Where was Faith when I needed her?

I attempted to remember the things that I heard her say to people in her own unique and God praying way. An imitation would be hard, and I didn't believe that I could actually do what she did and with that much grace in my own capacity. Gee! She was a prayer superstar or something! Since Tanya wasn't getting up, I got down on the floor with her and put my arms around her tight.

"Things are gonna be alright, and you don't have to do much except love that new baby. He or she is a gift from God. He will take care of that life. He will be that child's Father. Watch and see, girl. Just watch and see."

"Thank you, Jeena."

I didn't know that I did much, but at that point, I knew I couldn't be the other woman to any man anymore. Just seeing how hurt Tanya was, and Tony wasn't even her husband yet, changed how I saw everything I was doing. I was going to the hospital today to set things straight.

Right after leaving Tanya's, I drove to the hospital to face my doom. While on my way, I kept wondering how on earth I kept doing what I was doing without a second thought. The more I did it, the easier it got. I really made our relationship the norm for myself and pushed everything that would change my mind about it away from me just so I could feel good and do what I wanted. On the other end, Tina was getting beat and all because of me. I wasn't a monster, was I?

Tanya's face and her cradling her stomach like it was in pain hurt my soul. That baby in her belly didn't deserve that drama in seven more months. What if Andre's wife was pregnant just like Tanya? I was a fool. I real fool.

While driving down the road on the way to the hospital, I felt the serious need to stop somewhere, so I pulled into a parking lot. It was far less than halfway full. I scooted my little Saturn to the front of the lot and got out in a rush. I didn't know what was going on inside of the building in front of me, but I wasn't there for that. I needed a place to pray.

Opening the church doors, all the heads turned back to see me. They were in a meeting, well, at least, that's what it looked like to me. My eyes focused on the altar. Surely, prayer in my car would have sufficed, but even in there felt like smutty ground instead of holy ground.

"May I help you, hon?"

I stopped cold in my tracks, and looked to my right side. The lady that asked me that question was the lady I pushed in my dream! Hot dog! Prophecy like a mug!

"I need a place to pray, just for a minute."

She didn't respond, so I continued my anxiety ridden

plea. "Please, allow me to pray, a spot, just show me where I can go by myself," I began to cry from the bottled up emotion awaiting escape.

"No, baby," she said as she got up from her seat. "You don't need my permission to pray at anytime. Jesus is available at all times for you or anyone else, and I certainly can't stop it." Then she turned to the others who made up the small meeting. "Everyone, let's break for ten minutes, please." She looked back at me, and placed her hand on my arm. "Do you need to be alone right here specifically?"

"Yes. Please. Yes. This was the closest spot that I...I mean, I go here, but not as active my sister."

"Then you belong right here whether you are active or not if this is where the Lord sent you to be alone. A minister is through those doors if you need one." She pointed to the same doors the ushers stood by during the service.

There were no questions asked. She turned and left. They all knew my face I was sure, but not my name, unless Faith told them. I was never too friendly with the flock. When I looked back up, everyone, about 15 people, was walking out the side door leaving me face to face with the altar. I walked up to it. Yes, I knew that I couldn't see God, and why I needed to be here at the altar directly in front of the altar, I had no idea, but that was where I knelt and cried. It was the only place where I just knew God, through all my sin, would meet me. This was His house, and even though I couldn't see His face, I knew He would see me.

"Please forgive me, Jesus. I'm so sorry." Afraid to say what I was doing out loud, I whispered until my voice left and all of it came from my heart only. God could read my heart because He made it. I asked Him to fix it and please...

Save Me.

By the time I'd gotten up off my knees, I'd finished telling God everything as if He didn't already know. Everything that I'd done with Andre', I'd asked for forgiveness, including the way that I felt for him. It was beginning to stink. I smelled myself and finally wanted to come clean, never to do it again.

"Are you okay, baby?" It was the lady that I pushed in my dream causing those ropes to come down and get her from the rooftop.

"Yeah...yes ma'am. I had to pray for a moment in private, and thank you for allowing me in the sanctuary, you know, because I could have easily gone to the bathroom to do it or something."

"This isn't my house for you to thank me for anything. Do you need to talk to anyone else? You seem troubled about some things."

"No, no ma'am." I walked around her fast, and I didn't look back to even get another response. As far as my speaking about my situation with the lady at church at this point, I just didn't think that was wise. My dream told me that. Maybe some other time. Something about my story probably would have made her fall over dead, so the details stayed with me. With my luck, she would have ended up being Tina's aunt or Andre's distant cousin.

When I arrived at the hospital, I felt a burden leave because I was finally honest with someone about myself, and that was Jesus. Not like He didn't already know, but still. Secondly, I was getting ready to uncover something that would set my physical just as free. I was going for the gusto, and nothing was going to stop me. There was the space and opportunity for me to find out everything that I needed to know about everything. At the same time, poor Tina would find out about me, also.

My phone rang.

"Hello?"

"Girl, what the hell happened? Tanya done cut some man up!"

"Parri," I slammed my car door back shut and sat there, rolling my eyes in the process. "What's up, girl. Yeah her butt went and cut her man for finding him bunked over some chick in her bed."

"Are you kidding me?"

"Who told you?" I asked.

"Her."

"Well, Parri! What in the world? Didn't she tell you everything already?" I had gotten frustrated from all the stuff that Parri was asking me because she'd already found out from the main source and was just regurgitating it. I glanced up at the third floor. Please be there, I thought.

"What's wrong with you?"

She detected my anxious behavior already.

"Nothing."

"Nothing?" she asked in disbelief.

"Yeah. Tanya's pregnant. Two months, and I had to pull her off of her man before she cut him again."

"Say what!"

Whoops. I guess that part she didn't know.

"Yeah. So I'm not too happy about all that."

"No wonder she cut him up. I would have cut him, too, if I had his baby up in me, and he got another woman under my sheets."

"That's not a good reason, Parri."

"It wasn't a good reason to sleep with his dog ass either."

"What reason is that?" I asked confused.

"Love. Love and legs don't always mix ya know. Better know who to love with your legs closed, honey! Now look at her again - knocked up and nearly in jail."

There went that knot in my stomach again. I should've told her the truth about Andre' from the start. Maybe I wouldn't have slipped so far from reality. Parri always had these sayings or knowledge that she would rattle off from somewhere, but in the end, they would make so much sense. I could have used her truth a long time ago.

"Parri." She was still rambling, so I cut her off.

"What's up?"

"He's married." I just decided to spit it out.

"What!" She almost blew my ears out. Obviously, she probably assumed Tanya's man was the one hitched, therefore, I allowed myself to clarify.

"Not Tanya's man."

"Then whose?"

"Mine."

I knew that I shouldn't have left it at that word *mine*, but I did. After all that, there was complete silence. Then, she started again.

"Well, let's go find his ass and kick it."

"I knew." I had to cut her off again before the planning of a beat down started. "I knew ahead of time that he was married."

"Je-eena." She sang my name like she was at a funeral, and I was the corpse in the coffin.

"I know, Parri." This was my lowest point yet. "I'm sorry I didn't tell you the complete truth." I wiped my eyes from all the tears running down my cheeks.

"Did you really fall in love with him, Jeena?"

"Yeah, Parri, yes!" I responded frustrated emotionally and just worn out. "I don't think he is who I thought he was though, Parri. Please don't tell anyone about this because I am terribly ashamed of everything, no matter what it make sound like."

"Where are you?"

"Parri..."

"Where, Jeena?" She was serious, so I gave up trying to hide my location.

"At the hospital."

"Which one."

"The one down the street from you."

"Stay there. I'm coming. Stop crying. Just get out of the car in about ten minutes and stand next to it." She hung up the telephone.

I couldn't stop my tears. It was as if I was at church all over again in my dreams. Looking up at the sky, I looked for the sun, but the day was overcast. All the sunlight of any natural day was hidden. I wished that I could change everything back to that day - no that night - when Andre' dropped that business card in Capital City. If I could change things, I would've let it fall and remain on the floor. I even wished that I'd respected his wife enough at the point that I met her so that maybe I wouldn't be in this heartbreak that I brought all on myself. Who could I blame? Not God. I couldn't even blame Andre'. Shoot, not even Satan with his evil, monkey smelling ass! I only had myself to blame.

I kept a small Bible, one of those green half Bibles with the New Testament only, in my glove compartment. It was probably dusty because I never went in my glove compartment unless I got pulled over or needed to find out how to do something under the hood of my car. The Bible was actually just there as *the thing to do*, but I never cracked it.

"Lord, I meant what I said. Please take this feeling away from me. I know that what I did has consequences, but save me, not from the consequences necessarily, but from myself. I don't want to live like this anymore. But if you could take the consequences, that would be swell. Amen."

After that silent prayer, I took that small Bible out of my glove compartment, turned to the New Testament where Jesus spoke and tried to read all of them until...

Parri Knocked.

"I thought I asked you to get out of the car, Jee Jee," she called to me from my passenger's side window. "Let me in." Her hair was dyed a light brown orange type color which looked kind of nice against her complexion. I mean, it wasn't an orange kool-aid look, but it was just enough to give her some flair, not too much so that she would have to change professions.

"I like your hair," I complimented while opening the door.

"Accident." She dropped down on the seat.

"It certainly looks like you thought it all out. How was this an accident? It looks good," I stated, reaching out to grab a strand.

"That's because you hadn't seen the back."

My finger fiddled with a band of her hair, but she pulled away.

"At at! Don't mess with stuff you don't know a thing about. This thing is lethal. Take your breath away. You don't wanna see this at all. Weave will hide the other color in the middle. Gotta hook it up!"

"What other color, girl?"

"Nunya!"

"Forreal?"

"Man, Jee Jee, it's purple like a mug!"

"Say what?"

"I'm not saying that again. It might get worse. Have you ever heard of the bad lip?"

"No, Parri. There is no such thing."

"Well, I'm not gonna attempt to solve what you call an untrue mystery." She then twisted the front of her body in my direction and leaned her head on the head rest, eyes glued on me. By the way she was staring, I knew it was time to give up the 411, so I put my Bible on the back seat. "So what's up, Jee?" she asked quietly. "I'm sorry, girl, this had to happen."

"No, it's my fault. I didn't think I would do anything with him. Things just got the best of me and the best that became the worst began to happen."

"Are you still seeing him?"

"Yes, kind of. I haven't spoken to him to tell him any different since the last time I saw him." I placed my head on the steering wheel and rolled it back and forth. "I'm too sorry for leaving out that part when I spoke to you about it the first time, but that's truly why I was so upset at your house that day. It was because I'd slept with a married man, and now look at me. Parri, I just don't feel good about it at all."

"Girl, married men don't love you. They love your attention is all. They'll do and say anything for it. They love themselves. I thought we talked about this one thousand times when we always look and laugh at women who think a married man is actually going to leave their spouse for them. So rare. What would they say, hi mom, this is my ho. Blessings to marry her, please?"

"This was different, though, Parri."

"Then why is he still married?"

Silence.

"Then why hasn't he told his wife *hey, I'm divorcing you*? Why is he even sneaking around with you if this was so different? If he was dead serious about you, sneaking wouldn't be an option. He would be wide open with his stuff, taking you to meet the family and all that. Better yet, he would have divorced his wife and fast!"

I still couldn't answer, so Parri continued to dog me out.

"It's a game, Jee Jee. Don't ever sleep with a married man. They'll even make you believe they love you so much, then toss you away like rag dolls, especially when the wife finds out. All that time wasted. They stick to the woman with the ring and their money unless she's the one that skips town on his cheating ass. Then you're the one getting stuck with the playa' who will eventually dog your ass, too. Simple math and simple common ass sense, and I mean *ass* sense. Thing I don't understand is that you really didn't mind him getting inside his wife and you at the same time, Jee? Think about that mess, girl! She didn't' know about you, but you voluntarily kissed a man whose penis was stirring her tea amongst other things. Isn't that a bit gross to you, Jee? You just can't be serious about voluntarily even kissing a man while you know for a fact he's slobbing down his wife, Jee, and all over her body! Yuck."

All I did was cry. I ended up over in her lap weeping so

hard at the biggest mistake that I had ever made in history. Why did I even put myself in this position? The more I thought about it, the more I knew I needed to get out of it and fast. Parri was so right. That was the nastiest thing I could have ever done. And I thought I was the one turning him out. Really, it was Andre' getting his whole cake and shoving it down his throat.

Parri, who stopped talking as soon as my head hit her lap as I cried in emotional agony, pushed my head up and jokingly said with two snaps up, "Everybody ain't smooth like me, so stop crying. Fine don't mean freak 'em, girl. It might mean flirt, but that's about it in my book."

It was amazing how she always could separate her emotions from her physical. It was a science to me.

"But anyway! Why are you here at the hospital and things? Somebody you know sick?" she asked, acknowledging with the change of subject that she was overdoing the *this will teach you a lesson* talk.

"Not really sick. I need to find out what happened to a certain somebody." I fiddled with my keys while wiping my eyes at the same time knowing what was coming next - a bunch more questions that I didn't really want to entertain.

"A certain somebody, Jeena?" She cocked her neck over and tried to catch my eyes from the side, but I beat her to the punch. I turned the opposite direction and looked out my side window.

"Yep." Immediately, I got out of the car. Not to my surprise, her and her orange and purple hair jumped out, too.

"Jeena, is it him? Is he up in this hospital, girl?"

"No," I sighed slowly. I was gonna hate saying it, but while I was busy confessing, I figured I may as well say more. As I shut my door behind me and tossed my keys in my bag, I spoke up. "His wife. She's sort of sick."

"Oh, hell no, Jeena!" She almost broke her neck getting to my side of the car. I'd already started walking toward the hospital, and she galloped right behind me. I wasn't gonna listen to her continuous pleas though. "Jeena, don't go up in a hospital when his wife is sick telling her some bullcrap like this! Who does that? Do you want to kill her or something? This is not the time nor is it the place! Jeena, stop walking and listen to me with your crazy ass!" she continued to scream holding the back of her hair in an attempt to be sure that no purple is showing.

"It's not what you think, Parri. I'm not going to tell her all the crazy stuff." Honestly, I did think about confessing everything, but Parri was right. Now wasn't the time, but that couldn't stop me from telling her at least some of the truth along with all my other questions I had planned.

"Well then stop and tell me what else you two have to talk about? Shopping, nails...what? Sex!"

I stopped cold in my tracks. Parri ended up face to face with me, partially paralyzed by only thoughts she'd concocted of my answer to her question. I could only imagine what was going on in her pea brain. Her eyes were bulging, looking straight foolish with a bad hair-do.

"I need to find out if she was beaten."

"By who?"

"The married man I was sleeping with that's who."

"Oh hell no!"

"Oh hell yeah. And I need it to come from her own mouth." Again, I began to strut myself on toward the hospital, eyeing the third floor like my own life depended on getting to it. In a way, it did.

"How did you know she was even up here? Did he tell you?"

"No. That was the problem. He didn't say anything. I kinda bumped into some information when I was at the hospital the other day and well, to make a long story tiny, the night I made love to him was the night I think she was put in the hospital."

The hospital sliding doors didn't open fast enough, and Parri was still blabbing away at the mouth. Words were pouring out, and there was no bucket to catch them all. My ears kept reaching for pieces of the syllables but kept missing out on half the conversation anyway.

144

"Jeena, do you hear me?"

We boarded the elevator. I punched the number three.

"Nope. Please, Parri, you don't want to know more than what you already do. It's just that this whole situation is ugly, and half of it is caused by me."

Before the elevator even stopped, I released more information. I didn't know why I continued to reveal bits and pieces, but it just came out. "He scared the mess out of me at my place, Parri."

"What did this fool ass do? Put his hands on you, too!"

Before she even got to ranting worse, I spoke up. "I think he threatened me."

"How?!" The elevator stopped and opened.

"He did an I-wish-you-would type threat on me but without the words. He didn't hit me, but I knew he was serious. Nothing that bad, but..."

"Hold up." She grabbed me by my arm and yanked me back inside the elevator. Then, she had the audacity to punch the door close button.

"Parri!"

"We can ride. Tell me what part of an *I wish you would* is friendly, Jee? Huh? Tell me that? Just how was it *nothing bad*, Jeena?"

Right when the doors tapped shut, I rushed and hit the door open button. As requested, the elevator doors did as they were ordered to do.

"Parri, it's handled."

"Girl, don't let me go borrow Tanya's shank. Damn that! Ain't a sole on this earth about to threaten my friend. Get locked up!"

As we exited the elevator, Parri noticed the ICU sign on the door.

"ICU! What the hell is his wife doing on the death ward?"

"Would you shut up, Parri!" I looked around to make sure she didn't upset anyone on the floor that was waiting for their family member to get well or depart to God like Parri said. I yanked her closer to me and whispered. "She was in a pretty bad *so called* incident. Besides that, this is ICU and people go in and out, so she may even be moved today. I have to see. She didn't look like she was gonna have to stay, but she was pretty well beaten."

"So called incident? And you saw her! What do you mean you saw her? Are you spying on his wife or something? How did you just run up on all this information, Jeena? You *think* he beat her from what you said in the parking lot outside, but it sounds more like you *know* he beat her."

There went her mouth again. She was beginning to get a little bit too excited and loud, and I couldn't have all that.

"Parri, you have to calm down. I need to speak to the nurse. She knows Faith, and that way, I can get in and out easier than the rest of these people. You can't make a scene. I will explain later."

She folded her arms. "Well, you better. Got me all in the dark while this man's wife is getting ready to head for the light," she pouted.

As I approached the nurse's station with Parri standing at least six feet away, apprehension overcame me, however, I kept moving.

"Ahhhh! Lord have mercy, Jesus!"

A scream of agony rang out, and my heart tanked. Father God, someone must have passed away. It was the voice of a woman that sounded as if all the life was gone from her. It made me quake on the inside, but I continued on my assignment.

"Hi, it's me again. Looking for Faith. Is she here visiting Mrs. Tina…"

"No and oh… she may be upstairs," the nurse responded cutting me off, but doing so cheerfully. "The patient moved to the seventh floor. She's almost out of here! How have you been?"

"Good. Sorry I can't talk. In a rush."

"Take care."

"You, too."

When I turned back around, old guess who was still

standing there with her arms folded, looking pissed. I walked on by her,too, but unfortunately, she started to follow.

"Parri, get off of my heels." She was following so closely behind me you would have thought she was attached to my leg! "You're making everything ten times worse."

"Me?" she asked, shocked. "Me?!"

"Forget what I just said." I immediately withdrew my statement because I knew more words were getting ready to pounce from her mouth, so I quickly had to interject that one. Parri was very honest...blatantly and brutally. Therefore, though she was a good friend for the most part, she could quickly drive a dagger into your chest with no harm intended.

"Jeena."

"Let's just go to the seventh floor. You will find everything out. I need to do this." I faced her and repeated myself despite how frantic she looked. Good grief. You would think she was the one that slept with Andre'! "Really, I need to do this. This could help me. You don't understand. I'm In love with him here, not here." I pointed to my heart first, then my head. "Without concrete evidence, he could possibly tell me anything, and it would be harder for me to let go - no matter what my mind says or how he may have threatened me. I really don't want to be with him anymore, so I need this. I need to face him as if he is a monster, not my man, just to get my heart to stop cold turkey." My mind then went to Stay Black. That's who my mind wanted. My heart was just lagging a bit.

"Jeena, I'm cool. I'll just follow you. I got your back, but, girl, you need to learn... "

"That's why I need to do this! Stop preaching at me, too," I stressed. Parri can make a sister feel really dumb sometimes, geez! *Girl, you need to learn!* Well, duh, I just did!

Parri waved her hand toward the open elevator, and we both entered with other passengers going to the seventh floor...peacefully. When we got there, I noticed that the seventh floor wasn't as packed as the previous. There were a couple of heads here and there, but for the most part, it was non-active. As we walked to the nurses' station, we only saw one nurse. She didn't attempt to stop us at any point, so we made the natural move of requesting the room that Tina was in.

"Room seven eleven," the nurse stated. "Sign here please."

Sign? Must be a fake name because my real name wasn't going on paper for this particular visit. I grabbed the pen and wrote down Diana Jay. Parri peered over my shoulder like a hawk and then whispered, "You got that right. You ain't as dizzy as I thought!"

I tossed the pen into her hand, and turned away from the nurses station while whispering back at her, "Girl, I ain't crazy." What a nut would I have been to put my real name down with all the drama I was in.

"Just checkin'," Parri responded back.

I turned back around to see what name she signed, and it was signed Nunya Buziness Boo.

"Girl!"

"Shut your mouth, and let's go." She whispered, pulling me by the arm, and that was the best laugh of the day. That made me feel better, but for only a quick second because I suddenly heard his voice. My stomach bottomed out, and I almost shit on the pearly white floor.

"What's up? Girl, you cool?" she asked after noticing my absence of color and my knees buckle to keep from breaking wind. Buckling my knees didn't work. The gas seeped out quietly from my nerves gone noodles.

"He's in there," I coldly responded.

"Say what? He's in there with her?" She paused. "But ew...Jeena, you do that?" She asked holding her nose. "You need a laxative."

"We gotta go." I yanked her arm, but she pulled from my grasp and reversed the hold. This time she had me by the arm again.

"Hell no we're not!"

I snatched away from her in a panic. "Yes! Now!"

"Where are we gonna go? Run and hide like some chicken asses, or in your case, gassy ass?"

"We're going back out!" I yelled at the top of my whisper while pointing to the double doors.

Suddenly, the voices in the hospital room went silent. Oh God, and I wasn't calling to Him in vain. Quickly, I began to walk, nearly run, to the doors that were the barrier between me and those elevators. As far as Parri, I wasn't even thinking about her, but I should've been because when I glanced back, she was standing there where I left her - this time staring Andre' in the face. I ended up walking backwards to the double doors, and as Parri turned back to face me, my eyes met the eyes of both of them simultaneously, staring right back at me. I ran out...

Of Excuses.

My feet were hitting the pavement as if I had four bull dogs chasing me, and I was the running legend Jesse Owens. That all changed when I tripped up on the curb, fell to the dang ground and skinned up my palms and elbows. Without the time to dust off, check for blood or who saw me bust my butt while in panic mode, I got back up and took off again. When I got to my car, I fumbled for my keys and accidentally dropped them near my tire. Underneath the car, I went to scoot them out, and that was when I heard, loud and clear, Parri calling my name.

"Jeena!"

I couldn't face her, and I knew from the extra set of eyes on the very top of my head called instinct that she was racing toward me. It was time to go! My thoughts couldn't have been more clouded and my body so dirty, tired and hurt, not just from Andre' but also from that dog on fall! To make matters worse than getting all skinned up and embarrassed, I still didn't get a chance to see Tina and talk to her. I almost had my answer for sure, but it was too late. Andre' saw me. There wasn't even any telling what he and Parri said to one another while they stood there, her thinking *this is dude from Capital City*, and him thinking *what the hell*? What on earth did I do?

"Help me fix all this, please!" As I looked in my rear view mirror, I spotted Parri hopping in her car to follow me. She was gonna catch me if I moved any slower, so I made a break for it. A seriously illegal turn was made, and I was going down the wrong side of the road. Whatever. Forget the cops. Truth be told, I needed to be arrested so I could hide this nonsense behind some bars for at least 48 hours.

A spot cleared up in the traffic, and that's when I jumped my car back into the right lane. Parri got stuck at the light. At that point, I dumped my purse and everything spilled out on the car seat. I was searching for my cell. It was off. I made sure of it before I entered the ICU area.

Holding it up to my face, I turned that sucker back on despite it becoming my lifeline to my brand new lower level in Hades. Even if it rang, I didn't think I would answer it. There were no messages showing, and I was fooling myself to believe that there were going to be any either.

Andre's face, when I turned back to look at him standing only a good four feet away from Parri, was expressionless. I couldn't fathom what he was thinking when he saw me running, not toward, but away from him. How cowardly was that? What I should have done, I didn't do and that was confront him with the truth in front of his wife and Parri.   And Parri. That was my girl. No, she didn't have a relationship with Andre', but I deceived her, too. Shoot, she had her eyes on Andre' her dog on self, and what made it even worse wasn't us messing around, but the lying that came along with it. I lied to Parri's face over dinner at Captial City all the way up to now! I played Parri and Andre's wife, but most of all, I knew that the only person I truly played was myself. I was the only one having to lie, duck and dodge while it was everyone else, besides me and Andre', living a generally honest life to my knowledge.

Bump it. I didn't need any hard core proof of anything to get him out of my system anymore. I knew he beat her. It was over. Period. I was tired.

I began to dial. Faith.

"Please, Faith, please answer your phone." It rang a couple of times, but instead of hearing a live voice, I got her answering machine.   "Where is she?" I asked myself. I hung up and called one more time. There was a continuous ring. Wait!

"Hello?"

"Faith, are you busy?" I asked while placing my gear in neutral at the light. My car was getting more and more raggedy with each year that went by because of my failure to fix it. Neutral kept it from turning off. Good thing was that it would warn me prior to going dead by giving itself a little shake before the complete shut down. That was just enough time for me to press the gas to rev it up.

"No, what's up? You at work?"

I turned my music down.

"Didn't go in today." Before I continued, from the corner of my eye, I saw a nice ride pull up next to my small Saturn. The windows were tinted jet black. It was Andre'. "Hold on, Faith." I hit mute out of fear something might pop off as I stared over at his driver's side window. I knew his ride from anywhere, and I was in for the full out questionaire in the middle of traffic.

As I waited for his window to roll down with curses to follow, to my surprise, it didn't. The light turned green, and he drove. While my eyes followed the back of his ride down the road, I honestly couldn't believe this joker just drove off and didn't say squat after all those times I squat on top of him! I didn't know what to think as he drove away as if I didn't even exist, and I knew he saw me. I couldn't panic nor could I chill. I was stuck. Literally. My car suddenly died.

"Get out of the way!" Somebody behind me yelled, and immediately, my eyes lifted to the rear view mirror to spot some old bald headed dude ordering me around. Didn't he at least think that if I could've moved that I would have gladly gotten out of his way? A fashion statement it was not to stop in the middle of traffic at the light in a beat up car.

"Helloooo?" Faith sang. Oh, Faith! I forgot the phone call.

Unmute.

"Hey, Faith. What you doing now?"

"Nothing."

I sat back in my car and just shook my head. "I need a..."

"Jeena!"

At this point, I thought I could have just withered up and died. It was Parri, screaming like an idiot all outdoors, rendering my situation even more embarrassing.

"Never mind. I'll call you back."

"Huh?"

"I will, Faith," I responded, losing all train of thought in the process. "I'll call you back."

"I'ma be in church later."

Not good. I just knew someone was gonna give her the low down on me being on my bended knee, and then, lay out the scroll of questions about why it all happened to Faith who had absolutely no clue. Then that would leave Faith to calling me from the church bathroom or somewhere inconspicuous to get the low down on my breakdown when I would honestly like to be the first person to tell her.

"Don't go to church today. I really need to ask you something."

"Ask me now," Faith stated in a low *get to the point chick* voice.

"Jeena, talk to me!" I not only heard but watched Parri acting like a darn fool yelping through my window. How she got to my car so fast, I haven't the slightest idea. Did demons fly?

"No. Call ya' back. Bye," I stated to Faith as I tried to roll the window to Parri down, but whoops, all my electricity, car battery juice or whatever was gone. I opened the door.

"Move!"

"Make me move!" Parri screamed back at a driver that was giving her the hand. "Get out of the car, heffa! And the rest of y'all can go around! Look at all this road!" she yelled while pointing to the other lane, spinning her body around in the process. "Use it!" Then she looked over at me. "What the hell? Idiots! Can't they gather that this is a broken down vehicle?"

I exited my car, slammed the door shut and just stared at her with a *please slap the mess out of me* look on my face. I deserved it.

"I'm sorry, Parri. His name was Andre' in the hospital and Andre' in Capital City. It's the same man..."

"And the same Andre'," she interjected, "when I told you to check him out as well as Andre' when he slobbed my hand down as a *married* man which is something I don't flirt with nor do."

"And Andre' the married man when I fell in love with him."

"And Andre' when you slept with him." She paused, looked around and then scratched her scalp beneath all her purple hair which by the way she was no longer hiding. "Girl, he really ain't that fine."

I lifted my eyes to see her. "What is he then?"

"Damn married, Jee! That's how he looks, Jeena! Married!" she yelled. That's when she proceeded to shove me out of the way, open my car door and pop my hood. After that, she walked over to the back of her whip to get her jacks. "Had me all up in a married man's face in public at Capital City like a horny ass. I ain't perfect, but I did read the Ten Commandments one day in time, and somewhere in there God had an aka mind your business and don't steal stuff including spouses verse. I mean, what if someone saw me flirting with him? You sat there and let me! Not only that, you crawled up in his underwear later knowing he was married like a damn dummy. Now I know why you were acting all weird at the table. Scandalous."

"Parri, I don't have time for this."

"Oh, you got time. The one thing you got is time for this since you obviously had so much free time in your life that you ended up digging your ass into someone else's marriage. Oh yeah, too damn much extra time," she said, staring under my hood. "You need your engine cleaned, the one in your head and the one under your hood. Maybe they will both start to run right."

"You ladies need some help?" a gentleman asked as he slowed all the way up, offering his assistance.

"Hell no, and keep your ass going. Thank you for nothing." Parri responded calmly, barely looking up at him, as if she does this to men all the time.

"No, thank you," I stated, embarrassed as he drove off shrugging his shoulders. "You didn't have to speak to him like that, Parri," I said, totally against how rude she was to the passer by that wanted to help my broke down butt.

"Didn't have to talk to him like that? Yes I did! Get in the car and start it up, Jeena, so I can school your flunking ass. If he really wanted to help us, his googly eyes would have gotten out of his ride before those same googly eyes found their way beyond our clothes with a tape measure to my butt while I was stooping over your hood. His eyes had a conversation with my butt, not me. And then, what the hell does it look like? Doesn't it look like we need help? Dumb ass questions signals a dumb ass man. That was a conversation starter. Typical. Now that you are educated on that, it looks like you can learn to use a flat out *hell no* in your female male conversations anyway with the three ways you get into."

I started up my Saturn and let it run - right over her scolding of me. "Where do you find this stuff, Parri, in a book called how to read a man?"

"Girl," she said as she leaned over in my car, "I just make it up as I go along in life. Lessons aren't to be forgotten. They are lessons to learn and remember, just like a school lesson or a church lesson. Things happen to teach you, not to make you ignorant." She stood upright and shook her head up and down. "It's the truth, though. You have to be straight up on the rules for yourself and for them, too. Shoot, my daddy was a rollin' damn stone, sweetheart. Can't stand him either! That's really how I know so much. Watching dear ole daddy cheat on mama. I won't ever disrespect a woman or family like that by kissing and slobbing down her husband. You got to be kidding me. It hurt my mom, but it hurt me, too, when daddy didn't come back home after making some other woman happy. He became my worst nightmare because he always made mom cry so hard! Girl, you just don't know...my arms stayed around her while he wrapped his around someone else."

"Thanks, Parri. Thanks for everything." I followed her to the back of her ride so she can put her jacks back from where she got them. "I'll buy us lunch. My treat."

"No you're not. You got to get out my face. You're my friend for life, but that crap you did wasn't friendly back at Capital City. I don't have crap else to say to you right now. Lying ass. Get yourself together and then call me. What you pulled ain't cool by any means because you're supposed to have my back. You might mingle in marriages, but I don't. No, I'm not perfect, but damn that! I still get on my knees at night and whenever else I feel the need." Parri didn't flinch while she let me have it because she is straight up like that. "Call me when you get yourself together and find a better way to apologize other than lunch. Love ain't lost, but I was going to stick my neck out for you, and come to find out, you didn't budge for me and almost had me hooking up with oh boy. You were dead wrong, Jee. Get this stuff straight."

She got into her car and left, but before she sped off, she leaned out of her window and said, "Guess he ain't all you thought he was now, huh?" Then, she left me standing stupid in the middle of the street as people drove by still beeping at me. I just got into my car and drove...

Me, Myself And I Home.

All the way back home, my cell didn't ring. When I entered my condo, it felt like the twilight zone as the walls stared back at me. I was so accustomed to getting some type of reaction from someone when a bunch of crap went down that it scared me when I didn't. Then again, maybe I should have been the one calling and apologizing to everyone, but who was the everyone? I mean when I thought about it, the only true person that deserved the apology was Tina. I already told Parri I was sorry, and she left me cold in the street. Couldn't blame her either.

The calm before the storm had me ready to leave town. My world was crumbling, and I had no idea how to glue it all back together. My cell rang. Finally! It was Faith.

"Well, I didn't go to church yet, waitin' on you to call me back!" she exclaimed, sounding a bit perturbed, not even taking the time to say hello.

"Hello to you, too, Faith."

"What is it, Jee? What happened?" she dragged her voice like it was lugging a ton of weights on her vocal cords. "The drama you are causing in my life ..."

She need not say one thing more because she had no idea to what extent the drama truly was this particular time. "Nothing. Nothing happened. My car stopped in the middle of the street."

"You better be lying, Jee. You had me not go to church because your car stopped in the middle of the street."

Shut up, Faith, I thought as I yanked the phone from my ear for about fifteen seconds.

"No, listen. Whatever it was, it's nothing anymore, and I'm sorry I had you linger around waiting on me to call you back. I'm sorry. I forgot to get back to you. Go ahead. Go to church." At this particular point, I was frustrated as ever before.

"Jeena, are you serious?" Faith asked in disbelief. "Something really is wrong! I'm not going anywhere until you tell me," she stated. I heard all the concern in her voice because the tone went from *you get on my last nerves* to *oh my gosh my dear sister*!

"Faith," I started, but then I figured that I did need to ask her something in generality. Absolutely nothing specific. It was something that my younger sister knew about far better than me. "How do I know if I am completely at fault for something?"

"Jee, are you okay?"

"Yeah," I responded, sinking way down into my sofa while rolling my eyes, totally disgusted because I kept lying to her about my well being. "I just need to know how do you know with absolute certainty that God forgives you for the things that you do wrong, you know?" I decided not to ask her about Andre' and Tina. Regardless of if he beat his wife or not, he wasn't mine, and I didn't need Faith for that adultery part of the scriptures. Therefore, I wasn't going to drag Faith through the whole orgasmic spill if I could help it. Poor Faith would probably pause, mute and vomit to keep from wilting over like dying plant at the news anyway.

There was a picture on the shelf of me, her and mom altogether at the Grand Canyon one year sitting in the hot sun. Shoot, the sun was burning so much that day that the dag on devil had on shades with a fan in his ashy hand. We thought we were fly, too, with sweat beads pouring from our foreheads on down to our armpits. All three of us had on the same outfits with matching sunglasses, and in the background of the photo was the Canyon. Mom, she taught us a lot. Did I retain any of it? I learned how to wash my clothes, do my hair, make money and spend it all, but why didn't I learn how to choose a man? Better yet, why didn't the Word that she did teach us fail to stick like glue to me, but instead, overdosed onto Faith? I mean, she is always right! Always!

"It's because God can't lie," Faith replied to my question on forgiveness. "What He says, He says and does. There's no big trick to it. God doesn't lie and doesn't have to, and you have heard that one thousand times, Jeena, because mom used to walk around and say it all the time. What He says, even the impossible, He can make possible. That means the guilty are made innocent, something that courts and human judges simply can't do. He completely wipes away sin to remember it no more, like it never happened. Regardless of how you or anyone else feels, He is greater than your heart. Jeena, all you have to do is ask for forgiveness and try your best never to do it again which proves your repentant and changed heart, and then forgive yourself. Guilt comes with the territory because you have consequences to everything you do wrong, girl, but your guilt ain't got no power over grace and mercy. Jesus gives you that grace and mercy, even when you don't feel it. Just *know* it. He is greater than any feeling in your heart at all times. He is God, with our without your wrong doings, with or without your feelings. Faith moves Him, nothing else."

If a response is what she was waiting on when she stopped talking, it wasn't going to happen because I was sobbing terribly. By the time she got to the words *He is greater than your heart*, I had to put my cell on mute. I felt like a sucker weeping to my younger sister only because it was supposed to be me giving her advice and wisdom, but instead, I was wiping snot from my nose and streams from off of my cheeks learning from her.

When I gathered myself together, I asked, "How do you fix a bunch of stuff that you went about the wrong way?"

"Sometimes you can't. Pray, do what you can do to make it right, and let go of the guilt."

"If I asked Jesus to save me, am I?"

"Are you momma's child?"

I grinned, "Yes."

"Well then that's your answer, crazy! Imagine if you had a child. I mean really imagine, Jee. No matter what, you would love that child regardless. You would also forgive that child no matter what because your love of that child rules over any action. That's a simple way to know God forgives and still loves you through it all. He still wants us to do better though when we mess up. Don't get it twisted and think you can do whatever just because He will forgive you and love you through it though! God don't play that," she laughed.

"Thank you, sis."

"Okay so you can tell me anytime now," she sang, wanting me to tell her what was going on.

"I don't want to say anymore, but thank you for holding up on going to church and having a bit of church with me here."

"Girl, everybody in there already knows what's up, and if they don't, they're in the right place to find out. You know what's up, too, Jeena, but sometimes you like to go your own way."

"And my mind always drifts about everything and any subject."

"I know, Jee. God knows. Pray for wisdom, and when God gives it to you, use it."

"Alright. Will do." I said that about wisdom, but I wasn't so certain that God would trust me with such a golden thing. I might influence wisdom and turn it foolish at the rate I was going.

"Now, bye! I'm going to church!"

"Bye, Faith." I hung up. Sometimes, I think that God made her just for me, instead of vice versa. Thank you, Jesus, for my little sister.

I needed a drink, so I walked over to my kitchen to make, with my juicer, a glass of lemonade from some fresh lemons. Wow, I thought. The television remote control was hanging from the corner of the counter as if it was making an attempt to jump, so I picked it up and turned on the tube. Lifetime. Turned that crap right back off because I bet my real life story was somewhere on there, and I didn't want to watch the ending unfold.

When I finished juicing, I took a swig of my lemonade and then prayed that mug would turn into some holy water. That's when my cell went off, but I had to let it ring because some of the lemonade got caught somewhere between my trachea and my throat causing me to strangle. Just the cell ringing nearly killed me…or was it the bitterness of this juice that nearly took my life? It rang again, so I placed my glass down and went over to answer it. I just knew it was gonna be Andre'.

"Hello?"

"He beat the hell out of her. Girl, he beat the straight up

hell outta her, I'm telling you!"

It wasn't him.

"Parri?"

"Yeah, it's me," she stated, talking like she was on the run.

"What are you talking about?"

"I went back! Gi-irl," she sang, "I went back, jack!"

"You went back where?" I asked, too shocked to believe that she did what I thought she did. More drama had hit the surface of the earth that I stood on, so I began to pace backwards and forwards with the phone in my hand like mad person in the crazy house.

"To the hospital. I just left. Your *man* was gone, and she was up in there scared straight. Look, Jeena, I had my work clothes in the car and I changed into those babies! She saw me looking like a pro! I told her I was from the nutrition center, just stopping in on my way to the center by request of the doctor."

"Parri!"

"Jeena!" she yelled back. "It was only half a lie! I do work at a place like that! Anyway, when I walked up in there, she started a big old act up like she was in an accident, like some folks jumped her. So I said, are you sure that it was just a fist and not a fist full of something else like brass or anything else? By the way, I tucked my hair back in a pony tail so she wouldn't see my rainbow colored hair too well."

"No you didn't!"

"No I didn't what? Tuck my hair?"

"No, Parri, not your hair. I can't believe you went back up there!"

"Yes I did, and didn't have to duck from Andre' or any other man."

"Did he say something to you in the hospital when you just stood there?"

"No. I didn't speak to him either. For what reason would I have to speak to him though? I told you. Married men ain't fine when they're too friendly. They're freaks. When you ran out, I walked out. He just stood there before taking the stairs because he didn't come behind me. Shoot, I'm not the one sleeping with him. You two are. He ain't got no hold on me. Nigga touch me, he gonna get touched right back with a slap in his damn face."

"So she told you that he messed her face up like that?" I asked now biting my lower lip.

"No. She didn't have to tell me a thing. She didn't tell me that a fist went across her face *wasn't* what happened either. See, she got caught up in something else I said to her."

"What on earth was that, Parri? Stop stalling!" This was all too unreal to be true.

"I made up a story! I told her that I spoke to her man as he left, and that *he* said that the guys who jumped her used a pipe as well. Also that there was a woman involved according to what came from her mouth the night it happened."

"And..."

"She agreed! She agreed to that big bald faced lie that I made up! She even pulled more lies to cover for the one I just told out of the cracks in her black eye! This woman actually verified a lie that *my* ass made up on *her* man and her! Can you believe that? So in other words, he beat her ass and told her to lie about it saying it was some gang mess, and on top of that, dear Andre' is making up the story as time passes. Anything he tells the staff or she *thinks* he tells the staff, she's gunning all the way, ride or die for that moe-foe. I should call the cops right now and tell them to stop the chase because there are no gangsters in this beat down case to be found."

I couldn't say one word. I just dropped to the floor and folded my legs Indian style. "Hold on, Parri."

My coochie felt like it closed up. I let this foul joker sleep with me. As I thought back to the last night he and I made love, I caught the shakes. Then, I glanced over at my front door. This sick beast came over my place and made sweet love to me after he beat the hell out of his wife? Was he psychotic? It was too much for me to bear. The same wife that he kissed in front of me in the lingerie store? I wanted to vomit. They weren't having problems. Andre' was the problem because he was beating her down. The worst part about it was that her beat downs were for me.

"Parri, I made love to him that night," I stated as I held the phone back up to my ear.

"You mean the night he beat her down?"

"Yes." I paused. "I didn't know."

"You already told me that, Jeena. You told me at the hospital his trifling behind made love to you after he swole up her lips, eyes and cheeks!"

"It was beyond normal, too, Parri," I blurted out. "He was so loving to me. He was..."

"Get off of it, girl! He ain't worth the pain. He's not worth her pain either. And you damn right he was making love to you all natural like he didn't do shit because he's a damn sociopath!"

"Did she ask for proof of who you were when you were there, Parri?"

"No. Ain't that just crazy? She just treated me like kind of a friend. She didn't even get nasty with me like *who are you and show me your name tag*?"

"She must not have anyone..."

"To talk to? You got that right. Too busy fussing with that fist. Girl, I'm gonna tell you, don't let that man inside your place. Don't you do it. Change those locks or come and stay over here if you don't want to do that. If he beats her like that, then, what the heck will he do to you? Has he called you?"

"No. I saw him though. He didn't even look at me, just continued to drive. I doubt he will bother with me anymore. I'm sure he figures that I know now, and he's probably ashamed." The only reason I said that is because I was trying to make myself and her feel better about the situation, but in reality...

<u>That Joker Was Crazy, And I Was Scared.</u>

"I'ma call you back, Parri, okay. I have something to do."

"Okay, bye."

In my kitchen, four chairs sat empty at the table. I snatched one away and pushed it up underneath the door knob.

"Andre' can't be coming up in here on me about to tear my head off for being at the hospital. Shoot." I looked around the room for something to protect myself with. "I need some mace or something. Something that I can stun that flipping lunatic with from far away," I whispered to myself. My cell went off again.

I hoped it was Jesus calling to let a sister know that this was just a dream, but I knew that I was stretching that hope a little too far. Disgusted, I slid my feet across the floor until I was able to reach for the phone and pick it up. It was Andre'. Oh hell in the literal sense of the word. Panic wasn't even the word I would use to describe my emotion, but in the midst of it all, I answered.

"I thought you weren't gonna pick up."

"Well I did," I responded.

"How did you know Tina was in the hospital?"

"Why did you put her there?"

He sighed. "Baby, how do you figure I put her there?"

"You never told me about her being in there, Andre', so stop acting stupid. You said that she was out of town." He remained silent, so I continued, "And I want my key back."

"You got me all wrong, Jeena. I didn't tell you because that's my business. What did you need to know for? You never asked about her well being before so," he said, surprisingly calm.

"Your business? You came over here and made love to me, and wasn't that the same night Tina went to the hospital? Are you saying that beating your wife that night wasn't my business, Andre'? Your wife looks as if she could have died with how badly her face was blown all up. That beating that you gave her places me at the center of a damn crime, some flippin' ghetto ass scandal to ultimately have me be subpoenaed to court and questioned and all type of crap if they found out about us. I'm not happy about that mess! I didn't have anything to do with that,

Andre'! And yeah, sure we were having sex and it was wrong, but I would never condone you beating her like you did. Ever! What the hell is wrong with you?" I was screaming and didn't even realize it for a minute. He'd gotten me worked up, so during the silence that was taking over the conversation after my outburst, I calmed back down. It was over between us anyway.

"Who told you that was even the night?"

"Don't worry about it, Andre'." I wasn't trying to bring anyone else up into this affair, especially Faith. I wasn't gonna drop names because he had no idea that Faith, if he'd even met her face to face before by some strange turn of events, was my sister.

"Were you spying on me? You don't have to spy on me. Ask me whatever you want to ask me." His accent was thickening. I mean all of it was breaking out, and I had to listen hard.

"Spy on you, Andre'? If you haven't noticed, we tend to run into each other at not quite the best moments."

"Jeena, I didn't beat her."

"Well how on earth did her face get jacked up? By some other brother? She was in ICU for crying out loud!" I couldn't believe this. Parri had all the proof, and he was really gonna try and tell me otherwise.

"Man, Jeena, she has a hard time breathing. Asthma. She had an attack." He went quiet, and I waited on the rest of the story because ain't no way in hell or heaven asthma beats your face in. "We were arguing, baby. She hit me. I'm not proud of it, but I hit her back. I lost control, and I should have walked out and left, but I didn't. I don't want to talk about it though, Jeena. You just need to understand that."

"Understand what? Her face is swollen up like a damn water balloon - five of them! And it ain't from no asthma attack! Shoot, Andre', it was you that probably created the asthma attack from knocking her throat in!"

I could've cussed him from top to bottom, but I was already in deep water with God and didn't want to go deeper and drown. The point was to float back to the top, not tread the bottom with the crabs and poop.

"Man, Jeena...okay, okay. Nothing," he stated, giving up on the conversation obviously. "I'll bring you your key. I'll be there soon."

"Fine, and Andre'?"

"What?"

"Don't' fuckin' threaten me again."

He hung up. I grabbed a small screw driver and slid it in my pocket, and then, continued to ask God, Whom I talked more to than ever before, to forgive me for that word. I had to say it though in order to let him know that I was serious.

All these different stories about how she got in that hospital only proved Andre' needs to be locked up. Besides all of that, wasn't he supposed to be at work anyway? That was probably a lie, too. And did I *ask* him to come over soon? I should have called him back and told him to come over when *I* say come over, key or no key, so that I could have a witness. That was cool though. I had a screw driver to stab his eyes out if he threatened me again.

At that point, I felt that I had the upper hand finally. Everything was ending, the affair, my living arrangement with Andre', all my lies, home wrecking, and my past life. It was time to start fresh with a new attitude and crossed legs to match. I was gonna turn my life around and never repeat this mistake ever, ever again. It was horrible!

My phone rang. It was Tanya.

"Hey, girl. Are you okay?" Finally, it was someone who had more drama than me.

"Yes, and I just called to say thank you for earlier. Jee, I was getting ready to go to jail, away from all my babies."

"And that is what I know," I agreed with a chuckle. "Don't let a man send you there, girl." It was amazing that I sounded like I had so much sense when I spoke with Tanya about her situation, but I sucked at my own. "So he left for good?"

"Yep. It's just me now and my babies, with one on the

way. I'm gonna get my child support, too."

"You think he's gonna cooperate or fake the funk?"

"He won't have a choice. When the baby is born, I'm gonna woo him over here and get some DNA from the playa, if I don't sneak the DNA before I give birth. Then, I'ma sock it to him. Cheating on me. I'm not even gonna sleep in this bed anymore. Need a new mattress first," she said with a slight smile to her voice. She was better. I knew she was.

"Find your good conscience and sleep with it every night. That's my new motto, Tanya."

"My legs are gonna be shut."

"Mine, too! Hopefully," I whispered, and we began to laugh while I continued. "Doesn't it feel good to be free, though? I mean, no one to bug you or make you feel sad, just always happy by yourself."

"Hell yeah. But you know that's gonna get old, too, Jeena."

"Well, I'm gonna enjoy it while it lasts."

"What? Are you seeing somebody? Did I miss something?"

"Was."

"Why not anymore?"

"Ain't quite what I thought." Ain't quite what I thought was more like drag me to hell with a chain on my ankle so I can't get loose.

"I hear you."

"Hey, why don't you come on over, Tanya, so we can hang out for a minute, eat popcorn and slam our exes?"

"Girl, did you see my apartment? Can you say tragic? Gotta clean this mess up before I go anywhere. I will holler at you later, so you better pick up your phone. You know how you get with me when I call - think I want you to watch my kids or something so you just let the phone ring. I ain't mad at you, though," she laughed.

"I'll pick it up, Tanya. Later."

"Bye."

There was a knock on the door as soon as I hung my phone up. I knew who it had to be, and I didn't think that I was ready for it either. Hardcore wasn't exactly my best mode because I wasn't very upfront nor confrontational, especially to a proven woman beater. That's why I had Parri and a little bit of Faith in my life as my alter egos, but neither one was here so I was on my own.

"Be rational and stand your ground, Jeena," I whispered to myself after feeling for my screw driver. Then, I asked loudly, "Who is it?"

Though I thought it was Andre', I was wondering why he didn't use the key. But then when I thought about it, I did ban him from using the key just a short time ago so why would he help himself to use it.

I got no answer to my who is it, so I walked over and stuck my eye into the peephole. My instinct was right. Andre' was at the door holding his head in the air, and it kind of looked like he had his hands in his pockets. I didn't need any of this drama, and as a result of that, I even thought about telling him to leave that dag on key on the ground and walk away because I could pick it up later. Nevertheless, I opened sesame, after I walked the chair back over to the table.

"Thanks for bringing my key back, Andre'." I stated as expressionless as I could while looking beyond him.

"May I come in and talk to you for a minute, Jeena?" he asked while placing my key in the palm of my hand. He didn't appear to be angry or frustrated in a way that he could knock me in my face, so I let him in. I had my shank. Dang, I didn't want to cut a brother up like Tanya did, but this was a different situation. If he swung, I was gonna stab. Simple. I got what I wanted, and that was my key. Talk and then get the hell out, I thought.

I walked away from the door. "Come on in, Andre'. Just don't plan on staying long. I have things to do and expecting some company in a couple of minutes." I said that just in case he thought about trying something.

"No problem."

He entered, then, followed me to the couch. Before I even sat down, he reached and held me around my waist from behind. If he really thought that crap would work again, it didn't. That whole freeze up and then melt thing was over this time, so he can take his dirty paws off me. I just simply removed his hand and turned to face him.

"Don't touch me either. And you're standing too damn close. Back up and tell me what's up."

"I'm sorry, Delilah, baby," he stated moving a couple paces backward.

D who? Delilah? Man, at that point, I wanted to change my middle name to anything but that hair stealing trick! I never knew why my mom named me such a thing, but she did. When I got older, she said that at the time she thought the name was pretty and didn't realize who it was when she named me. She learned the Bible at a later date, and that's when she sighed a big oops.

"Don't call me by my middle name, Andre'," I stated in pure disgust, rolling my eyes and clearly not needing his company. "How about," I started again as I sat down, grabbed a magazine from my coffee table and started flipping through, "you tell me what you need to tell me so that you can leave. Sorry for what?"

"I'm sorry for not telling you about what happened between me and Tina. That doesn't go on all the time. It's just that the frustration got to me and..."

"Frustration? What frustration? You got frustrated enough to pound her face in, huh? Can't you see the mess you caused, and not to mention you having my key as if I'm involved with the whole thing when I was really just involved with you for a minute, not knowing that all this..."

"And look, she was in ICU for asthma, not her face. Jeena, I've been pulled your way so much that..."

"Don't call me out like that, Andre', or you can get out right now! Don't dare make me the reason for your doing what you did to her. It was your own choice. I have nothing to do with your fists."

"I made a mistake."

"Yes, you did. You damn right. I made a mistake, too."

"That's what you call us?"

"What else? Andre', I *did* love you. I don't love you anymore. How the hell can I love someone like you? You ain't a lover. You're a woman beater and damn near threatened me with your fucked up hand, putting blood all on my neck..."

"Jeena, please. What I did to Tina won't ever happen to you. I love you, and that whole thing was a mistake. I didn't want you to ever know because it would change how you see me."

"No, Andre', that shit you did to my apple changed how I saw you!"

Before I continued on my cussing rant that I was obviously unable to stop, Andre' started to cry! Tears! This brotha was weeping for real! Why he was crying, I didn't know, but the only reason that I could think of was that he was caught with her blood on his hands. Wasn't that the old saying about a man? They didn't cry out of regret for their actions, but only because they got caught. The other half of the saying was that it always takes years for a man to truly be sorry for the things that he did. Didn't know how true it was, but hey, maybe this was the time to see. Whoops, his spill wasn't over. He continued.

"I told her I was seeing someone, Jeena. I didn't tell her who, but I just told her. And uh...she attacked me, and my instincts retaliated. I stopped after I started in on her though. I just almost stopped too late. She ran out of breath after I hit her and shoved her off of me. That's when I rushed her to the hospital. Afterwards, I came over here. I needed you that night, Jeena."

"What did you just say?" Out of all the crap! "Are you serious? Did you even wash after beating the blood out of her mouth?"

"Yes." He held his head in his hands.

And this fool answered me!

"I wanted to tell you what happened, but couldn't and kept it from you. I'm sorry, Jee. I love you."

He reached out and touched my hand, and surprisingly, I let him because I was stunned stiff. Then he leaned over and kissed me, and no there wasn't a kiss back. My lips were in flipping shock at the fool fact that this man thought things were alright because he cried, said I'm sorry and kissed me.

"I didn't mean to hurt you or Tina as I have. It's hard loving you, Jeena, and not being able to not have you as I need you. I care about you."

I didn't want him to finish. It was obvious that screws were loose, really hanging by the metal, because he would go from one extreme to the other. Kill you to love you. Really, I just needed Andre' to leave. Dip. Peace out.

"Stop talking, Andre'. It's okay. You can stop crying because we can't be together either way." I had to ignore my feelings because I knew he was aiming at getting me all riled up over his weeping. Instead of continuing to sit on the couch, I stood up and decided to walk him out - one hand shoved in my shank pocket for emergencies only.

He began to plead. "Please, Jeena." His hands gathered themselves around my waist once again, and once again, he could cool off because it wasn't happening. "You can have your key, but come on, Jee. I'm asking you please. Don't you remember when I told you that I chose to love you?"

"Yes. Yes, I remember."

"Well, that doesn't stop."

"Unless we make it stop." I stated, directing the comment to us being alone together as if we were supposed to have some real type of relationship. In hell maybe, but not here. Not anymore.

He took one last stab at placing his soft, insane lips on top of mine...

Until The Door Spoke.

"I'm sorry, Andre'. You have to go." A little disturbed because I didn't know who in the world was at my door despite my lie to Andre' earlier about someone stopping by, I scurried over to it and stared through the peep hole.

Immediately, I looked back over at Andre' standing there like he couldn't believe that I was giving him the boot, and then, I turned back to check out the man standing happily outside of my door. Stay Black. I forgot I told him to come over, and if I was a white woman, I would have been beet red! My heart sank at the thought of Black meeting Andre', but then, what better way to get rid of one man than with another man, I thought. Kill the relationship. He needed to repair his wife's mangled face, and I needed to keep myself out of this drama for good. I opened the door.

"Hey, Black," I spoke to him as if I was not shocked that he was standing at my doorstep. In his hand, he had food, and lots of it, from one of my favorite Asian restaurants. Without even looking directly over at Andre', from the corner of my eye, I watched as he slowly walked toward me and Black. Of course, my hand remained on my shank. Me and Black weren't officially a pair yet, but Andre' didn't know that, therefore, I fought to keep my mouth shut. My heart wanted me to explain for some asinine reason, but my mind just wanted me to shut it up and let things flow so Andre' could hit the door. That's what happened. All Andre' did was walk by us and leave. No good-bye. No nothing. Good. Get the hell on.

"He was just leaving, Black," I told him. Stay Black was staring at Andre' as he walked by like he was getting ready to be 'bout it 'bout it. "He's had a hard day, Black, that's why he didn't speak."

"That's your man?"

"No," I moved from the door and beckoned him inside.

"Never was. A friend. An old, very old friend."

"Cool." He waltzed on inside. "I know I didn't call first, but I knew that you weren't at work. That's why I decided to bring some food here so we could chow down. You hungry?"

"Yeah! I haven't really eaten all day. Had some drama."

"Was that what you needed me for? Drama?"

Awe man! I forgot that I asked him for that favor! "No, Black, that's all taken care of. Forget about it. What are you doing off work so early?"

"Came to see you," he responded, sticking a straw in my cup and a fork in my food. "Make sure my girl's okay and to also make sure I could get back in here like I did the first time without you telling me off."

"I'm sorry, Black! For all those times I treated you like scum." I sipped my drink, thinking of all the times I was cold as ice. "I dissed you pretty badly. How can I make it up to you?"

"By eating all that food, man! That broke a brother. I'm not all green with money. I am flower boy."

"That's alright. My flower boy."

"What was that?"

Did I say that out loud?

"Nothing." I wanted to bust out laughing because I meant every word, but he didn't need to know all that. He was all mine. "Thank you for hooking me up with your shoulder last night. I needed that."

"Is everything alright now, Jee?"

"Yeah, things are better now."

"What do you say about me staying over tonight then? We can chill out, watch some movies, ya know?"

While his head was down, I watched him chew on that food like it was going out of style. He was starving. I remembered when I used to nearly loathe him, and at this point, he appeared all too different to me. He didn't know how much I wanted him to stay over with me tonight. I was afraid, however, to mess up a good thing just starting.   Emotions. Where Andre' made love to my body, Stay Black was beginning to touch me in my soul by barely doing anything at all. Just listening. That was deeper than I ever imagined. The fact that he cared about me and what was up with me, I couldn't help but want to share with him. It was a different feeling with Stay Black, a God send feeling. The right replacement for the wrong one. It wasn't even about looks or the physical touch, but could've easily fallen that way at any given time. So to answer the question could he stay?

"Yeah, you can stay. What movies you got for us to see?" I asked upbeat and as and free as a bird.

"I don't. We can go get them."

"Cool."

"Who was that, though, for real? Bro didn't say nothing," he asked referring to my ex-Andre'.

"I told you, nosey. Nobody. Just somebody." I shrugged my shoulders.

"How is nobody," he asked with a mouth full of food, "a somebody?"

I got up from the table and took my food with me because separation was needed for the joke that was gonna come sailing from my lips. "Similar to you. A nobody and a somebody all wrapped up in one!" I laughed.

"I tell you, Jee. You always got jokes."

"Uhm humm," I hummed in agreement. "Thanks for the food, though." It was too much to eat, so I put mine in the fridge. A little more weight gain on the butt was what I needed but not that much. My next man was gonna have to pinch on and be satisfied the little bit that I got.

"I should take it back to the restaurant and get my money back. Calling me a nobody and a somebody. That's a slick way of telling somebody off. Yeah, I should take that food right back," he joked.

"How?" I shut the refrigerator door, placed my hand on my hip and glanced his way. "You can't leave."

"Oh," he said as he stood up from the kitchen table and turned to face the front door. "Doesn't that look like a door to you? You holding me hostage or something?"

"Yeah, my hostage."

"Now since when did Miss Jeena become so needy?" He started walking over to the garbage can to dump the rest of his food.

"I'm not." Before I completed my answer, I thought back to what Andre' said to me on our first date about knowing what you want. "I just know what I want."

Right after those words came from my mouth, I felt like I caught a hot flash. In a rush of nerves and attempting to run away from what I just said, I went over to toss myself down on the floor in front of my television, afraid to even look Black in the eyes. "Wanna just watch some of my movies I have here?" I didn't know what else to do after my foot went and clogged my mouth, so I had to change the subject back to cinema. That didn't help.

From behind, I felt the silence in response what I said about wanting him, and it felt like he was burning a peep hole through my clothes. Putting myself on the spot was like sucking cow manure through a twisted straw. It stunk plus it tasted like foot.

"Man, Jeena, get up. We're going to the movie shop down the road. Those wack movies you got up in here...all ten of them! We won't be watching from that stash."

Stay Black just proved he was punctual. I knew he heard what I said, but thank God he was man enough to take it, but place it back down until the time was right to address it. Obviously, he was a great judge of opportunity unlike myself. Either I move too fast, too slow or altogether the wrong way.

"Don't hate on my collection," I responded.

"Better keep buying to make that a full out collection. More like scraps."

"Shut up." He couldn't talk about me having jokes.

After lifting me from the floor, Black grabbed my hand, and we went to rent. But when we got outside...

"You want me to ride on that? What happened to your

174

car?" A sista wasn't tripping or anything, but ain't no way I was hopping on that. He had a moped. There was nothing wrong with one, but I wasn't sitting on something without a trunk and a hood with four wheels to keep me a bit more padded.

"Come on, Jeena. You ain't too big nor too little for this. You can slide right up behind me. I had to drop my car off, so it's parked right now getting fixed up. Giving my ride a new style...black."

"You getting it painted?"

"Yeah, among other things, so in the meantime, I got my lady right here." He hit the moped on the side. "Come on," he said, cocking his eyes to the back of the seat. "She won't get jealous."

"I hope not." I was getting ready to do something that I had never done before...

Trust Stay Black With My Life.

We got beeped at and cursed out all the way down the road to the video store. Everybody that drove nice whips behind us nearly blew my ears out going down the street. Black wasn't phased. Me, not only was I scared straight but more embarrassed than I'd ever been in my life, minus the whole episode back at the hospital atop breaking down in the road while people cussed at me and Parri. By the time we arrived at the movie shop, I was ready to hop a taxi back home.

"When I asked you to go slow, Black, I didn't mean that slow," I said, jumping off his moped. "See, you're forever trying to be funny, stupid," I called him, busting him upside the back of his head in the process. "Going two miles an hour down the road."

"Hey! Watch that. I'm a sensitive black man. Tenderheaded." As he got off the moped, I'd already

175

strolled in the entrance, leaving him right back there to catch up. The store was overflowing with folks. Who would have thought that on a Monday people needed a movie to watch that badly, especially when most folks with computers could download. They must not put the time in, such as I. Download what when I could drop a dollar without the headache of learning the trade. Technology was not my thing. The click of the mouse was an awesome task at times. I hated computers and was a regular old fashioned yet modern day cell phone toting chick.

"Time to find a couple of movies," I whispered to myself. Up against the wall were the new releases, and down the aisles were the oldies but goodies. I spied Jason, well, Friday the 13th, all the way up to Boomerang and then Eve's Bayou. I went to pick it up.   "Hmmm..." I flipped it over and back like I'd never seen the cover nor the movie.

"Eve's Bayou?" he asked, finally having approached from behind.

"Yeah. What's wrong with that?"

"Nothing. That's a pretty good watch." He took the movie from me. "Man, the first time I saw this, I was trippin at homey in that mirror scene with his wife. Artistic like a mug. Never saw anything like that in a movie. Spooked me out."

"Spooked you out?"

"Well, not spooked. I ain't no punk or nothing," he said as he handed the movie back to me and shrugged his shoulders. "We can do that."

"Oh so now you give me the okay for what I can and can't watch?"

"Can't win for losing. Boy, I tell you. A man say something, there's a woman to run it over like road kill."

"That's my job, big daddy. Let's go."

He grabbed my arm before I was able to move one step.

"Hold up. You got your movie, and now I gotta get mine. This might take some time, sweetheart. Follow Black."

"Okay, but hurry up. I gotta go to work in the morning, and I want to get finished with at least one movie."

"Call in sick again."

"You gonna pay my bills?"

"It ain't even late yet, Jeena, so two movies tonight is no sweat." He grabbed me by my hand. His fingers fell in between my fingers, and honestly, I didn't know that I was gonna enjoy holding hands with him like that. I mean, I wasn't a school girl. Holding hands? Come on now. That was so elementary to get goosebumps over, but I was feeling it. It felt good. I thought back to Andre'. We only held bodies. Never hands. This...this felt nice. "Come on with me. Gotta check out some Scarface or some manly type stuff."

Along he tugged me without my resistance, and we hit the *manly* section alright. Terminator to Predator. I wasn't gonna front. I did like myself some Predator. Alien vs. Predator was my stuff.

"Let's get this one," I requested, while I tugged at his hand.

"Predator? You like that?"

"Yeah, I like Predator. You wanna?"

"Let's do this. I hope you got some money."

"Yeah, I sure do. Keyword...mine. Not the cash register's," I responded.

"I'm just playin', Jeena, baby." Then all out of the blue he leaned over and kissed me twice, once on my cheek and the second time on my neck. "I got you, sis." He then looked away and proceeded to put the movies on the checkout counter.

Whew, did that throw me! Kissed my body all over some movies! Deep down, whether I wanted to admit it or not to myself, I knew Stay Black meant more with that *I got you sis* and kiss than some movie rentals. He wanted me to feel like I belonged with him, and at that moment, it worked. A dumb kiss on neck and some swag got me panting.

When we got outside, I glared at the infamous moped that caused me to get cussed out all the way here. Now, where I lived was nothing but three blocks away from here, but on a moped, his moped, it felt like an eternity.

"Come on and put your helmet back on."

And that was the other thing that I left off. I had to wear that big heavy thing on my head. I didn't feel too cute at all, but hey, I would rather have worn that helmet than have a huge block of concrete hitting my forehead.

I snatched it from him jokingly. "You just better get me home in one piece."

"I will. One whole solid piece."

From there, I hopped behind him on the bike and waited…and waited and waited. I hopped back off.

"What's wrong?"

"Man, don't embarrass me, man," he sighed. "Jeena, we might have to walk."

"Walk what?" I spun around looking for a dog or cat or something and failed to find one. "A pet, a dog or something 'cause I don't have a leash and really not into the whole pick up poop thing?"

"No, Jee. My moped, it's dead. I'ma call my boy to come and get it for me. He lives down the road. He'll have it for me tomorrow no sweat. He built this bad boy over for me."

"Ha!" At this point, I wasn't trippin', because everybody has a bad day. "It's cool, Black. You callin' now?" I saw him get his cell out.

"Yeah. Ain't leaving my whip unattended."

What the heck, I thought. I didn't have any plans. "You sure we can't get dropped off. Think your friend will mind?"

He didn't answer because he was already on the phone yapping at his boy. As he explained the situation to the other party on the phone, I sat on the curb with the movies in a bag tossed over my shoulder. Slumping my shoulders, I grinned with my head down not believing what was going on inside of me.

As I glanced up at him chatting away about his broken down moped, Stay Black was getting more and more fine as the heavens. His dead moped, all out of nowhere, looked like a Benz, and his hair didn't look all that bad anymore either. Even his voice was telling me a different story about his life, things that I wanted to learn about and know. I hadn't even seen his body yet, and didn't even need to look just yet because it didn't even matter. The way I was feeling about him, it was going to be like fantasy island when I got underneath those rags for the first time. Nothing but mouth watering goodness. My head fell back in between my legs, and I spoke to my vagina aka Gina.

"This is a nightmare, Gina. What in the world am I doing? What is wrong with meeeee and you? We have to talk about some things before you go making decisions that I can't live with - seriously," I sang silently. The man I once despised was the man I was diggin', not believing I was actually sitting on a curb stranded, undressing and tasting Stay Black after all the drama and sin I put myself in. Temptation must be the hardest habit to break because now was not the time for me to be falling in love with another man so soon. I needed to take things really slowly, like constipation slow. Sit and wait.

"Alright. Sorry, Jee. You don't mind walking with me do you? It's nice out here. You don't live far, and I know those legs of yours can carry...unless you want me to carry you all the way back?" He paused, I supposed waiting on me to respond, but I hesitated. My mind wasn't all there at that point. "He's on his way now. Just lives up the street. Come on," he spoke softly while he knelt down beside me.

I knew that he must have thought I was either crying or angry at the walk home situation because of my bodily expression which was curled in a ball. He would have never guessed that I was actually taming my namesake Gina, just spelled differently. Black had no idea how he made Gina feel right now, and real Jeena was fighting the whole idea!

I lifted my head. "Of course. I mean, I don't mind the stroll. I haven't been for a walk in a long time." I stated, getting up from the curb. He then took the bag of movies from my fingertips.

"I got that."

"I can handle this little bag, Black."

"I'm the man here, so let me handle that."

"Fine with me."

We started. I'd never walked this road before, physically on the concrete nor emotionally with Black. I knew that by the time we got back to my condo, the sun would probably be setting because Black's feet were moving quite slowly as if he was in absolutely no rush. Because of this, I had to slow my normal, fast stroll to stay back with his.

I was more nervous than a kid in a spelling bee. I'd never felt this way before around Black - ever. Jesus! If my stomach doesn't chill with the knots I'm gonna stool on the curb! My nerves are shot. Just the thought of having sex with Black got me all messed up. Going from hated homeboy to sex object wasn't at all normal for me, but nor was a man actually caring about me, the real me, without me giving up the goods.

"Are you feeling better, Jeena? You still haven't told me anything about..."

"About?" I asked while kicking a rock ahead of me as if it were a soft ball. I was hoping that he didn't get on the why I was crying the other day on his chest subject.

"About the other day when you were crying on my chest."

Dannnng!

"It's a long story, Black. I really don't think you wanna know, therefore, I don't think I should spill the beans."

"I just know that you need somebody to talk to, and it won't help holding it inside."

My rock rolled over in front of him, and he gave it a tap back to me.

"How would you figure that?"

"You needed me to stay."

Duh, Jeena! I *did* ask him to stay. Practically pleaded! My mouth and my foot had met again. Why me? I decided not to panic while cornered by the comment, but like a fighter in the ring, I fought my way out.

"*Needed* you to stay? Black, I don't necessarily need anyone. Come on now, this is me, Jeena, remember? Don't get it twisted. I can hold my own."

"You can cut that out, Jeena," he stated, shaking his head like no this girl ain't trying to be hardcore. "Stop that, Jee. You may be able to hold your own, but I held you that night."

Now that hardcore Plan A had officially gone to the dogs, it was on to Plan B which was completely change the subject.

"So you lived here all your life?"

"Jeena, you ain't no stranger to me. Who cares? Stop trying to change the subject."

When I stopped responding, he stopped walking, tapped my elbow and had me turn around to face him.

"Reason I'm asking is 'cause a brother doesn't just wanna know. I *need* to know, Jee. Just because you tell me what's going on with you doesn't mean that I will put it in the streets. I don't run my mouth like I'm one of your homegirls gone wild. I'm a full grown man. It's safe here. I care enough about you to keep it that way. You can talk to me."

At that point, I knew that he was dead serious, positively knowing that the reason he wanted to know was not because he wanted to pry. He was beginning to feel deeper about me just as I was beginning to feel deeper for him. Besides, this was the first time that we actually hung out besides back at my place when I cried a river, and things were going good now. At this point, I guessed honesty was the best policy. Love me or hate me. Lies didn't get me anywhere but hurt before, so I could try the truth. I trusted Black enough I guess.

"Black, my answer to your question isn't too good." I twirled my fingers together in my hand and waited on some slack, but Black gave me none. I continued, "I was in a relationship with someone, Black, and I got hurt really badly. I put my feelings on a platter, and he had the blade, axe, and whatever else. Well, really, I can't even blame him. I knew..." I stopped dead in mid sentence because I was talking too fast, so fast that I almost blurted the main *married* issue out without the build up that I needed.

I began to walk again. This time, Black kept up with my

pace. I swore his ears had gotten bigger, too. The better to hear you with, my dear, I thought back to the children's book with baby girl red and the big bad wolf. This was not even cool. The man that I really wanted to be perfect for now was getting ready to hear the worst news imaginable, making me terribly imperfect and a home wrecker all the way around! I couldn't have dug a better grave for my love life any deeper.

"You knew what, Jee?" he asked, pushing me to finish the sentence.

Could lightening hit me now or what? The perfect time to drop dead had always been when you're busted, but that just never seemed to happen!

"I knew that I would fall easily for someone because I'd been alone for so long. The only problem was that I got my feelings tangled up in something that I shouldn't have. I wound up not liking him as much as I thought eventually, and the bottom line was that I slept with a married man."

There. I said it. I kept my eyes on my two feet that seemed, at that particular point, to drill holes into the concrete.

"You were messing with two guys at the same time?"

Huh? Two guys? Oh...wait a minute. My bad.

"No, Black. I mean, the man that I was with was married, I knew it, and I made the worst mistake of my life being with him in the first place. That's what I was crying about, and really, Black, please believe me that I'm sorry about all my mistakes, including mistreating you. I've grown and not into wrecking homes, despite what it may seem because I wouldn't want that to happen to me and my family."

When I was finished yapping a mile a minute, Black, well, he said nothing. All he did was motion me to continue walking with him. I couldn't believe this mug! He didn't say a word. Nothing! What the freak! Man, this was too much to handle. I was willing to put one hundred on it that I look like home wreckin' champ of the decade. I'd come to find out through Parri mainly that the only person who loves the home wrecker was the man she was sleeping with. To everyone else, she was a whore, thus

Black's thoughts of me maybe.

"Black," I called with no luck, but then he answered.

"I hear you, Jee, but I don't have much to say about that, you know. Sure would hate if someone knowingly came in and busted up my thing with someone I married though. Hard core cold stuff there. Gotta be clueless, selfish or just plain apathetic. That stuff right there is family, children, time and all destroyed for some sex. That's what split my happy home up as a child, some other man on my mom," he stated as he stared back at the movie shop before we completed turning the curve and saw his friend at his moped. I had the good nerve to run back there and hitch a ride with the moped mechanic, but I didn't. I had to grow up and face what I did and not run away like a scared chicken as I did in the hospital.

After Black just put my face further in the mud, I realized that I could have hurt far more people that what I'd already hurt. If there were kids involved, how much worse! Then there were Tina's parents who possibly knew she was beat up, not to mention the time she spent out of work, the emotional strain, mental mess...all because of me and her husband. From the side of my teary eye, I saw Black. Silent. He never went in detail with the story, but apparently, the hurt came through his mom. Unlucky me, I was the mirror image of her! A woman with issues who simply didn't consider anything beyond herself. I just knew that Black wasn't about to be my man now.

By the time we got to the area where I could see my front door, in a nutshell, I was through dealing. My arms were already folded in defense mode as I awaited losing Black from my life, too. It never failed. I would always lose the man I needed, only to end up with garbage that I tended to fall for repeatedly.

Although Stay Black eventually continued to talk about other things other than my confession, I was barely listening the whole way back. And those movies, he could forget it. They weren't gonna be watched by us. Maybe by him at his place, but not us. I didn't feel the need in dragging my emotions any further with Black as it would seem he was over me by now. Maybe my thoughts were all wrong, but they outweighed any other hopeful thought I had at the time. Oh shoot! I just remembered I had to drive him home tonight, further elongating my slut hoe embarrassment.

As soon as we got to the condo, he stopped me at the door. I paused. I couldn't even look at him for God's sake. This was absolutely the worst I'd ever felt I my entire life. Failure. 360 degrees of pure failure backed with a tramp stamp.

"Jeena, were you in love with him?"

"What?" I asked in disbelief. What the hell kind of question was that all out of the blue? "Are you serious, Black? Did I love him? Why?" I popped back with an attitude. My attitude was more a defense mechanism than anything else because I wasn't about to feel even worse by crying, therefore, I grew tough woman skin. "After that long, old walk home," I stated in a highly irritated manner, "did you really have to go and make me feel worse by telling me that's what happened to your family? Not that I don't care, but dang, it's something I'm not proud of, Black! You made me feel like ... snot soot."

What the hell snot soot was, I didn't know. I only said it because I didn't want to say the word shit being that my new leaf is turning. Slowly, but it's turning, thus, slip ups were bound to happen in stressful situations. Anyway, Stay Black just stared back at me like duh, so I kept piling on the dirt.

"You know what, Black," I stated as I looked back at him as harshly as I could, but I was at a loss for words. Fucker. Just that last time cursing in my brain, Lord, please forgive me...again! Agh! I wanted to pound myself in the skull! "I felt like you dissed me back there? I mean, you asked me to pour my guts out about what I didn't want to say anyway, and then you just go and make me feel worse. On the real, that was kinda cruel."

"Can we go on inside now?"

I pointed to my front door. "Where? Inside here?"

He lifted his head and let out a huge breath. "Yeah, Jeena. We need to chill that's all."

"Chill?" Say what?!

"Yeah...and it wasn't a diss, Jee. Let's just go in and watch the movies," he stated, obviously disappointed beyond what I would have imagined. Whatever. I was tired of my mistakes biting me in my butt. Just so tired.

Though I hesitated on letting Black back inside, I wanted another chance for us with everything, no matter how my anger tried to get me to deny it. One more chance. That's why I opened the door for the both of us to go and calm the situation down.

We walked in. As soon as I hit the floor, the air circulated a bad trash can odor that could make someone gag to pure death. Gross. I hadn't dumped the thing in two days, so I guessed that was my bad.

"Excuse me, Black. Suddenly, my trash can has a lot to say. I need to go and dump it right about now."

"No, no. It's good. I'll take it for you. Right out back? Is that where the dumpster is?"

"Yeah, thanks."

"No problem." He tossed the movies over in the living room and came to take the garbage out of my hand after I had a difficult time pulling it out of the trash can. I thought it was only two days worth of garbage, but it could have been more.

As soon as he exited, I turned and stared at myself in the mirror making sure that I didn't have a big old long booger or something hanging out of my nose or some freakin' face tragedy that would make my night a bit worse than my day. Nothing found, so I fled to my bedroom, changed clothes, came back out and made sure my room door was slammed shut. My emotions were in a haze, and I definitely didn't want that haze to guide me into my bedroom and through the woods in an attempt to quick fix the bad attitude I had with Black on the way back.

By the time I got back out into the living room, Black was already sitting on the couch with the movie that I picked out in his hand and appeared much more relaxed than he did at the door when I jumped down his throat for what I knew was no real reason. It was obvious that my situation vexed him greatly, so instead of being the one with the attitude, I decided to identify with his situation and lay my pride low. What I told him on the way back home probably hit him in a deeper way than what I imagined, and that was by no fault of his, just based on his past experiences as a child. I'd never been on that side of the coin, so I had no idea what it felt like.

When I was in the bedroom, I'd changed into my yellow and orange jogging suit pants and orange tank top. This was the one that I normally wore to the gym whenever I went which wasn't often, thus, I was coming up slack on Parri's *join me on my get fine diet* plan. Parri was a monster in the gym. Forget a diet! Leave the letter T off, and it was more like die in your workout! Along with the weight control with what she ate, she would match that with great cardio and weight lifting to the point of death. I was a sideliner with a huge water in my hand half way through.

Anyway, back to my jogging suits. I had two others in the same style, one blue and purple and the other black and gray, but tonight I felt yellow and orange. After pepping myself up mentally to forget the whole diss situation from earlier and get a nice movie night happening, I walked up behind him on the sofa and covered his eyes with the palms of my hands.

"I know it's you, Jeena," he sighed.

"Well, how did you guess?"

"I'm up in *your* place chillin'." He got up from the sofa, but continued talking. "Waitin' on you to put this movie in the player while I go dig in your refrigerator to make up some of what you got in there to drink for the both of us."

I smiled.

"What you smiling at?" he asked.

"You, Black. Thanks for ignoring me at the door. It was pretty bad what I said on the walk home and at the front door. I was just on the defense because I just didn't know how to accept..."

"It was nothing," he interjected. "So what do you want to drink?" he asked as he placed the movie in my hands.

"How do you know that I want you in my fridge?" I asked jokingly.

He continued to walk in the direction of my ice box.

"Because you don't want me near that DVD player."

"Why don't I?"

"I don't know how to work it."

"What?!" I couldn't believe it.

"Nope. I still have VHS, Jee. Ain't nothing like old tape. All the movies on VHS ain't even on DVD yet. Can't sell out on the VHS so fast. That's Swag 101. Old school beats out new school every time, right? Look at deejays still hustling for vinyl in a digital world."

I busted out laughing! No he didn't say that he was still rocking the VHS. They're practically antiques! I hadn't even seen one in ages.

"I'm not gonna hate, so excuse my laughing. I'll handle the DVD while you hit the fridge, but don't think I even believe you right now, Black, about not knowing how to use one of these things."

"I don't even know how to take one of those bad boys out of the case, but the drink right here, I can handle. I'm telling you the truth."

"I hope you drink cranberry juice or kool-aid because that's all I have," I stated, sliding the DVD into the DVD player and hit play, "unless you want to use a juicer."

"I'm dipping in the kool-aid right now. This man don't mix with cranberries. My question is where did you get this big ole thing of red kool-aid from, Jee?"

It was big. Gigantic even. Got it from this sweepstakes type entry thing I won at the grocery store, and I haven't been able to drink enough of that kool-aid yet. It mimicked three milk cartons full except in a big can. The grocery store delivered it to me, and I've been attempting to drink it ever since.

"I won at the grocery store, and that was the prize. Well, it wasn't the grand, but one of the prizes. You know how they do with the optional prizes. The grand prize was a car, but I bet no one won that."

"I bet your phone calls doubled, too, from all those telemarketers they sell your phone number."

"Nope. I gave them Faith's."

"Your sister?"

"Yep, and they wouldn't stop calling her! She was the one that called me and told me that I won. She wasn't too happy about the phone number thing though. She changed it. No worries."

"Word?"

"Word."

"Man, please. I would've called 'em back, gave them your number and then laughed in your face."

"Shut up, Black!" I laughed.

"Here we are. Two big kool-aids. Hey, where you going?" he asked as I jumped from the chair at the same time he was walking toward me in the living room.

"What's kool-aid without chips, man? Where have you been? You can't drink kook-aid without chips. It's like peanut butter and jelly or biscuits and syrup. They match."

"I feel you. I feel you."

Out of curiosity, I stared over at Black while I reached under the cabinet, feeling for the bag of crunchies I bought last week. "Black?"

"Yeah," he answered, sipping that probably way too sugary drink he just made.

"Do you have a serious or less than serious girlfriend or anything? I've never, ever seen you with one whenever we cross paths, and you never talk about one." Just because he held my hand and kissed me didn't mean that he wasn't doing it to the next female no matter how nice and kind he was being. I just wanted to be sure this time that the man I wanted was totally and completely free.

"I guess that means that I don't because if I did have one, you would have both heard and seen."

"So you're saying," I started, standing back up after

finding the chips, "that you aren't a player, and you sport your woman like a pair of Jordans on your feet?"

"No. I'm saying that I would sport my woman like she's a part of my heart. I wouldn't play her because, in essence, I would be playing myself if she is with me. That would make me a fool and us a mockery. Why would I do that to not only her but myself likewise? In other words, I would take care of her better than I would take care of shoes. Shoes I walk on, not my woman." He sipped on his kool-aid. "Can't have people sitting back laughing at me and my woman because if they're laughing at her, dang that's a super bad reflection on me. Hell no, I wouldn't play her. If she's mine, she's mine. If anything, I'll make every woman in the world wish they were her as long as I'm with her which would end up making me look like the best man alive. We reflect each other."

Well shut me up! That must be a page out of his Swag 101 philosophy. Swag on, Black! Swag on, brother! I knew he had his beliefs and could sound like a small time philosopher at times but that was exactly what I wanted to hear. Knowing Stay Black, he truly believed everything he said and lived by it.

"Wow, Black! You sound like you know what's up."

"I've had enough time as a single man to think about life, and soon I want to put it to action. See how it all works out."

"Have you ever been in love and all before?"

"Not quite, but very close."

"What stopped you?"

"Every time I wanted her, she was taken, unavailable, or something just wasn't right about me, or for that matter, her." He slightly grinned while I handed the chips over to him so that he could bust them open. Every time I would bust chips open, half of them would spill out. Only had one bag tonight, so I couldn't afford to lose not one to the floor.

"Are you still waiting on her?" Yep, I asked the dumbest question of the night. I wanted to know, but then again, I didn't want to know. I knew that it was selfish, but I wanted to know for sure that I was the one he was talking about for a fact, not just assume it was me because of how he gushed about me from time to time. Thing was, I'd never given Black anything to love about me, so I had doubts along with my hopes he was crushing on me that hard. Sure, Stay Black flirted with me a lot, but not like he spoke of this mystery lady. Whatever the case may be, if things went far deeper with me and Black anytime soon, at least I knew his philosophy on relationships.

Bottom line, I had come to find out that he was really a nice guy, and not bad looking at all anymore, especially now that I have looked beyond his fight the power ways and my superior blindness. Black had the most gorgeous eyes in the world, and his eyebrows were perfect. He didn't have long fingernails like he was competing with my amateur French tips, and he spoke with sense and not sex - so far. I was accustomed to other types of men, but Black, I never heard nor saw this side of him. Ever. Either this was too good to be true or finally my dream coming true.

The answer to my question about him waiting on his lady love went unanswered, so I kept bugging him about it. Sometimes, I was just a pest like that.

"Is she why you didn't try anything on me the night you stayed with me?" I joked outwardly, but extra serious inwardly and sneakily prying for my benefit. "You're still too stuck on her?"

"Don't you think it's time to watch the movie?"

"Oh it's like that! You're gonna kick my question to the curb!" Obviously, I'd created some tension which made me believe whole heartedly that I was that girl. Me. Yeah, Black had been waiting on me.

"Yeah," he replied softly with a sigh, not willing to reveal anymore information to me by making use of the force called self control. Instead of discussing his unknown love, he continued to speak in the calmest, sexiest voice while he darn near undressed me with his eyes, "Yeah, Jee, it's like that. Let's do what we came here to do."

Just what the hell *did* we come here to do, I asked myself, and just then, my kool-aid went down the wrong pipe at the split second thought of me and him butt naked on the sofa watching Eve's Bayou.

"Is my kool-aid that bad?" he asked as he put his cup down to pat me on the back because I was coughing nonstop.

"No," I continued choking, still finding the time to answer him. "The Kool-aid is great," I stated giving him the thumbs up. "I think I swallowed wrong."

"You okay? Your eyes are red and watering up."

I was so embarrassed. "Yeah, I'm okay." I reached over to the remote and pressed play. Got the attention off of me and my halfway dead from choking behind. This would have been the wrong way to leave the earth, so, "I'll be right back, Black. Don't laugh!" I smiled, and then left him alone in the living room, awaiting my rebirth.

When I reached my bathroom, I went haywire. I coughed as hard as I could to get the mess out of my windpipe and into the proper area, wherever that would end up being to prevent the cough from continuing. Finally, after about fifteen more seconds of nightmare, the cough cleared.

"Breathe! Breathe! This is just your friend from back in the day! He works at the flower shop, and rides that moped around all day long for now. His dog on hair is more flick-ted than yours." I reached up and yanked my hair every which way but out in frustration, then turned the water on and drenched my flushed face. "This is not gonna happen." I was mad insane. "I don't like him that much! Not Blaaaacccckkkk! What is wrong with me?" I screamed silently because I knew the truth of the matter. When Black said let's do what we came here to do, my own thoughts went bump and grind. The real long and luscious bump and grind, too! I had to get a grip.

"You alright?" It was Black calling from the living room.

Dang! The sound of his voice made me grip the edge of the sink with both hands. I let out a long breath. I had to figure out a way to ruin the night because there was that ruin a friendship factor going on tonight that wasn't about to happen. My emotions were going nuts for some literal nuts, and I wasn't going out like that. Not after the mess I got in with Parri, God and everyone else.

"Yeah, I'm cool. I'll be out in a second! Pause the movie!"

"I don't know how to pause this thing, Jee, I told you."

"It's not that different from a VCR!" I shouted. He was so silly that it was attractive to me. Just nice and silly. Thank God for giving me something good to compare to bad. I finally knew how to appreciate good and hold on to it tight after feeling like a piece of dirt. I wasn't about to let Black go. If we remained friends, that was fine. On the other hand, if anything under heaven made us come together in the right way, I knew that it would be good and last. I wouldn't push it. On top of him or off of him, I wasn't going to push it.

On my knees atop my bathroom rug, I told God thanks in a silent prayer, and stood back up. I was ready. I was ready enough not to make the same mistake more than once. Therefore, I took several deep breaths and clenched my fists, ready to fight for some redemptive actions to take place within me.

"So help me God." I opened my bathroom door while thinking that connecting with God in the midst of temptation wasn't a bad idea, but then temptation struck again at the bathroom door, standing live and in color. Nearly caused cardiac arrest in my poor chest! Hadn't I been through enough stress? Dang!

"Black! Don't stand up next to my bathroom door like that! Why are you back here? Lord!" I yelped, stunned silly.

He started laughing hysterically, probably because I'd been looking straight up ignorant since the night started.

"I could've been taking a dump, you know? That would've been foul, so stop cracking up." I stated, beginning to laugh with him.

"My bad," he replied, still laughing and backing up with his hands up in the air like he was being arrested. He finally put his hands down to his sides and started walking back over toward me.

Cut. My mind began to wonder. Why on earth do I always get stuck near or in a bathroom with a man that I am attracted to? The same mess happened with Andre'. At that point, I slid away from the bathroom door, out into my bedroom. That bathroom thing was severe bad luck the last time. Wasn't even gonna happen this time.

Black stopped in his tracks and looked at me oddly when I moved away from my personal use it station.

"What's wrong with you?"

"Nothing. Just scooting over."

"Are you sure?"

"How many times do I have to tell you yes, I'm fine?" I asked him, rolling my eyes like I was highly irritated, but on the real, just trying to shake bad thoughts out of my head and throw him off a little.

"You gotta tell me until I believe you, Jeena. You've been kind of on the sensitive side lately, and now you're jumping to the side like I bite."

In one split second, I felt Black's hand around my waist and then his fingers went in between mine. It felt like ice was trickling down my spine and my central nervous system was about to snap into a million pieces. I wanted to stay as normal and as friend like as possible but at the same time, jump all over him. This whole hand in hand thing should not have been happening. It was too much for me at this point.

"Are you still in love with him, Jeena?"

"Black..." I really didn't want to go into that mess that we talked about on the way home. Strike one on Stay Black. He was too persistent.

"Jeena, just let me know. Yes or no." He grabbed my other hand.

When he grabbed my hand, my whole entire bed came into view, and my vagina began to panic. I was so used to it, you know, liking a man and then enter the woods and clear the trail, but I didn't want to do that again. The way I thought I could play with Andre' before, got me in love with Andre' and hurt at the same time. To tell the truth, I didn't know how to answer Black's question, but I did know that if I didn't want to love or care for Andre' as much as I did, I would first have to say it.

"No. No, Black, I don't love him anymore. That's done." I needed to move further away from my bathroom. It had to be a freaking jinx.

"Do you think it'll be hard for you to fall in love with a man like me?"

Well, damn. Where did my tongue go? I couldn't feel it. I didn't answer out loud, but my mind was like *what do you think*? Screw it. I was scared as hell. Friend to more than just friends in less than one second. Actually Black was more like foe to more than just friends. I didn't know about this.

He continued, "Jeena, I don't care about what you did. I care about what you wanna do with me. Some people mess up, but as long as you don't love him anymore, we're good. You're that woman I was talking about Jeena. You know that. You've always known I was feeling you like that."

"Black," It was time for me to get up off of it, and let Black know the same thing I just let God know. "I wanna try and live right this time." Then, I cut my eyes over to my bed, unmade and all. Black saw me and then he looked back over there, too.

"Jeena, the last thing I want you to do is live wrong." He turned back to face me. "But I do want us to get it right together. So if you know in your heart that something is wrong, I won't ask it of you. I'll wait until you think it's right. Been waiting this damn long to get you."

As he spoke, I noticed that he never let go of my hands. He was still there, as passionate as ever, with his hands holding mine as if he never even planned on releasing. Any other man would have slung my hands down at the notion of me trying to live right by not cocking my legs open and then probably push the issue so far only to steal every attempt to alter my feelings to fit theirs. That's what I was used to back when I first started dating years ago - being made to feel guilty for not wanting to be guilty.

That was how I learned how to keep a man happy while dating. Do what he wanted while I lost myself in the process, knowing right but ultimately doing wrong and loving it eventually, until now. I didn't like it anymore.

Andre' was the last straw. I did the same thing with him when I offered him my key just to please him. I was tired of pleasing and sleazing, and my morale had hit a new married men low. I needed to be fixed because I was just as much to blame for my condition as any man on earth because, fact was, my choices were my fault – Andre' included.

At that point, I finally knew what a man would do if he was really true. Remain. Remain right there with me no matter my decision about the bedroom. I didn't know how to react or what to say to Stay Black's acceptance of my decision except...

"Thank you."

Black, then led me out of my bedroom, while remaining locked tight to my ten fingers. Since he was in front of me, I glanced back at my bed. What I should do is change the mattress, I thought, but those craps cost entirely too much. Since I didn't have a middle finger that was free, I stuck out my tongue at it instead. Finally, a time where I felt no...

Pressure.

By the end of the night, Eve's Bayou had become the greatest movie of all time. As for Black, he was the best man of all time as he sat there and watched it with me while I laid in his lap. Honestly, I was shocked I didn't feel any drool slap me in my face from him having fallen asleep. He actually stayed awake while he held my hand the whole entire time. Wow! I was used to a man holding my breast or rubbing all up my legs while I pushed back or either enjoyed the paws.

"Ready for Predator?"

I turned to face him. "You just couldn't wait could you?" I joked.

"No, no...Eve's Bayou...what did I say? It's the junk, but Predator. That's my stuff right there. Grew up on that."

"Yeah?"

"Yeah."

I sat up and because I wanted to be a good hostess, I asked, "Well, do you want some more kool-aid? I know that you made it last time, but I'll hook you up this time."

"Yeah," he paused, looked away for a brief moment and then, came right back to my eyes. Hesitantly, I looked elsewhere and then got up off of the couch, but couldn't go anywhere because he was still holding my hand. When I turned back around to tell him to stop trippin' and let my hand go, he stood up in front of me, leaned into my space and kissed me gently on my cheek right next to corner of my lips.

As my eyes entered into his gaze, the space that he entered into just a second ago that I referred to as mine, suddenly became ours. My lips met his, without a kiss. Instead, they grazed across his, and I swear my lungs collapsed, I promise to God in heaven! Dead on arrival with the heavenly hosts doing CPR. His lips felt like...dang...I couldn't think. Then, softly, I kissed his lips. He let me, and then, he moved my hands behind my back while still holding my hands in his. Then, Black kissed me back.

Oh my good Lord, I thought I was getting ready to sinny, sin sin again! I wanted to touch him, but when I tried to pull my fingers from his, he tightened down on them just a little to let me know that he wanted them to stay there. Therefore, I relaxed them. That's when he began to kiss my neck, and at the same time, I could have sworn I was in some sort of lamaze class because my breathing got harder. I couldn't even keep my mouth shut. My breathing turned into short passionate exhales, and his kisses transformed into what I wanted with and on me always.

I had to pull back because that bedroom was about to call

me over, so Black stopped. He also brought my hands back in between us.

"Black," I spoke, not saying anymore, but only motioning my eyes to the bedroom like *yea-yuh*, I think I have a mind change!

"Leave that bed alone, Jee."

"Leave whaa?" I responded as my thoughts caught a case of confusion.

"The bed. Kill that right now."

What? I was gonna just die! Literally, I had no response. A man who seriously didn't want any of my lovely lower lady was standing before me. But wait, he must be limp, I thought. Had to be. Either that or I just turned back into a sling it out slut giving it out on the sort of first date.

"That's habit, Jeena."

"Isn't that what you're asking for?"

"Isn't that what you said you didn't want?"

Ouch. That hurt.

"Jeena, I want *you*. When I get you and really know that I have you, Jeena, then I want to keep you. You don't have to give me what I might want right now, Jeena, baby. Just give me what you can." He then looked over at the bedroom. "It's hard as hell declining on that, but I don't want to be what every other man was to you. I want to be that different thing for you and you for me. Excuse the way I'm gonna put this, but sleeping with a habit ain't shit of what making love is. I know, trust me. On top of that, no disrespect to my mom, but I don't want a woman like she was to my father either. That's all she wanted. Messed us up. She is my reminder of what I don't need."

Black began to smile, reducing the seriousness of the conversation. "Besides that, all I wanted was a nice kiss."

"Was it nice enough?"

He pushed his dreadlocks back away from his face, and let out a deep breath. "I know you're about to get some more snacks, but I gotta get up out of here before things get too nice. I don't need a wishy washy woman who can't keep her own word to herself, and you don't need a man who won't help you do it, be a better person, and vice versa. That's what it's all about, right? On that note, I'm gone before Thunder makes the lightening flash," he stated referencing his other head.

He leaned over and gave me another kiss. "I'm gonna go ahead..." he paused and began to rub his head, kinda like he was drowning in a pit of shame. "Will you give me a lift? You know my ride..."

Oh, I supposed he'd forgotten that I had to take him home in order for him to get there fast or else his feet would do it for him the turtle way. "Yeah, I see that you kinda forgot about your moped being back at your boy's place broke down." I grinned. "I'll take you home, but only if you come really close to me so I can tell you something in your ear."

He leaned in. "What's that?"

"I want you, too, Black." Then, I kissed him once more. "And thank you for helping me do what I made a decision to do. It's hard as hell though."

"That's what your man is for. Hurts me more than you, believe that."

"You're my man now?"

"Yeah, you're my lady. You've always been my lady."

This was exactly what I was missing. This could actually turn into what was called real love. No rub my body talk just yet. Only real love.

"Well, come on then, baby, and let me take you home," I joked.
"I've never truly seen where you live either, so now will be my chance for me to bust up in there."

"Whoa!"

"Whoa?" I placed my hand on my hip and looked back at him like *huh*? "Whoa what?"

"You really don't have to go up in there tonight."

As Black responded, a big frown grew across his face as if going in his house would be the last thing he would ever wish from me. But uh, if he could hang out in mine and shoot the dog on breeze, then I can bust up in his and pick up a dog on dime!

"Why not?" I gathered my stuff, itching to see what I could see at Black's. The more he was trying to hide, the more I wanted to see. "Being that you are my man and all, and that makes me your lady and things like that, I think I deserve to see how my man is living, right? Dirty, crusty drawers mid floor and mold in the tub," I continued, gliding back by him and then pinching him on his cheek. "Don't you think so, baby?"

"Jokes! Got jokes. Don't pinch a man's cheek, especially in public."

"Come on." I beat him out the door.

"I really should walk back."

He stumbled outside with me, and we left.

When we got to his spot, I finally stepped foot in the yard that I'd dreaded for so long. Have mercy. As far as the actual house was concerned, it was pretty decent for a flower boy. All out in the yard, however, it looked tore up! That was what I was so accustomed to seeing - the outside - and because of the way it looked, I never felt motivated to go beyond the curb in front of Black's house. The best thing for me to do was just drive on by, each and every day.

There was not a lick of grass was in the yard. Just one small, dizzy looking bush yielded life in the middle of all that gray, ashy dirt that drowned the poor property. Wait, there was another bush peeping off from the side of the house that looked like it was stolen from someone else's yard on the down low. Knowing Black, he sneaked it off of some deserted property.

Such a shame, this yard was. Couldn't even tell the ant piles from the good walking ground. When I would pass by while driving, I always turned my head away from Black and this drought mess. If he managed to catch my eye, I would speak with a hand cock over the stirring wheel like hi, bye and keep it moving. Then, as always, he would do something goofy like blow me a kiss or mouth something to which I would never wait on his lips to stop moving to interpret his words. I was terrible, sure, but he was just as goofy as I was horrid. Once, I even caught him tossing grass seeds everywhere to no avail while he was trying to get me to catch some pucker up love he blew at me from the street. Again, we used to be such a shame. Who would have ever imagine me and him? Not I.

Enough about the outside though because to my shock, the inside of Black's place was sleek! He had a completely open and spacious home with a grand entertainment system, and yep, there were his VHS tapes. That mug wasn't lying! He had no idea about the term modern world. They were neat though, stacks of them in alphabetical order. Next to them was the VCR. Lovely, polished, and old. His furniture was man black as usual for a guy, and it smelled like genuine new leather. He must've just brought this stuff in here because the entire home smelled new! It was laid out like a pimp's pad. With one glance in his small hallway, I nearly fell over when I saw three disco balls for hall lights reflecting light off of four civil rights photos representing the struggle! That's when my mind floated to the bedroom. Not. Don't even want to see it, I thought.

"I'm gonna go now." I had to interrupt that flow quick.

"Yeah, you should." Black said looking like a nervous wreck.

"Your house is very nice, Black. It's much different..."

"Yeah, I know. I don't let most people on the inside. You're the first female in some time now. I was fixing up the inside, do the outside afterwards. Takes money which is something that I don't have a lot of on hand. A brother like me has to save." He looked a bit ashamed or embarrassed. I felt like I was the cause of it.

"Black," I walked over in front of him. "Money doesn't make nor impress me when it comes to someone I like. Sure it helps to have money, Black, don't get me wrong because it's played for a woman to have to take care of a man, but," Suddenly, I felt extremely small, like it wasn't the time nor the place for preaching to someone about the guy girl rules as it was obvious he worked hard to try to have something nice for any female to feel welcome. As I looked around, I spotted those VHS tapes. Maybe the reason he really had them was because he was saving from scratch and only spent money he had to spend.

I turned back to him. "Black, please say that you didn't do this all these years because you think that you have impress me or anyone else?"

He put his head down. "Yeah." Then, he raised it again. "I thought maybe I could get my arms around you then if I had more nice things."

"Don't buy me anything," I told him softly. It hurt me that all of this was for me. "If I can only have you, Black, I really don't even deserve that. Remember that, and see you later."

As I walked out the door, Black yelled, and my whole face fell to the ground.

"Gotcha!" he laughed, holding pack after pack of his abs. "I been feeling you for a while now, but outside of that, a brother still needed some furniture! Now the leather was the added lady bonus on the side! I ain't no scrub like that to be buying furniture and crying and mess behind anybody. Don't even think that! I might have chased you, Jee, but uh, my acting classes back in the day paid off for the look on your face right now!"

"And you got me about to cry, Black!" I turned around in awe, eyes bulging and teary, at him making me shed all my emotion thinking that he was all sentimental.

Black, then, walked over to me as I stood in all my stupor. "I still want you, baby, especially now that I don't have to buy you nothing."

"You got me, Black, but don't think you ain't coming off of that wallet sometimes no matter what I just said! Lying butt. And I bet you got some DVDs up in here, too. Wait until I case this joint."

He kissed me on my cheek, and then I hopped down the steps.

"You're right, too. I do have some DVDs - all in my bedroom! My bad for lying all that time, but Jee, you believe anything," he continued to laugh, unable to spare me my ignorance.

I could have punched him in his throat. Jokester. A cute one though.

All the way back home, my heart felt like I'd been completely missing out. The one that I rejected, I ended up needing and wanting to have with me, always around me. I wanted everything between us to fall right, no matter how it felt. Bottom line, rebound off of another woman's husband was quite possible, and I wanted to be sure that it wasn't what I was making Black - just a rebound. Sleeping with him was not in the game plan. My vagina needed a break. It truly needed some Lysol and a mop with a full polish and wax.

Truthfully, I was afraid of that word karma when it came down to Stay Black. That was the word that meant all the dirt I buried someone else under would bury me in my own life. The way that karma was supposed to happen in my case would be me falling in love, marrying whom I marry and then, bingo! He cheats on me and beats my behind while at it. My thoughts were that my karma would end up just like what I believe Andre' did to Tina.

Another word for that karma thing is God's vengeance. In this particular case, I didn't know what would end up happening or when, but I knew something would possibly go down. All I could pray for was mercy. What I knew for sure was that I didn't want to go back to the way I was for these past weeks with Andre'. It felt good to live right, well better, once again.

As I stepped back into my condo, I walked in to meet a visitor.

"Andre'?" I was stunned. He must have made a copy of my key which I hoped was illegal so I could turn his butt over to the cops. I marched over and placed my keys and cell on the chair, without even giving him a second glance. "Get out. You can't come here anymore."

"Let me know what's up with what I saw."

"What you saw? Saw what?" I stopped and glared at

him like he had an absolute absent-minded problem. "I thought we discussed this, Andre'. Go home or, for that matter, to your hospitalized wife. I'm serious. Get out of my house, or did I forget to tell you. We're done."

"Who was that cat?"

"What?" I threw my hands up in disbelief. "Okay, you need to go. I don't belong to you. You have a wife, and she's laid up in the hospital beat down and bruised, scared to talk. No, my bad," I corrected myself. "She will talk, but it won't be truth. She only lies to keep your ass out of jail! Well, Andre', baby, I'm not her. Don't question me in my place. You don't pay any rent in here, and you're not supposed to have any legal way in here anymore either!"

I was furious. My ass was already cussing again, dammit.

"Jeena," he called softly. "I love you anyway, girl. You gonna let me go over some cheap brotha that you have to take home. This wasn't even about Tina was it? You was with somebody else. You want another man in your crib, huh? Cutting me loose."

"Andre'! Get the fuck out!" I didn't want to hear his crap nor did I owe him an excuse, conversation or sex for that matter. This fool had really lost all the damn mind he had left coming up in my house like he is ruling me.

He stood up from leaning on my kitchen table, came over and made an attempt to hold me, but I pushed him off.

"Jeena..."

"Andre', get out or..." I peered at my cell, getting ready to go for it to call the cops, but Andre' pulled my arm so hard that I felt it snap. "Andre', stop!" I commanded while holding back the tears from the pain, but he didn't let go. My arm, at this point, was pulsating because he had it so tightly. Quickly, I thought about Tina, and the more frightened I got. The more I pulled back, the tighter he held on, and that's when I knew that I was in for a fight.

"Where you going, Jee? Cussing me out and all that," he commented with a smirk on his face while holding my arm high in the air. "You act like you don't know me anymore." Then, he yanked me closer, my nose right up against his, and there was nothing gentle about this touch. It was like night from day and summer from winter. This was the other side I thought wasn't ever gonna happen to me, but karma walked right into my living room with an eff'ed up Caribbean accent.

"Didn't I tell you not to mess with me? Huh, girl? You got all that lip. Talk now. Go ahead and flap those jaws. Answer that simple question, didn't I tell you? I stood right up here in this kitchen and told you not to play around with me by seeing another man."

"Andre', what is wrong with you?" I cried. "Please let me go!" As I gained more strength, I yanked away from him, but this time, ripped my shirt in the process.

"That's the lady I know. Ready to drop those clothes for me."

"No, Andre'!"

He started smiling as I nearly stumbled over the rug in horror. I wasn't used to being handled like this, especially by someone I legitimately had feelings for, so I started doing the only thing I could do - rationalize with the not so rational person.

"Andre', I did care for you and still do, but you have to leave my house. I want to be with someone else. You...you're all wrong and your wife – you have a wife. If you were single then maybe I could live with it all, but this isn't right. None of it is called for." What I was saying was just a stall tactic. I wanted to dive for my cell, but he wasn't gonna let me do that. The one time that I needed my landline, I didn't have it hooked up. Unfortunately, he knew that much, too, so I couldn't even fake a dial.

"Now you tell me, what am I supposed to do?" he asked like he was a flipping fool.

"What, Andre'?" I didn't know what the hell he was gonna do, but what he *needed* to do was get the heck on out of here!

"What am I supposed to do? I put it all out there on the table for you after reconsidering your dressed up ass when you walked in Capital City, cheated on my wife, told you that when I chose to love somebody that's what I do and now you think you can just leave me? I could give a damn if I had three or four of you desperate hoes. Fact is, you're mine. So now," he paused to wipe the sides of his mouth with his fingers, "you convince me why I shouldn't break some sense into your skull, huh? Better yet, tell me why I shouldn't beat your ass until you leave this earth because, shit," he stated as he took a breath once again, "I can make that happen when I damn well please? Were you trying to use me, Jeena? Is that was that was? All that nice sex and shit, and then, you were gonna try and mess up the life I made, weren't you? Blackmail my ass? That was the real reason that you were up there to see my wife, huh? Try and hem me up in court with her? Take my money, get me locked up? Have me paying you so you can keep your mouth shut? Dead people don't talk, Jee. Blackmail that."

What the devil? This joker was crazy! Stone loco. I had no choice, so I took my chance. I dove for my only lifeline away from him which was where I tossed it when I came in - on the chair. Before I could get my fingers curled around it like I wanted to, his fist took me in the opposite direction. My whole body stumbled onto the floor while my mouth filled with blood. It began to pour from the sides of my lips as I wiped my mouth with my wrist, confused as to why Andre' had gone and punched me square in my jaw. He was truly about to kill me.

On all fours, I tried to move and figure out what went wrong and why he was doing this to me. I was frantic. Everything my hands touched, I threw, trying to aim right at him. Sadly, everything I hurled missed. Blood continued to pour out of my mouth as I rubbed my tongue on the inside of my lip. The blood was coming from a huge gash starting on the side of my mouth and stretching to the middle of my bottom lip. I stumbled over onto my back still dazed from the blow, and on my elbows and feet, I pushed myself back until I hit the wall. Andre' wasn't even chasing me. He remained in that same spot, going through my cell phone numbers.

"Is this who that brother was coming up in here today to

take my spot? Stay Black?" He tossed the phone down. "Well, he didn't look so black, Jee. He got a key like me? You putting it on him, too? I didn't sign up to share any parts of you."

I didn't answer. Couldn't. My shirt was bloody and so was my floor. The bat that my mom told me to keep with me at all times for protection just in case something popped off was up underneath my bed. Thank God for ma because I needed it now. Damn near needed a rifle to blow this fool's brains out, but I'd have to settle for the bat to beat them out instead.

Because he thought I was still dazed, when he turned his eyes off of me, I jumped up and ran into my bedroom. At that point, I heard him coming after me, but I slammed the door shut, locked it and went on the hunt. Tears began to roll down my face as I fell to my knees and searched like a wild woman for my bat. I located it on the other side of my bed, so I jumped across the bed and tumbled on the other side of the floor to get to it.

"Jesus, please," I cried, and then I heard him hit my bedroom door. Immediately, I ran to the side of the door ready to knock his ass out when he came through, but then hesitated when I thought about climbing out of the window. I felt that though I wanted to clock this dude, I knew I couldn't beat him if I didn't hit him hard enough. What if I missed?

That quick thought made me dart to the window with the bat in my hand, but he hit the door again, obviously weakening the hinges as the door shook. Then, he did it again. He was gonna get in. I couldn't even concentrate on the window, so I clenched my bat tightly and headed back over to my bedroom door. Once I got back, the door shattered at the lock and flew wide open. He stood in front of me enraged as hell, but before he could see it, I swung that bat so hard that his knees buckled at the impact of me busting him in his gut. After that, I tried to hit him across the back of his skull to nullify his ass, but he caught my swing. I knew that if I was to swing high, more than likely that would have happen, so I kicked him in the face while he was slightly bunked over and holding the other end of my bat.

Where my strength went, I didn't know, but I felt like I

needed to run before I couldn't fight anymore. I gave my bat another tug to try and wrestle it from his grasp, but he pulled the other end of the bat harder than my strength gave me, and I fell over into him, tearing into his face with my fingernails. I didn't know about Tina, but I was gonna try to hurt this bastard as long as he was in my face. Before I could take his skin off again, my feet were off of the floor, and he'd already slammed me back down to the floor on my back. All the wind inside me left.

"Jesus, please help me," I whispered, tired and out of every ounce of energy that God allotted me. There was a picture of Faith on my dresser. She was grinning from ear to ear holding the Bible in her hand, pointing at it with her other hand like nothing on earth could make her happier. I understood everything about God at that point while I was lying there on the floor. "Never again, Jesus. I won't. Please! I'm sorry. Just help me," I pleaded, but God didn't even make the thunder roll.

"You know why I'm beating your ass for you? Because you need it beat, Jee. You think you're smarter than me in this game you're playing. I put this shit together though, Jee. You think you the shit and can get a man to do what *you* want because your legs are wide open. Like you can make me delusional." He wiped his nose. "You ain't that good. Stop fooling yourself. And you damn sure can't beat my ass - not even with a bat, bitch."

I didn't answer. He wasn't searching for an answer or any sort of reply from me. He was digging for my pain.

"Oh and here's one. You throw your body at me and then want me to treat you like my wife. Surprise, Jeena," he stated sarcastically, "This is how I treat her ass. Wait though. You think it was Tina, don't you? No, my real wife wasn't Tina. I married her because the wife I had didn't want me no more because I slept with Tina's ass behind her back. Never could get her back the way I had her when we met, and I needed her to forget that shit. She wouldn't though, so Tina, with her scheming ass, gets what she deserves after setting me up to ruin my marriage. She told my wife everything. So hell yeah, I pretended to love her ass

207

so I could beat her ass after losing all I had, the woman I really loved. And I beat her ass every time I think of my ex-wife. Her being in the hospital really ain't got shit to do with you to be honest." He rubbed his face where I scratched him. "What the hell you scratch me for? We just doing what we normally do. You don't like it no more, me on top of you?"

I sucked up as much blood as I could from my mouth and spit it in his face. Eat that you wanna be rasta. He then smacked me again. I retaliated.

"Well I'm not Tina! And I bet she wishes everyday of her life that her mistake wasn't you. One day, I hope she beats your crazy ass!" I screamed tearfully.

"She wanted me. She got me, just like you. Shit, you damn near broke your back to pick up my card after confirming I was married in the first place. Immoral ass. Hot in the pants. Well, I got your hot. Listen to this - when I leave, stay on the floor, with your door mat ass or I'll beat you down there again."

Before he left, he kicked me twice in my stomach as my last warning. My insides numbed out and then...

I Drove.

With my busted lip, I drove. When I got up from where Andre' left me curled up holding my stomach on the floor, there was more blood than what I thought. I couldn't continue to cry either because of all the anger I had from not being able to kill him for what he did to me.

I approached Black's house and slowed up, tempted to stop and ask if I could stay there, but I didn't. I was warned not to contact Black again while Andre' was kicking my insides out before he left, and I didn't want to cause any trouble for Black. He was a good man. Because of my hesitation at stopping and getting him involved, I pressed the gas and kept going because I knew Faith was at home. She had to be. It was nightfall, and she didn't go places unless she had to at night. She was at least ten minutes away, and the streets were empty so I could get there in five.

As I glanced at my mouth in the driver's side mirror, it was growing, and I knew that I was going to have to have it stitched up. It looked awful and throbbed as if it was ready to give up and fall off. Pulling up in the driveway of Faith's house, agony overwhelmed me, both inside and out. I wasn't prepared to speak nor did I know what to do when I got up in there, but I knew Faith. She wasn't gonna be happy, but what sibling would be elated seeing her sister busted up by some guy? This was the worst thing that I had ever done and the worst thing that has ever physically happened to me at the hands of a beast. A married beast.

Exiting my car was the hardest thing, and that's why I sat there, literally staring at her front door with a big Jesus Lives sign hanging from a nail underneath the peephole. Oh how I preferred Jesus just making a special trip down here again to patch up my face, reverse all my decisions and send me back with everything fixed again. But no. All things have a beginning and an end, I thought. That was just my luck.

"This must be my end." I opened the car door and placed one foot outside of it.

"You got a quarter, ma'am, or some spare change or some food?"

"Jesus!" I slammed my door, nearly taking my ankle off in the process. Some man came strolling up to my car asking me for something in the dead night in front of my sister's house! Lord, this can't be you, can it?

"Excuse me," he kept talking while knocking on my window.

My eyes scurried across all my locks making sure I was secure inside and his butt outside. Then I continued to stare back in his face with *what the heck do you want* wrinkles on my forehead.

"Mr. Marcus, don't do that! I already gave you some change and fed you. I told you not to mess with my company when they drive up. Bye, Mr. Marcus! See you tomorrow."

"I'm sorry, Ms. Faith. I just wasn't gonna be around here tomorrow for your kind generosity. Got to go across town. Didn't want to ask you for more, that's all."

"Well, why didn't you say so? Here," she stated, leaving the door and returning in three seconds only to step off of the porch with her long, thick robe on in the heat of the summer. "Here," she repeated like she was out of breath. The man went up and took some money from her.

"God will bless you, Ms. Faith."

"He already has. Where's your Bible?"

"Right here." He pulled it from his pocket and showed it to her.

"Good. Don't die without reading it. It has directions to heaven."

He laughed. "I hear you, Ms. Faith. And Jesus will lead the way!"

"You got that right." Faith then cut at sharp glance over at me. "Well, get out. That was just Mr. Marcus. He won't hurt you. He's just a little lost right now, and it's up to God to lead him. I feed him on the way."

She didn't see my face. Too dark. I slammed my door after getting out of the car and slowly walked up to the front door. In my pocket, I had some extra bills, so before I went inside behind Faith, I ran and gave Mr. Marcus the money in my pocket. Just three dollars.

"Thank you, ma'am."

"I'm sorry. You just scared me," I responded, looking down and to the side so that he wouldn't see my face too well.

"I know, ma'am. That was my fault. Ms. Faith told me about that." He grabbed my hand, held it tight and tapped it. "It won't happen again...me scaring ya'. God bless ya'."

"You, too." I stared at his hand on mine until he let it go.

It was amazing how somebody so alone and hungry could be nicer than somebody so rich and full. Before he continued on his way, I grabbed his hand back. "Thank you."

He laughed. "Now you're scaring me. Folk don't grab at me much, and I mostly can't help anybody with anything so I don't understand your thank you to me."

"It was for your blessing. You said God bless you. I need that right now because I'm a wreck."

He didn't say anything back to me after that except smile with his eyes. Then, I left him and went on inside. He didn't know that blessing was worth so much to me, especially when I felt so much like a curse. I truly hoped God did bless me out of this mess.

Faith still hadn't seen me yet, even though I was sitting on her rocking chair. Yep. She had a rocking chair like a little old lady and she was younger than me. It rocked, too! I didn't know where Faith had disappeared to, but she wasn't in the living room where I was and didn't come out until about five minutes had gone by.

"Well?" she said, finally poking her head around the corner, "You came over here all late, and I suppose you want me to come out here with you when you can come back here where I am and tell me..." All of a sudden, her wise cracking ceased. I didn't even have to look her way. I knew that she finally saw. She ran over and dropped on her knees in front of me, pulling that long five hundred thread gown up and around her waist so she wouldn't fall over. "Jee Jee! Jeena, what happened to your face? Who hit you, sis?"

I couldn't help but cry. I cried and cried. Those tears just started flowing, and it felt so good to finally let out all that pain and fear that I carried over here.

"Jeena, tell me what happened. Come on, sis, please. Oh God, oh Jesus, please Lord," she'd already started praying as she curled up underneath me, rubbing me all over my hands, then, she tugged on my shirt where blood had dripped all over it.

That made her run to a first aid kit that she had in her kitchen. Who kept a first aid kit in their kitchen without kids? Answer - Faith. The thought of her cleaning me up almost made me laugh when she began to wipe my face, tears and all, until she saw my fingernails. They were bloody, and she reacted.

"Jeena, shut up crying and talk!" she shouted, and then right away, I got quiet like she was my own momma. She squeezed my wrists. "Did somebody fight you or did somebody rape you or both? We are wasting time sitting here with you not talking, sis. Lord, help me not kill somebody tonight because my sister...somebody hurt my sister," she whispered, shaking her head.

I didn't reply right away because my thoughts were continuously of every possible scenario to put into storyline for Faith, but then, I got tired. I was tired of making up scripts in my head and lying to people, including myself.

"I was sleeping with somebody's husband, Faith. When I tried to break it off, he didn't want to, and he thought he was due what I normally would do with him. So he hit me, just like he hit his wife."

"What? Jeena you can't be serious." She didn't do much else at that point but stare at me, almost like she didn't even know me. "Did you know he was married when you started to mess around with him?"

"Yes."

"Was that the man on the phone that day I picked it up?"

"Yes," I responded, and it seemed as if with every word I spoke, more tears rushed out. "I'm sorry. And," I wiped my eyes. "I'm sorry about crying about something that I did to myself."

"Don't worry about that crying anymore, and you didn't do it to yourself. You were attacked." She let go of me and placed her hands in her lap. "Go ahead and cry. Crying just gets the ugly out, Jee," she sighed.

I wanted to smile at that. It was what momma used to say. Crying gets the ugly out, and that was why your face looks all ugly when you do it. When all the ugly gets out, it leaves more room for the pretty, momma would teach us. She would say that crying was good if somebody hurt you or if you fell and hurt yourself some sort of way. It would get the ugly and the hurt out through the ugly face when you cry. It wasn't until I got older that crying just wasn't cool, so I learned to hide the ugly when I could. I kept my cries inside so that whatever happened didn't have to show. It sounded corny, but the more time went by, the more I wanted to fall back on what momma said because slowly but surely, the ugly seemed to stay in and made me worse a person than if I would have just cried.

"We gotta get you to the hospital."

"No."

I tried to push myself back from her as she sat on the floor in front of the rocking chair, but when I did, it just rocked me back in front of her. Useless. She caught it, holding it still.

"No?" she asked in disbelief.

I thought about my lip looking all deformed in the near future, and then changed my mind. "After I use your bathroom, we can go."

"Don't wash up, Jeena. We need you to go how you are for the police report."

"Police? I'm not going that deep," I paused and stood up from in front of her. "I just need to get my lip stitched up. That's all. I'll be fine. I'm not going to the police."

"Jeena."

"I don't want anybody to know!" I shouted in a frenzy. "I just don't want anybody to know, Faith!" My screams echoed through the house they were so loud. All my screaming then turned into tears once again. Faith just remained stooped there in front of that rocking chair as I tried to pull myself back together. "I'm sorry. I just can't right now, Faith."

"Go ahead to the bathroom," she stated. "I'll throw on some clothes."

I already knew who did it and didn't want to make it any worse on myself by letting the world plus his wife know that I was the whore on her man. I didn't want to be that person anymore, and everything that I knew about the stigma of being the other woman began to sink in. My secrets were about to be leaked, not just to those who I trust and trust me, but to the world. People would hear about it that didn't even know me personally, and then family, their friends and I would be labeled for life. Police? I would never tell. I had to keep it quiet. This had to stay where it already was - between us. Me, Parri, Faith, Andre', Stay Black and...

Unfortunately Tanya.

While in the bathroom cleaning up my hands and face a little, my cell rang. I made sure I looked at the caller ID before I picked it up. Tanya.

"Hello?" I answered on speaker.

"What the hell you doing sleeping with somebody else's man? I mean, what was with you allowing me to cry on your shoulder, and you're doing the same thing that heffa was doing to my man?"

Tanya was in a fit of rage, so I had to cut her off.

"Who told you that, Tanya?" I took the phone off of speaker.

"Parri! All that crap that you give me or used to give me about how I live? Jeena, you're a hypocrite!"

"I'm sorry." Staring at the ceiling was all that I could do with my busted up lip still hanging and oozing blood the more I stretched it to talk. "I was wrong, stupid, dumb and crazy. I messed up, Tanya. I didn't mean to hurt you or deceive you about the type of person that I really was." I could only imagine how she saw me. Like the scum of the earth. Probably like I was the one who was sleeping with her man. I was a hypocrite, but that didn't mean that I couldn't change.

"Man, Jeena, don't you know how much that hurts? How could you do that to her? Are you even a woman or do you just not care?"

"At that point, I wasn't being a woman or caring about anyone but myself, Tanya." That's what dogs do. The proper term for it was a female dog, or the animal behavior biological term, a bitch. They bunk over for every male dog that comes by. "I stopped, Tanya. I got into fantasy and then tried to mix it with reality. I messed up. Please forgive me, and I didn't mean to double talk either. What I stated to you, I meant. For some reason, I didn't connect the situation to myself until now. Sorry. I apologize for turning into the type of woman that would hurt another. I'm not perfect, but I wish I was." I stared up at the ceiling. "I really wish I was perfect."

There was a pause. A long one. Tanya was one to point out hypocrisy all the time because she didn't live right hardly ever. She was always excited when she got the chance to point a finger instead of the finger pointing at her, so she took full advantage. Not like I didn't deserve it.

"I guess I shouldn't be pointing the finger. Look at me. At least you stopped. I need to stop effin' around with guys and focus on my kids and my life like mom said."

"You will. Just like me. I really am sorry. Tanya, I'm changing that part of my life. Please keep this quiet because it's nothing that I'm proud of doing."

"I'll keep yours like you've kept all of mine. But you know I had to dive in on you."

"Thank you, and I needed it. I have to go though, Tanya. We'll chat later."

"Bye, girl."

I hit the hang up button. Telling Tanya about the mad beating Andre' gave me all throughout my living room and bedroom was not going to happen. I was just done forever with doing anything like that again, so help me Father God.

I got to the hospital looking a wreck despite washing up my face here and there. My lip was still gushing blood and dripping on every piece of thread it could find. It was so huge, much bigger than what it was when I left home. Mercy. I was ashamed to even show my face.

"So what happened here?" The female doctor asked, approaching me with latex gloves as she examined the wound.

"I fell down some brick steps tonight. My heel broke, and the fall was long and hard." I was glad Faith stayed in the emergency waiting area. I didn't need her in here. Just her presence would have made me feel guilty for concealing what I knew to be the truth. I knew the doctor already knew that I was lying because she was noticeably looking for more scrapes from the brick steps I said I fell on, but she really couldn't do much about it if I stuck to my story. That was what I planned on doing until this whole mess was over.

"Well," she began, taking a deep breath. "You need some stitches. We'll be right back to sew you up. We gotta get you numb first. Expect swelling. I will sign a work excuse for you because you won't be going. Check back with your doctor in a couple of days if swelling continues with signs of infection such as more pain, fever and puss. I'll be back, but Ms. Ray?"

"Yes?" I answered.

"Get away and get some help."

I didn't say one word as she walked out. When she came back, she checked the rest of my body before stitching me up. No broken bones etc. I knew there weren't. Just a broken heart in more ways than one and internal pain that wasn't gonna make me flinch until I was out of this doctor's sight. The doctor couldn't feel that kick Andre' gave me, and I wasn't gonna explain it despite the fact that she kept asking me questions about the fall. I looked like a busted lip broad. I even felt like one. Maybe I should turn him in, I thought, for me and his wife. Honestly, I didn't know what to do but stop, just stop, and hope that it all would go away.

On the way back to the house, Black was calling me

constantly to check to see if I made it home. I couldn't answer. Every time my phone vibrated, I looked at Faith nervously. She was eerily quiet the whole way back. I didn't finish telling her the story about me and Andre' either. She would probably gasp when I told her whose man he was, so not to waste anymore time, I did.

"Faith, it was Tina's husband."

The whole car swerved, and I grabbed her arm to yank her back onto the right side of the road.

"Tina who?" she asked, and I could tell by the tone of her voice she was daring me to say the Tina that she was counseling Tina.

"The lady that you were in the hospital with that day when I came to get you."

"What in the pits of hell, Jeena, did you just say? You knew who she was that day?"

Faith's face was beyond belief.

"Yes."

"Is that why you were crying so hard on my shoulder?"

"Yes."

"Jeena," she sang as she pressed the side of her head against the window. The good thing was that the car stayed in the lane. "So wait... when you saw her on the bed in the hospital, you knew what really happened to her?"

"No, not then, but I figured it out."

"How?"

"Things just didn't make sense is all. I didn't know he was gonna beat me like he did her."

"Jeena," she began as she slowed the car into the driveway of her house. "Why?" She appeared horribly confused as if she just couldn't imagine what would possess me to do a thing like I'd done. "How on this earth could you do that, Jee? You even deceived me! How does that look, huh? I'm counseling the woman and you...my sister...are having sex with her husband. What were you thinking?"

I opened my car door. "I don't know. I didn't think that I would fall in love with him, but I did for a short while until I found

217

out about Tina. Well, it was when I saw her face in the hospital. I couldn't shake the fact anymore that what I was doing was wrong after I'd already convinced myself that it was partly right."

She got out of the car, totally pissed off. "Stop, Jeena. Just stop."

"Don't tell mom." I walked to the other side of the car to take the keys from her.

"I won't tell her because it's not for me to tell. You're staying here tonight, though. Don't even think about taking these car keys because if homeboy is there waiting on you, believe me, I'm calling on him when I find out. It would be best for both you and Tina if you ask me."

"No, Faith, I can't stay here. I'm leaving. I have to stop somewhere, at a friend's house."

"Who, Jee?" Faith asked, obviously frustrated. "Who at this time of night looking like lip gone elephant?" She continued especially tired of the drama that I had gotten myself into. "No more secrets. Just flat out tell me. Where do you have to go now?"

"Stay Black."

"The guy that you hate."

"No, the guy that's my best friend. It just took me some time to figure that out."

She threw her hands up in the air. "Call me when you get there. At least I know of him to be a nice guy."

"Okay." I felt my lip. "Does my face look that bad?"

"No, just your lip." There was a pause. "Jee, pray." She gave me a hug while continuing, "And remember that I love you anyway." She looked up at the night sky. "But love doesn't mean that what you did is okay because the effects and consequences of what happened don't just disappear. You hurt people, and now look at your face, Jee. It comes back."

"Thank you, Faith. I know."

"No problem, big sister."

"You should have been my big sister."

She shook her head at what I stated. "Big or little, the

218

fact of the matter is that we are sisters. I'm here, always here. Just like you would be here for me." She then started walking toward her door. "Just get to Black's house and answer your phone when I call. Don't forget that I know where he lives."

"Gotcha, Faith!" I hopped back in the car and hit the road.

After leaving, I really tried to go back home alone, but failed miserably. The only reason I didn't go back was because I kept feeling Andre' was gonna be in there ready to beat the daylights out of me again. It wasn't like he had a wife at home waiting for his return or that doesn't know he beats the living blood out of women. That's why turning back around and sticking to my original plan of going to Black's house was what I did.

I didn't want him to see me like I was, but it beat having to become a younger sister to my younger sister. Our roles were reversed somehow, and I honestly couldn't take it. Her giving me advice all the time was a big sister's tragedy. I was thankful for the advice, but how tired it made my life look! What sort of example did I set for her? It was obvious she took no notes from me.

Before I got to Black's place, I called. It was about midnight, just a little bit after. He answered the phone.

"Hello?"

"Black, will you please let me in." I heard him stutter something, but that was cut off when I abruptly ended the call. I pulled into his driveway and got out of the car. Before I even got up to the door, he was there, rubbing his hand through his hair with no shirt on and some jeans. Dang! I paused. My feet didn't even move anymore, and I felt my brain leave my head, grow legs and walk back to my car. My feet, soon after, began to follow. No matter how hurt I was, a brother's flesh was looking kinda nice at the same exact time mine was looking rough and raggedy.

"Hey, where you going?" he yelled at the sight of my turning around.

"I left something in my car," I hollered back. "Just leave

the door open." Rushing back to the car, I thought aloud, "What the heck am I doing? If he was falling in love with me, my face will certainly change his mind!" On that note, I slung my whole body back inside the car and pulled out a mirror that I would normally leave in my glove compartment. I didn't want to use the rear view mirror because that was too obvious that I was checking myself. Therefore, I held my head way down, as if I was searching for something on the floor board then peered at my reflection. "I look busted!" I whispered. "My lip is bigger than dag on Jupiter." Quickly, I moved my eyes toward his window and screen door. I wasn't able to see anyway. It was too dark. I got back out of the car. "Face it." Slam went the car door and up to the front door went I.

When I went inside Black's house, I made certain I shut the door behind myself and locked it up really good because I was paranoid though still making the suave stab at being cool. Black fell back from the door onto a stationary position on his sofa, half dazed, yet awake.

"I've been calling you all night. You didn't go straight home or something? Just wanted to make sure you made it back okay. Can't have you getting mugged or nothing on my account, right? Wouldn't be able to live that down, Jee."

"Yeah," I had my hair falling around my face to hide that lip. "I got home good. Just needed to come back over here to see you." I didn't go over and sit down next to him. A literal mouthful of hesitation was holding me in my stance, and Black noticed.

"Jee," he called, moving from his comfortable half asleep position to a more erect and awakened posture. "Hold your head up. What's up, girl?"

I couldn't find it inside me to respond.

"Jeena," he said again, this time arising from the chair and proceeding over to me as if he knew for a fact something was the matter.

Before he reached me, I spoke, "I got beat up, Black." He stopped cold in his tracks, and I continued, "He busted my lip and kicked me in my stomach." Finally, I lifted my head, and he saw the swelling aftermath, stitches and all. "I just got back from the hospital. Faith went with me."

"Who, Jeena?" he questioned me as he placed his hand on my face, right next to my lip.

"It's numb, and," I pulled my face back away from his hand. "I just need to be somewhere other than around where I live and around my little sister. Man, Black, I'm embarrassed," I stated quietly, shaking my head lightly with tears welling up in my eyes.

"Who hit you?"

"Andre'."

"Who?"

"The guy that I was messing with."

"The man that left your crib today as I was coming in?"

"Yes," I confirmed. Black wasn't stupid. He already

knew.

"That was that other lady's man?"

"Yeah."

"Why did you tell me it was nobody?"

"Because I didn't want you to know." I moved away from him, already ticked off that the more information I concealed, everything seemed to somehow reveal itself anyway. "It wasn't your problem what you saw earlier today, and it's still not. I didn't invite him in, Black. He had a key." My stomach turned nauseous. "He must've gone somewhere and made another copy of the key because he left it with me as he was leaving out. After I dropped you off, he was back inside waiting on me, asking me about you."

"Dang, Jeena, you call the cops?"

I shook my head to symbolize no.

"Come here." He took me and held me tight. "You don't have to walk away from me nor be embarrassed. Stay over here tonight." He left me in the living room while he went back down his hallway. He returned with a big t-shirt that had a drawing of an afro pick on it complete with fist. "Sleep in this back there in my room. I'll stay in here. Uh...there are some towels in the closet. Only like two of them, but they're clean though."

"That's fine, Black." Before I left him to go and wash up once again before bed, I paused and told him the rest of what Andre' demanded out of me. "He told me not to see you again."

"What?" He stopped preparing the sofa bed he was making for himself. "Whoa, brotha' ain't got shit to do with me and what I do. Tell ole boy..." he paused, "No wait. Let's go."

"Black, please calm down." I could tell he was about to bust three veins and some skulls as he grabbed another t-shirt that he had lying around near us in the living room.

"We ain't stayin' here. Don't let no fool ass dude put you out of your spot, Jeena. I got this."

"What do you mean, Black?" I asked, totally out of it, not putting two and two together.

His eyes got as big as a lemur, and he answered, "What do you think I mean? I'm stayin' over there with you. Bro, got a key, right? Let him walk in on *me* tonight and beat *my* ass. He told you to relay a damn message to me when he can relay that shit himself. Make my ass stop talking to you." He continued to get his stuff together and shrugged his shoulders like he was a boxer. "Man to man, Jee. That's how we do. No cops necessary except for what he did to you. He just made this personal with me."

"No, Black," I put the shirt down. "I'm not going anywhere. *We* aren't going anywhere. There's no sense in it. This crap will all blow over. He got his anger out, unfortunately on my face, so I just wanna leave it."

I was going to literally blow my own head off! Not knowing how I was going to keep this situation contained anymore, everything was about to unravel like a scroll, left to cover the streets of Miami with me as the star of the show.

"Baby, look, you still can't let him do it. Now, you either call the police for yourself, or let him come tell a brother what problem he has with me. Ain't nothing but simple math and logic. Solving a problem that definitely needs to be solved, Jee."

"Black," I couldn't finish because there he went stopping me in my flow.

"What, Jee?" he asked highly irritated with me which was very much noticed with the high pitched tone. "You plan on living here with me?"

If he only knew how much I wished I could, but I didn't answer.

"I thought so," he responded to my silence. "Let's go get your place back. We can change the locks, Jee. Until then, I'm there." He walked over to me, slowly and more calm. "I know what's up. I see it in you. I'll be cool as long as he is. I'll also get the locks changed myself, and I won't even go to work tomorrow." He caressed my cheek and kissed my busted up lip. Disgusting. It was only a peck though. I couldn't even look at it, so I could only imagine what he had to think about when he kissed it. "I'll stay with you."

"Thanks, Black, but you have bills to pay, and you can't just take time off for what I got myself into. That's just not right, and it's fine if I stay over here until tomorrow."

"I got me," he said, starting to bring the hot temper down to cool. "Don't worry about me. Now, where I need to be is..."

"Black, I'm sorry." I interrupted.

"Me, too. I'm sorry that you got yourself into something like that. I'm here to help you out though. I'm your man now, remember?"

"You always have been, huh?"

"Yeah, Jeena. Just waiting on you."

"Man, I'm so sorry, Black. I'm just so stupid about everything! I'm frustrated. Ouch!" My lip! Saying the word frustrated hurt like hell fire! I guessed that frustrated word couldn't be stated until the stitches came out or my lip felt better. The numbing meds must have already started wearing off.

"Did the doctor give you something for pain? It doesn't look that bad, Jeena. How many stiches?"

"Six."

"Ha! Jeena, six!" he laughed trying to make the upset

223

atmosphere better. I stared back at him like I could punch his Adam's apple down his esophagus. "My bad," he continued, changing his response to my stitches.

"And you can shut up, Black. That crap hurt in my lip."

"I'm cool," he grinned. "Just messin' with you. I just know you won't be hit again, and your lips will be just fine for me when they heal. Come on. You can clean up in your own casa. You'll be good."

"Yeah?"

"What I say?" He cocked his head back and stuck out his chest.

"Thanks, Black."

I could've married him that day. That was how a man was supposed to make a woman feel - secure, not afraid.

It was no joke when we got back to my condo because I didn't realize the amount stuff that had gotten broken nor the amount of blood that I dripped across the floor during the fight. Scratch that, not the fight. In better terms, my beat down. I took a breath and just sat down when I got inside, in disbelief that I was just here getting the life beat out of me. The only thing that felt real was the lip on my face and the horrified look on Black's face when his eyes scrolled the territory. All he continued to do was walk around and stare at the blood and the broken Lladro that my mom had given me which was scattered about in the circular blood puddles. No, it didn't look like a gruesome murder scene, but it came close, with myself again as the star of the show.

As I thought back to what happened, I didn't even want to go back into the bedroom. Just didn't want to see the place where he stomped me. My bedroom was my place of serenity and sex, well, what used to be sex, and now the memories were all scarred, in need of replacement. I couldn't imagine what would happen if momma popped up with dad to catch wind of what went down. Not good. They would have flipped cold out, and then my busted lip would have sent dad into a rage that would possibly land him in prison.

Black was still walking around like he didn't know what to do, as if sitting down was not an option. After a while, he began picking up the broken pieces of glass from my floor, and I finally got up and went for the broom to sweep the pieces that were too small to get. I also got a bucket and a wet rag to start wiping my walls. I wasn't trying to rush. I had all night long. My cell rang.

"Hello?"

"Do I need to come over there or are you okay?" It was Faith. "Where's Black?"

"He's here. I'm fine." I wasn't gonna tell her where I was exactly so that she would flip her lid and come over and stay with me, too. I really didn't need that. The only thing I needed from Faith were her prayers, the really hard ones that will meet mine at the feet of Jesus.

"Okay, Jeena. Call me if you need something. I'm not trying to be pushy either, but I still think that you need to forget about what everybody else sees or thinks about you and call the police on him. It's not all about what happened to you tonight, Jeena. It's about the sole possibilities of what that crazy nut might do in the future. Every second that goes by might involve something bad with you and him, and the police need to at least know."

"I'll be fine, Faith." I looked up to the ceiling to hold back the tears because I knew deep down inside that she was right, but I just couldn't fight the feeling of my business being out there like I meant to do what I did. Setting out to sleep with a married man wasn't my plan despite how it looked. I made a bad choice, and I didn't know if I could stand living with it anymore. It wasn't something that I was proud of at all.

"Just pray for me to make the right decisions from now on, Faith. Pray with me for that. I do remember one thing in the Bible...wisdom. Pray that I get that from our Father, so that even in my temptations, I know how to get out. That was my mistake, Faith. It was really hard to choose getting out this time. I remember momma saying what's the purpose of you knowing right from wrong if you aren't going to choose right? I messed up is all. I really did. I just need to know how not to do that again."

"I think you already know how to do that - or not do that again - now. I'll pray with you about all this, sis. You need my hand just like I need yours. I love you."

"I love you, too. Goodnight."

"Goodnight."

When I got off of the phone, I noticed that Black had already made his way down my hallway. That was the place that I had to go. Instead of placing my phone down, I kept it on me. I'd gotten paranoid about letting it hang loose like I normally did just that quickly after getting beat down, but I supposed that was what trauma would do. Change you.

Deciding to walk back behind Black to see what he was uncovering in my bedroom, I took a deep breath before reliving what took place in the location where I rested my head for peace. I didn't even think that I could sleep in that room again. All I'd been doing was thinking about how he came in there after me after punching me to the floor like a raging lunatic! Psychopath. What Andre' needed was a straight jacket and a prison reality check.

I saw Black sitting on my bed when I got back there. My walk back felt like an eternity. With every step I took, I remembered him coming after me, to the point where he hit the door. It was mangled. So much for a lock. It didn't do a bit of good.

"All this happened after you took me home," he stated in a low voice. I didn't know if it was an actual question or if he was just bringing himself to believe what his eyes were seeing. He wasn't even looking up, just gazing as if he was imagining my attacker attacking me.

The bat that I used to hit him with was on the floor, bloody. It wasn't his blood on the bat though, but mine, more than likely coming from all the blood on my hands from my lip. I wasn't lucky enough to draw his blood.

"I hit him with all I had in his gut, thinking that I could

knock the wind out of him enough to take his head off with the second swing, but when I went to swing again, he caught me in midair."

Black didn't respond. I glanced up at the window that I was going to dive out of and didn't. I should have taken that opportunity, but I'm sure I wouldn't have made it. Plus, I thought that I could be freaking She-lady and tackle that monster. Lesson learned. If it ever happened again, I would run and only fight if necessary.

I stared down at the floor and recalled how he kicked me in my stomach. Thank God I wasn't pregnant. I knew that I would have lost a baby because that kick landed square on my uterus it seemed like. I already knew that I would have to go to the gynecologist later after not wanting to divulge information for a full fleged exam in the emergency room.

"He kicked me here," I said pointing to the reproductive area.

"Jesus!" Black clenched his eyes shut tight and covered his entire face with the palms of his hands. From there, he just rocked back and forth on the bed holding his head, not letting go, which meant he was either furious or couldn't believe it.

"I tried to get out of the window, but I got too scared and thought that I could beat him. I should have done differently, but I was..."

"Naw, no, Jeena, come sit on this bed. No should haves. Get some sleep. You gotta go back to the doctor, and I'll handle your doors, um...tomorrow. Yeah, I'll do that. Lemme just get me some stuff so I can stay out there on the couch. He's not coming in here tonight." As he stood up, I stopped him from walking away.

"It's become bad luck for me to let you leave me. You can stay in here with me if you don't mind, Black. Nothing like that, you know, nothing inappropriate, but I would appreciate it if you stayed in the bedroom."

He looked around and then answered, "No problem. I'll hit the floor."

"Plenty blankets on the shelf."

"I'm gonna need a pile of them on this hard pile of wood."

"Just kidding. I have an air mattress."

"You do?"

"Yeah, I do. Girls have sleepovers."

"My bad."

I went and got my air mattress. It was big, green and hopefully comfortable for his backside. I hadn't used it in ages. It was pushed beneath the oodles of comforter sets I had that I had gotten on sale or as gifts.

"I got it," he spoke as he walked up behind me. "Just go clean yourself up, get relaxed. I got this, as long as I don't have to blow it up with the wind God gave me."

"No, you don't. There's a pump underneath the cabinet in the kitchen. Help yourself."

"Yeah, good. Okay," he stated in agreement with my words.

I watched his eyes graze me really quickly, like he was checking me over.

"I'm okay, Black. Just gonna go wash up a little bit." Me and my big lip, I thought. Don't wanna lay down in hospital germs. No telling who or what was there before me.

"You do that." He tossed the mattress underneath his arm. "I'm gonna go and make this sucka rise."

Bad choice of words I thought as I headed into the bathroom for a great shower. When I got in, the water felt so good against my dry skin. When the water hit it, it soothed everything that had gotten inflamed from stress and torture. I released even more tension as I let my tears mix in with the streams of water on my face. Sitting in the tub, the shower filled it up until it was over three fourths full, then, I shut it off. Letting out a deep breath helped me calm myself down, enough to slow my crying.

I could have died, I repeated over and over. All it took would have been for Andre' to hit me in the wrong spot and that would have been it. I placed my forehead on the top of my knees and thanked God repeatedly. My life flashed before me, and I didn't want to put it at risk ever again for as long as I lived. As I sat there, a knock alerted my ear drums from my bathroom door.

"Yeah," I said, while at the same time, trying to clear my voice from sounding so sad. It was difficult putting on a facade of calmness when there was an internal wreck going on.

"I need to ask you something. Pull the curtain."

Thank God it was Black. My heart had started to pound about two hundred beats per minute at the thought of the knock being a crazed Andre' who'd suffocated poor Black and dumped his body out back in less than ten minutes.

"It's pulled." I wiped my eyes and waited on the bathroom door to open.

I heard his feet. They were bare on the floor, and he stopped at what sounded like the toilet where he took a seat.

"What do you want to ask me, Black?"

"Are you tense?"

"Too tense. I'm just trying to make my body calm down. I have never in my life felt so shriveled together, like my body is trying to hide from another hit. It's hard to explain."

"I know. I got hit, really beat down a couple times."

"You have? When?"

"When I was a kid. I wasn't soft or nothing like that, but being the jump joke in school by a bunch a kids wasn't fun. I got a few licks in, but they got me. I learned how to stiffen up and pound back harder. Untouchable then."

"I didn't know it hurt so bad afterwards."

"You probably feel worse than I did when I got hit. I never had a grown man beat me down when I was a kid. The beat down would have probably felt ten times worse. I've never been a woman either behind a man's fist so..."

"It hurts is what I can tell you," I responded, thumping the water.

"If you don't mind, I can help you. Turn and place this towel over your body. I'm not looking," he stated, placing a towel against the shower curtain.

Hesitantly, I took the towel from around the curtain, let some of the water out of the tub and turned around so that my back faced him. The towel covered the most important parts. Then, I pulled the curtain back. I heard when he got on his knees and moved closer to me. He reached beside me and made the hot water run slowly again in the tub.

"Don't want you to get too cold."

His hands touched my neck, and his fingers helped ease some of the pain in and around my shoulders. I slowly dropped my neck down, and it felt like Black placed pressure against all the rights spots near my spine. My back began to relax, and my body felt overwhelmed with relief. The steam Black made with the hot water flow was making a natural massage on my stomach as it crept full circle around me, and at last I thought, thank you, Father, for a nice, not nasty, touch. When he was done, Black simply got up and left. I had gotten so relaxed that when I did get out of the tub and into my bed, I fell straight to sleep. The last thing I felt was Black as he kissed me on my cheek...

Goodnight.

That's what I had - a very good night. I awakened a couple of times during the night to make sure that Black was still there and that Andre' wasn't dangling over my bed with a knife to my throat. Good thing was that Andre' was nowhere to be found.

As I leaned over to pop Black upside his head and tell him good morning now that the sun started shining through, I noticed that he was already up. The sheets that he had slept in were all folded, not neatly, but folded in an odd guy kind of way. I gave him an E for effort, not an A for amazing, but at least he folded. Glancing over at the time on my alarm clock, it was seven o'clock. Crap! I had to call in to work, but at least I had a true excuse this time.

"Good morning." Black came back into the room with a bucket of paint in his hand. "If you don't mind, I borrowed your car so that I could run to my boy's shop and..."

"No, Black, I don't mind." How could I have had a problem with that? Black was my knight in shining armor. Do whatever you want to do, Black! I let a man like this slide for too long, I thought . "Whew! I smell. Teeth and tongue time." My breath was loaded!

"I hear you way over here," he said, fanning my breath away as if it really reached him.

"So what are you sayin'? Shut up," I said, throwing my pillow at him and only missing him because he ducked. His shirt was off again. Stunning. And I thought I was a dark skinned man lover. This beautifully beige man worked really well. I could propose to this man right here, right now, with my busted up face and all, I thought. There was no way I was gonna let him go. Not ever again. I looked at his body one more time. Oh heck no! I do, preacher, I do!

"That's that Sugar Ray up in there. Quick, fast...gotta move fast from that breath," he joked. "Whenever you get ready, we can go out and find some new locks, alright?"

"Yeah, that's cool, Black. Ten minutes, just give me ten." On to the bathroom I went to get ready for hopefully a good day, but when I got there, things were swollen. All swollen and dry! Good Lord! The best thing was that I had meds and lip gloss. It wouldn't make me look like a glamour queen, but it would work.

"How on the face of this planet am I gonna accomplish this feat?" I asked myself holding the toothbrush aiming and ready at my mouth. "Here goes." I started brushing, and boy was I going slowly until I knew I wasn't gonna bust those stitches loose. Then, it was smooth sailing. My tongue felt like new money by the time I was done. The pain wasn't even that bad in my mouth nor my stomach. Happy was an understatement because if I'd awakened to a gut filled with agony, I would've known there was a serious problem.

I washed up again in the shower and got myself together, wanting another one of those excellent massages from Black. It wasn't because I needed it, but because it made me feel so good on the inside. You know how a massage was supposed to make your *body* feel good? Well, Black made *me* feel good, inside and out. I needed that because I finally felt cleaner, more innocent than I'd felt in weeks.

Digging through my drawers, I yanked out a red shirt and some blue jeans. A while ago, I bought some brand new sneakers that I couldn't wait to wear, so I figured today was the day. Yeah, they were fitting the outfit kinda nice.

When I finished dressing, I tackled my hair. I started to try and put a bunch of candy curls in it but gave that up to put that baby in a ponytail. Nice and easy. Whoever said a woman can't be sexy with a pony tail and a stitched lip ain't seen Jeena Delilah Ray today, I thought jokingly. Somebody had to tell me I looked good, and that someone was going to be me.

"Need some help?" I asked exiting my room. He was scrubbing the rest of the blood from the wall.

"No, just chill."

"Man, it's my bloody mess. Toss me a rag." He tossed it over to me, and I caught it like a champ. "Oh and I don't have no diseases."

"Ain't nobody said you did. Nobody said anything like that. But in case, a playa is strapped." He held up his hands so I could see those big thick gloves.

"I got you. At least I know you're a man who protects himself because if I did have something, oops on you." I winked at him. "Glad you love yourself. Kinda sexy."

"How's that?" he asked as he struggled getting a mark off of the wall.

"If you love yourself then that means that you might just love me, too, enough to not bring me some crap that could kill me or make me itch, burn or smell like a dead animal."

"Oh that's your philosophy?"

"Now it is. Gotta watch how you do and not just what you

say. I got that lesson stone cold in the gut last night."

"How does your stomach feel, by the way?"

"It's better. Not nearly as much pain as when it happened. I can only make a good assumption that nothing is damaged down there that bad because the pain eased off rather quickly."

"That's real good. Now let's go and get some breakfast. A brotha' hungry, and your fridge is empty," he stated, removing those dirty gloves, tossing them over in a bucket.

"I know. I eat oatmeal, cereal, cook eggs and toast or fruit in the morning. If you want bacon, grits, pancakes, or even a steak biscuit, this isn't the fridge to look into."

"Oatmeal, Jeena? Toast? Who eats toast?"

"Yep. Me. All the time."

"Not this morning."

"Where are we going?"

"Get some waffles."

"Really?"

"Syrup down, baby."

"Well, let's do this then! Are we sneaking in a hotel to get that free breakfast buffet deal they give to the guests?" I asked jokingly.

"A brother's not rich, but a brother's not broke either. Plus I'm not going to jail behind some Jeena junk like that."

I laughed, "Jeena junk? I don't do that, Black. I'm playin'!"

"No you ain't."

At that, I pushed him until I shoved him out the door, myself behind him.

The all you can eat breakfast bar was full, and the restaurant was empty which meant more food for us. The buffet smelled extra good, and the cheese potatoes I was about to attack! I remember when I fell in love with those things. At eighteen years old, when my family and I busted up at a breakfast bar out of town for the pre-family reunion, I had my first taste and was hooked on them ever since.

"You wanna do buffet, right?"

"Uhm hmm! Yeah! I didn't eat all night long."

"Yeah," he stared me down. "You're looking a little hungry there. Catch that." He leaned over and pointed at the side of my mouth.

"What?" I began to fiddle with my mouth to figure out what he was talking about.

"That drool."

"Black! I thought you were for real!" I said as I slapped him on the arm.

"You think too hard, Jee, baby. Way too hard for a man like me."

When we sat down, we ate and ate. My poor lip was over worked. Bump it. If Black loved me looking like this, he was gonna love me for life! Old age and all, with saggy breasts and a broth butt.

Black had some grits, eggs, bacon, sausage, a big glass of orange juice, toast, two biscuits with jelly and a bowl of fruit with some French toast on the side of his waffles. As for myself, I added fruit with my potatoes, two pieces of toast and waffles. In comparison to my plate, Black's plates equaled too much food for one stomach. He ate what he had though - all of it!

Once finished eating and on the way to the parking lot, Black was rubbing on his stomach, and I was wondering, what did Black think I looked like? He hadn't commented one way or the other, thus, I was curious.

"Black," I called him as he walked ahead of me to open up my car door.

"Yeah?"

"Look at me."

He stopped and looked. "Yeah?"

"What do you think I look like?"

"With the busted mouth or without the big jaw?"

"With the big, busted face, Black." Geez, jokes!

He didn't answer right away, but instead, came back over

to me, kissed me on my beat up face and said, "You're still beautiful to me." Then, he backed up. "Because if you weren't, you think that I would really be out here with you?" He lifted his arms and stressed the fact that we were in public.

"Oh, now you're wrong for that! So you're saying if my face was just a little more draggin' then you would hide out," I asked, hands on hips.

"Only 'til the swelling went down," he replied while he looked at me dumbfounded. "You asked, baby."

"Remind me not to ask next time."

"Just jokin'. Problem is, half these people probably believe I knocked your head in. Did you see all the stares I got up in there?"

"Yeah, I bet you did!" Whatever! Jokes were definitely something that I had to get used to hearing on a daily from Black.

On our way to the hardware store, full of food and all, it was time to get new locks for my doors. There were so many that I didn't know what I was looking at nor how much it was gonna cost. I'd never had to do this before. Atop the locks, I had to buy a whole new door, but that could wait because a sista didn't have the money. That bedroom door money went to the emergency room. I would have to hit momma up again to make that door purchase today, and that wasn't happening this time because I wasn't about to explain why I needed a new door.

"This one should do right here. What you think?"

"I guess. I'll trust your judgment on that one. Get the best lock for my buck. One that he can't simply pick his way into."

That was the one. We took it home, and Black hooked it up. I didn't realize that he was such a handy man. A flower boy just wasn't thought of as being handy but more pansy, more grooming and brushy, but not handy. I saw fast that his daddy must've taught him more than his rather loose mom did because Black was a stand up guy.

While he was putting the lock on, I decided to check my cell because it had been turned off all morning. A message. Oh, there were two. The first one was Faith. If she wasn't a stone cold Christian, she would have probably cussed me clean out after I heard the tone in her voice. *"Girl, where you at! You and Black ain't there, and when I went by your house, your car was gone, too! Jeeeeennnnnaaa! I'm gonna call the authorities, girl, and momma...."* Whoa! Not momma. I hung up and dialed her number.

"Pick up! Pick up!"

"What did you say?"

"Nothing," I responded to Black. "I'm on the phone with Faith."

"Hello?"

"Hey, Faith. I'm fine! Did you call mom?" I asked frantically.

"Yeah, she just wasn't home."

"What!" My heart skipped a beat. As I felt my chest, I swore I was going to need a doctor and a defibrillator. Faith always had to tell! Tell ma, tell ma! I wished she would leave ma out of things for a change, but noooo!

"I didn't leave a message about you, but I did tell her to call me."

"Faith! Don't get mom all concerned about all this," I begged.

"Well now that you called me back, I won't. Stop being all shady acting, Jeena. You're hurt, and I'm not gonna just sit back and worry with no action."

"Faith, stop acting up. You know I've been with Black."

"How? Just how was I supposed to know that when all early in the morning, I'm banging on his door, your car isn't there, and he ain't answering!"

"He's working on my locks and stuff now at home."

"Did crazy contact you yet?" she asked referring to Andre'.

"No. He won't, so don't worry about it. He got his kicks off of me last night. He's probably thinking that I've already called the law."

"Yeah, well, I found out where he lives. Called Tina."

"What!"

"I didn't say anything about anything, and she doesn't know about you two. I got the address through other means of communication besides talking about your busted lip. Didn't even mention the word sister or the name Jeena. I just needed to know in case he tried something again."

"How is she?"

"Who, Tina?"

"Yeah. Is she okay?"

I felt horrible, like a real fart but with legs.

"She sounded so-so. I'm just glad she's out of the hospital. They just released her."

I was about to take her spot, I thought. "That's good. I gotta go, okay? I'll call you tonight."

"God bless you, sis"

"You, too."

We hung up. I turned my phone back off. Whatever. I couldn't handle anymore drama, and no one else knew how to contact dear old mom. Thank goodness. It was gonna be me and Black from now on without stop ins from mom or dad to soak in my bloody lip. I had to kick the drama to the curb, get my face back, and learn to live right. One step with Jesus at a time.

Placing my phone down on the couch, I tiptoed over behind Black and squeezed him around his waist.

"I let a good man like you walk around me all this time?"

"Yeah, you did. So what you gonna do with me now? Use me to fix your locks and let me go?"

"No. I have some more stuff for you to fix around here actually."

He picked me up and then placed me between him and the door. "So you're gonna use me to fix what else up in here?"

"My heart. It was busted, and it needs somebody who specializes in it."

"I ain't Jesus, but I'll do my best to *help* you get that thing mended. How about that?"

"Sounds good to me." Marry me, I thought. Just take me and whisp my behind away. Dang, his body felt good. Never even tried to feel it before like this. Whew! One, two, three and so on counted my fingers as they thumbed through his abs. I needed to stay in church thanking God for all this wonderful-ness that I could potentially have for the rest of my life! "Are you staying over here with me again tonight?""You didn't get tired of me snoring?"

"No, I sure didn't! It let me know that you were still in there with me. I'm still freaked out a bit about the other night, so snore on if you have to."

He looked down at my fingers on his abs. "You better back up off me, girl, before you make a brother forget that you've been traumatized!"

"Isn't that the point?"

"All that teasing." He moved my hands and continued with the door. "Hey, partner contacted you yet?"

"I don't know. I don't think so," I responded, remembering that voice mail I didn't listen to. I just really didn't want to be bothered. "I do have a message on my phone that I didn't listen to, but it was by choice."

"Don't be scared, Jee. Keep the message if it's him though. Turn him in with that, proof of him stalking you after he hit you."

I looked back over at Black. "It's easy for you to say. My reputation is at stake. It's not like I tried to run my name all in the mud. People will see me as a whore, and I know that's what I was. *Was* is the key word. I don't want to be seen like that anymore. No telling how his wife is gonna drag my name if she found out. I want to tell her that I wished to God I never met him, but I just can't. I'm afraid of how much hurt I will cause her, and she is innocent. I'm not evil, and I don't even have anything against her. My preference would be for her to just pound me in my skull with her fists until she gets too tired and that probably still wouldn't equate to her pain."

"At least you know you're wrong and not boasting about it

like you did something so good. Man, I've heard some ladies who are proud of doing the do with other women's men, and then some. It shows your true character, Jeena, how you only blame yourself. A real woman, not a fake broad who justifies that shit like my moms did. Excuse my language. Every time I think of what she did to us, I get beyond pissed off even now."

Can you say mature, too? How many faces did Black have?

"Since when did you know so much?" I asked.

"I don't. Being alone and keeping to myself so long gives me time to take in things of the past to learn from them and put more effort towards my future. I don't like to waste time. Learned appreciation from losing what I loved so much, and that was my mom, my family. I was in therapy for that nonsense, Jee. My dad took me every week, and the pain got better. Now that I'm older," he continued, stopping to look at me from head to toe, "I know what kind of company and people I want in my life. Maybe even for a long time."

With the way he was looking at me, seducing me with his eyes, it was obvious that he had more on his mind than having me around as only a girlfriend. Was he really hinting at being ready to settle down with a woman like in wife form?

"So if you were to get that woman in your life for a long time, what would that be like?"

He came over and took me by my hands again. "It would be like you and me, the new Adam and Eve, but not that ignorant to throw away the world we have together for a single piece of fruit on the side. My long time woman would be my wife, my jewel, my gift and I hers. I would help my woman just as much as a woman may help me." He looked at me passionately. "That's how I want my relationship to be. Togetherness. If I do nothing, then my wife can help me do nothing, right?" He laughed. "We chill together, we work together, we clean together and we love each other, together. You know what my father told me?

"What?"

"After he became a preacher, one of the things he said

was that in all the helping that God told women to do as helpmates, he never told men to stop doing anything. We cook still, clean still, but a man with a good wife now has someone to share in it, help him, give him an extra boost. That's all it is. People make relationships too hard. We're supposed to work together and play together. Simple as that. Can't expect a good relationship when two people are always on separate duties, right? It's called spending time, learning each other. Falling in love over and over again." His lips met my lips, and he kissed me like I was the only woman in the world. Stay Black had already made it to the point of settling down, and me, well I was just getting there. Finally, I really wanted to be there, and be there with a good man. Sure, if things remained like this, becoming Mrs. Black would be no problem for me. Absolutely no...

<u>Problem.</u>

After sweeping me off my ten toes, Stay Black continued to fix the door until he was satisfied with the outcome. I knew it was ready when he backed away, tossed the tools and old locks on the floor and stared at his work like it was a masterpiece.

"There. It's all done."

"Lemme see." I stepped in front of him, and yep, that big time bolt lock worked like a champ. Now all I needed was a guard dog, alarm system, stun gun and mace, and I would have been set. "It works well!" I smiled, twisting it back and forth.

"I'm gonna run over to my house. You wanna come with me? Gotta get some mail I left over there that I need to send off as soon as I can. I left my work clothes over there, too, so if you don't mind me borrowing your ride again. Maybe you can take me to get my moped today. That's the least you can do to pay me, right?"

"Ha! Yeah, I can do that."

"Alright. Gonna be alright?"

I looked around one more time. Should be all secure, I

thought. Got my butcher knife in the kitchen, ready to make a stab wound. I was set. "Yep, I'll be okay."

"Be back." He shut the door behind him, and I reached over to lock that sucker. I was finally alone and more secure than I'd been just 24 hours ago. Life was beginning to look up. It had no choice. My mind was made up, and there would be no turning back.

The cell. I wondered who was on the other end of that second message on my voicemail.

"I'm not gonna listen to it." I walked to the window to see whether or not Black had already taken off and he had. "Well, at least I'm not alone for too long. He'll be back, and Andre' should be at work. Plus Tina is released from the hospital, so he should be busier than usual with her. Hopefully, she locks him up."

I was so sleepy that I could drop to the floor. Though last night I slept good, it was the waking up in the middle of the night a couple times that stole some time from me, so I decided to take a rest. With my bedroom door still hanging off the hinges, I went into my room and slept. I would hear when Black came back through the door, and I had my bat again, laying right by my side just in case.

Mid dream and startled, I woke up and looked at the clock. It was around three in the afternoon. "Black?" I called, but got no answer. I supposed it was going to take a bit longer than what I thought for him to get back. "Ouch." I'd caught a migraine. "Great."

Every time I opened my eyes and let the sun come in, my head hurt worse. I never felt a major migraine before, but I guessed anything could happen after a beat down. Therefore, I simply laid my head back down and tried to get more rest. As I spread my arms across my bed sheets to try to get into a relaxed state again, I noticed that my bat was missing. Where did it go?

My heart nearly skipped a beat as I leaned my body over

the side of the bed to see if it dropped off. It wasn't there. To the other side of the bed I rolled, but it wasn't there either, so I got up. "Where is my bat?" I questioned myself as if I needed to answer back. "What?" I stated confused as ever as I flattened out the covers on the bed feeling for it, but nothing.

"Come get it."

At the sound of the voice, my eyes began to float in tears as I turned toward my closet which was on the other side of the bathroom.

"Come on and get it," the voice repeated, taunting me.

I went breathless and paralyzed. Trying to block out what he told me after beating me failed as it popped back up in my head. *Don't make me hurt you again, Jeena.* It was Andre'.

"Jeena, baby, I'm not gonna touch you again," he stated to me, his body appearing drained and his eyes glossy like he was high or out of his mind as he showed himself from behind the wall.

"Andre', I just need you to understand that I'm changing my life. Don't hit me with that, Andre'." My eyes stared at the bat he was tossing to and fro in both his hands. I couldn't survive another beating. I just didn't have the strength.

"Why y'all like that? You offer up the goods until you feel like you don't want to anymore. Can't terminate a contract. You remember all that stuff I bought for you, made you dinner after hours."

Father, help me, Jesus. All he gave me was roses and the cooks made the food! He was gone nuts if he thought that was deserving of any type of assault!

"I didn't even have to say much to you. You had your legs open before I even told you I loved you. This whole thing wasn't my fault. You asked," he sung, "and I accepted. My rules now, Jee Jee."

Suddenly, he walked over to me, and I fearfully fell backwards off of the bed and onto the floor. When he reached me, I wiped the tears off of my eyes so I could see him better, without the blur.

"Don't cry, baby. But if you're gonna cry, lemme give you something to cry about." That's when he raised the bat and hit me dead center of my thigh.

"God!" I screamed, agony leaving my leg to lung then out of my mouth, but it didn't do any good. The pain pulsated through my entire leg unlike any other that I knew. "I'm not sleeping with him!" I screamed, but it didn't matter. Andre' was gone, and I didn't recognize the man that stood in front of me. He'd become a complete stranger.

"Now you can't open your legs until I tell you to," he smirked. "Oh don't worry. Your leg's not broken. I hit it just hard enough to give you a definite problem for a couple of days."

This fool's crazy. I gotta get the heck outta here, I thought. Frantically, I started calling for help, to the walls, windows, doors, and the air, but no help came. I wished so bad that I could beat him all across this room, but my leg felt fractured. While down, on my right arm, I tried to scoot myself back as I attempted to stabilize my left thigh with my left hand.

"Where are you going? You tell the cops I hit you the first time? I told you to keep your mouth shut!"

"No! No, I didn't!" I screamed, covering my face with my arm, afraid that he would hit my head with the bat next. "Andre', just go! Leave! I didn't say anything to any police because I thought we could forget it. I thought you would..."

"You thought I would what? I didn't think that you would have oh boy change the locks on me. He stayed over here in *my* bed last night. I earned this bed, sheee-iiiiiit!"

As I heard Andre' sing the word shit, I knew there was no stopping him. "How did you get in here? Are you high?"

"You forgot you had a sliding door. When I came in the other day, I made sure that I could get in and out." He flicked his nose with his thumb. "You got a problem with that, Jee?"

"What do you want, Andre'? You are married!" I screamed, spelling it out for him. "Married, married, married! God, please, just make him leave me alone! I will never again in my life," I cried with tears streaming down my cheeks, my eyes glued shut as I yelled at the top of my lungs. I was wishing that he would disappear before I opened my eyes again, but he didn't. Instead, when I reopened my eyes, he'd knelt down in front of me, within inches of my face, causing me to slam my back against the wall as I tried to create more space between us.

"Why don't you love me no more?"

Why don't I *love you*? You beat the hell outta me and your wife, that's why, and because of your first flippin' wife, whoever the hell she was! I should have spit in his flippin' face right then and there, but while my thigh continued to throb, I answered.

"I thought it was love. You may even think you love me, I don't know! Thing is, I know the difference between us then and us now clearly, and it's not cool, Andre'. We need to stop lying to ourselves," I responded somberly, even reaching to caress his face to dismantle the fog in his fuzzy, fizzled out brain. The caress didn't work. He knocked my hand away.

"So you a lying ass?"

I lost it.

"You don't love me, Andre'! You are beating my ass and breaking my legs! That isn't love, Andre', and it ain't even spelled the same!" The more I looked into his eyes, the less it seemed he even saw me. He was looking somewhere, but that somewhere wasn't at me despite the fact I was directly in his face. There was some sort of disconnect, and it confirmed everything about Andre' being a madman.

My heart skipped a beat from all the irritation, fear, stress and anger. On top off all my heavy breathing, I felt like I could have passed out at any given moment. "Stop double talking and acting like you don't understand anything, please!"

He started laughing. "You're right. That's the game, baby. I am double talking, right?"

Surprisingly, he threw that bat down on the floor, and I made that my turn to dive for it first chance I could get. Therefore I waited on my opportunity while he continued yapping his mouth off.

"Look at you," he said, tilting his head to the side examining how I was positioned on the floor. "Don't lemme see that brotha' round here anymore," he commanded in a deeper voice. "And I don't need a key. You're gonna let me in," he continued to taunt. "Gotta love a ho', though. Ain't nothing or nobody like you."

"You can't come here anymore, Andre'," I stated, choking back tears, but as soon as I stated his name, Andre's hand gripped me around my neck and lifted me up off of the floor. I started to lose oxygen as I attempted to hook my hands onto something near me to hold myself down, but I found absolutely nothing to help me save my life. My leg could barely stand with the other one as they lifted up off of the ground.

"What was that? I can't hear you. What? You choking up?" he taunted while having a great time watching me struggle to get some air. It was getting harder and harder to breathe, and the more I fought, the less oxygen came my way. The room felt so hot, and then finally oxygen.

"Get your hands down, money!" It was Black. He turned the corner and knocked Andre' directly in the back of head causing him to fall to the floor. Thankfully, Black caught me before I hit the floor, too, and then, put me on the bed. Before I could even blink, Andre' was up off the floor, and Black was tackling him up against the wall, Andre's head denting it in the process.

"Choke me like you choke Jeena, man!" Black shouted, staring Andre' into his eyes. After that, Andre's feet left the floor from Stay Black lifting him up in the air and then slamming him right back down onto my hardwood floor. As his body hit, I was hoping that the floor broke and sent him through the ground so I could bury the bastard. That didn't happen.

"Get the hell back!" Andre' suddenly commanded.

Black immediately backed up, clenching his fists while addressing me, "Stay down, Jeena, and get out of the room." There was a clear sense of urgency in Black's voice, like the rules of the game had changed.

"I can't because I think he broke my leg." Then I zoomed in on a pistol hanging from Andre's palm. Watching as Andre' pushed himself up off of the floor, wiping his face with his shoulder, I thought my life was about to be over.

"Big man!" Andre' smirked, waving the gun from side to side. "You ain't no punk after all." He then glanced at me and started to laugh. "What you fightin' for her for? Her legs ain't no more good for you. She can't do what she do anymore, man. I tried to break those loose ass legs, partna'."

"Put the gun down, man."

"Put the gun down? Playa, did you see how you just dropped me, brotha? Noo, I'm a lover, not a fighter," Andre' stated, glancing at me, "but I beat her ass though."

"Sure about that, homey?" Black's chest swelled up as if he forgot about the metal Andre' had in his hand that could easily un-swell that mug.

"For sure," Andre' answered, still looking directly at me with his finger on the trigger, aiming at Black. I just looked away, not able to accept the fact that Andre' had full control of the situation now. There was no telling what he would do. He continued, "Ain't that right, Jeena? I beat your ass in more than one way. But yo', man," he stated, turning his full attention back to Black, "I'm gettin' outta your way. Keep her."

Andre' held his gun up in the air as if he was surrendering, but then he walked by the bed, my face felt like it shattered from him busting me in the face with it. Blood flew out of my mouth as I felt my stitches come apart, and saw Black lunge for me. That's when the gun went off, sending me into a state of screaming. Black got hit with a bullet, dropped on his knees and squeezed the sheets on the bed tight without taking his eyes off of me.

"Black!" I cried, but he didn't say a word back. All he kept doing was squeezing and pulling the sheets. Lord God, please don't let him die, I prayed immediately. Not knowing where my cell was, I saw Black's cell hanging off of his pants. I reached for it.

"Stop!" Andre' yelled, waving his gun. His eyes looked frantic, almost like he didn't know what to do next. "I didn't mean that, Jee. He came at me! Now, I hit you, I admit that, but dude came at me!" he exclaimed, hitting himself across the chest.

I pretended to die when he yelled the word stop. That was all I had left inside, the only drop of hope to help me or Black live. I dropped my body as if it was dead from struggling from the hit to the face, like I'd passed out cold. When Andre' saw me leaning off of the bed motionless, he nudged me with the gun. I felt it, but I didn't move, knowing that I could hold my breath for two minutes. My prayer was that he left before time was up for both my breath and Stay Black.

Black, suddenly, grabbed my arm, and I almost gasped for air to let him know to hold on, but I still heard Andre' in the room. It sounded like he was wiping down things. Prints. He was afraid of leaving fingerprints. Little did he know, I wasn't dead or dying. The only thing that I could do to alert Black was to give some resistance to his tug on my arm. Please, Jesus, let us live through this, I prayed.

Finally, I heard Andre' leave. I heard the sliding door open and shut. Black's cell phone came back to mind, and I snatched it from his waist. He fell to the floor completely lifeless once again.

"Black, please! I'm trying!" I rushed to dial emergency, and cut off the operator when she picked up. "Hello, please come. My boyfriend has been shot, and the shooter's name is Andre' Dickson. I live at the Youring Condos at nine forty-three. I'm hurt, but he might be dying. Please."

The operator kept speaking, but that was all I said. I reached for Black's hand and rubbed it because that was all I could do to give him hope.

"We will make it, Black. We will." The only way I was gonna let go of his hand is if ...

He Died.

After passing in and out of consciousness, I woke up in the hospital with a massive migraine. It felt like my whole brain was hanging out of my skull with a bunch of witches sticking needles in it for the joy of torturing me. I figured that I must have actually passed out back at the house because I was clueless as to what happened on the way to the hospital. Either that or the emergency workers put me to sleep. I didn't even remember any police officers, if they even came, nothing.

Reaching up to touch my face, a big bandage covered my left eye. Actually, it covered the whole left side of my face as I continued to rub down toward the lower end of the bandage. Panicking from the thought of my face being seriously damaged, I searched for a way to get up and away from the tubes in my arm, but as soon as I lifted my head, a sharp pain slashed through the back of my neck and down my spine. To make things worse, there was nobody else in the room with me. My thoughts then went to Black.

"Black," I mumbled. "Please, God, don't let him be dead." Buzzing for the nurse over and over again, I waited for a response while becoming frightened of the real possibility that Stay Black may have lost his life over my drama. It played out like a movie in my mind until the nurse came around the corner.

"Where's Black?"

"Who, ma'am? Calm down," she stated, reaching for the IV and the pole that I'd managed to yank as close to me as possible in my failed attempt to get up from the hospital bed.

"Where is he!" I shouted, about to rain tears down my cheeks.

"Please, ma'am, calm down some. The gentleman that we brought in with you is in another area. He just came out of surgery and doing fine. We are trying to find out what his name actually is in order to..."

"That is his name! It's his *real* name. He was shot by somebody because he was protecting me. Did you get the man who shot him? I told the lady on the phone his name is Andre'. Andre' Dickson. D-I-C-K-S..."

"Are you saying that Stay is his first name and Black is his last name?" she asked puzzled.

Didn't she just hear me? I took a deep breath. "Yes! It is legally his name. Ouch!"

"Don't try to move," she requested, placing her hand on my shoulder lightly.

"I know. Just please. Is he really alive, and you're not just saying he's doing fine because I'm all battered in this bed?"

"Yes. I am being honest with you, Ms. Ray. Mr. Stay Black is healing. Don't worry."

"Did they arrest Andre', the guy that shot him?"

"I don't know, ma'am. I'm sorry. That's the business of the authorities. My only job is to keep you from harm. They are coming back to question you in the incident later."

I gave up. "Thank you." I just laid back in a slump, and the nurse left the room after re-examining me.

This was all my fault. I'd gotten myself involved in more than just chaos but an attempted murder that Black didn't deserve at all. Shutting my eyes, I imagined me and Black. If only I'd heard him much earlier than now, the things he said to me in the past when his pitch for me was at its finest. Please, God, keep him here. I was blinded by stupidity, I prayed. If You need somebody to take, it needs to be me. It was my fault Black was shot because he was protecting me.

"I spoke with your sister today."

My eyes popped open. It was a woman's voice, and she knew my sister? When I got a visual of her completely entering the room, I watched her closely as she strolled in, like she was on a cocky mission. She had a bandage on her face, but her hair swayed down around her shoulders like silk. Her attire was mock free. Designer. I could tell she had money and lots of it. As I looked at her hands, one thing stood out. That big, what looked to be a four to five carat, diamond dragging her finger surrounded by other diamonds. It was Tina, Andre's wife.

Oh dear God. Just days ago, the roles were reversed, and I was gawking at Tina as she lay in the hospital bed from punches to the face. That thing that monitors the heart rate must have been about to break because that sucker had to be going a mile a minute by now. My mouth became dry as the dust on car in the heat of the summer on a dirt road, and my palms were soaked in sweat. Tina must've found out about me and Andre'. She must know something, especially after talking with Faith. Faith! Since me and her lived in the same city, she was always first contact for my medical emergencies. Oh Father, she must be terrified. Had she even been here? What did she say to Tina, I whined on the inside, but on the outside I was in disbelief.

"She got a phone call about you while she was on the telephone with me." As Tina spoke, she cocked her head to the side and stared at my face. "She told me that her sister was admitted into the hospital, so I decided to come up since I was in the area being that Faith did so much for me in the past. Faith will be up here any minute."

"So Faith doesn't know that you're here right now?" I asked, terrified to go more direct than that only because I was still feeling my way around, not knowing if she knew about me and her husband or not. Faith promised that she wouldn't tell, and I believed her. In all this commotion though, anything could have slipped out.

"No need to look all dazed, Jeena, and confused," she stated placing her keys on the side of the unused white sink. "It's so amazing how we've both grown to come and love the same people, you my husband and me, your sister. She was so helpful to me when I was down and out, and you on the other hand are so different from her." She leaned back on the wall. "You took full advantage. In fact, you're the reason for my marriage and myself getting beat down. Did you know that, Jeena? Do you care, Jeena?" she asked, lifting herself from the wall and walking closer to the bed. "To put an answer to that questionable look on your beat up face, yes. I knew he was sleeping with you all along. Men have a tendency of slipping up. Poor Faith doesn't even have a clue about you and Andre', does she? You wouldn't tell her something like that, huh, Jeena, being that she's a straight up and down Christian. They tend to look at the best in people, but I bet you saw the worst of yourself when you were around her, didn't you? Such a liar." Tina proceeded calmly, quietly glancing around the room, and then, back towards the door. Finally, she turned back to me. "My butt got whipped into the hospital as another excuse for Andre' to leave and, of course, be with you. Can you at least admit that?"

"Why didn't you say something to me sooner? Tina, I..."

"Why would I?" she smiled. "So I could get all mad and worked up. No, that would be dumb and defeat the purpose when I was too used to him and his ways. Besides that, why say something to you," she continued as she bent all the way over, so close to my face that I smelled the mint on her breath while she spoke, "when I knew he was gonna beat the hell out of your ass for me?"

What the...? She knew? Tears fell from my eyes. My heart was beating like it was gonna come out of my chest. As I cried, Tina didn't move away from my face not one inch. She just stood over me, nose about three inches away from mine, and watched tears race down my cheeks as if it was entertaining. Tina was cold. Ice cold. Then she started laughing.

"Don't cry. That'll teach you, baby." She moved further back toward the top half of my stomach, reached in her purse, and placed a red rose on my chest. "But you know what, Jeena?" She said, moving her purse on the side of my bed, stretching it open wider as she continued talking. "I'm so sick of you tricks getting my ass beat. Now I love Faith, but," she glanced back at the door, "before she gets here, I have something else to deliver besides that rose."

"Nurse!" I screamed, but it was too late. What I thought was a well put together Tina began to unravel while pulling a huge knife out of her purse, shoving it as hard as she could into my chest!

All my crying stopped as I attempted to pull her hands from the knife that she was baring down with on my chest. The harder I tried to keep the knife from going any deeper, the weaker I got, so I balled up my fist really hard and busted her crazy ass in her left temple with my knuckles. She nearly fell to the floor, completely dazed, but it wasn't enough. The nurse wasn't coming fast enough either, so I didn't know what else to do but scream and wonder why I wasn't dead already. In the movies, a stab to the chest gave only five seconds to live. Real life was obviously different.

The knife was still poking out of my chest, but I stalled on trying to pull it out, afraid of making a second cut on the way out which could make things worse. Tina lunged back at me, but I gripped my IV pole in between me and her as she tried to grab the knife once again.

Finally, the nurse came through the door, but the distraction the nurse brought me when she came through allowed Tina to get her hands back on the knife in my chest. That's when she ripped it back out to slice the approaching nurse across the face. Blood immediately poured from the nurse's face, and she ran back out screaming.

Tina then stabbed me in the same leg that Andre' fractured.

"God!!" I screamed at the top of my lungs. From there, I started to black out. Before I got another chance to defend myself from her knife wounds against my body, three men came in, one in white while the others in security gear and stunned her with one of those things that send shock waves through your body. Tina hit the floor screaming, the rose from my chest rolled onto the floor, and...

I Died.

252

Or so I thought. From what I heard from Faith, who ended up seeing the blood bath seconds later in the hospital room, it took me a while to regain consciousness after I went through surgery. The doctor told me that I could have died if it weren't for the concrete fact that when Tina stabbed me in my chest, she missed my heart. She didn't go as far in as she thought nor did she target right. Too many movies made her aim for side chest instead of mid chest. Thus, my breast ended up ripped to shreds, but at least I survived.

Word was that Tina flipped her gang beat down story on Andre, thus, he got a domestic violence arrest on top of him getting nabbed for attempted murder when it came down to myself and Black. Tina's case was open and shut, but she had to get a psychological evaluation because that was honestly some sick stuff she did in the hospital room.

Faith finally got to do her duty and call my mom and dad which had them on the first plane out to be by my side. Unfortunately, the story came out. All of it. Parri and Tanya even ended up at the hospital with everyone else listening to the full out unedited version of my fight for love, lust and in the end, my life. The only part I left out was how I made love to the moron. They all forgave me, including Black after we were about to talk over the phone from room to room.

As for myself, I found my favorite scripture. Crazy, but true. Since my encounters of the worst kind, I became as in love with the Lord as my sister! My favorite scripture goes as follows, from the time of my attack until this very day, after taking that Holy Bible out of the drawer at the hospital while I healed:

Before I was afflicted I went astray, but now Your word do I keep [hearing, receiving, loving, and obeying it]. You are good and kind and do good; teach me Your statutes. The arrogant and godless have put together a lie against me, but I will keep Your precepts with my whole heart. Their hearts are as fat as grease [their minds are dull and brutal], but I delight in Your law.

It is good for me that I have been afflicted, that I might learn Your statutes. The law from Your mouth is better to me than thousands of gold and silver pieces. - Psalm 119:67-72

That beat down I got from Andre' and that psychotic killer visit that I got from his wife, Tina, pushed me over the edge. As long as God lets me live, I vowed that I would never touch a married man again, and I would always remember, keep and live in the Lord.

Yes, me and Black ended up together in all the right ways under the *Son* until we got hitched, even with all my scars. I found out that lust is a beast, and love is honorable. What I thought was love nearly got me killed. Did I learn my lesson? Sure. I might have made stupid decisions, but I didn't want a repeat.

My wedding was a fabulous, yet simple, event. Everyone who joined me out of my turmoil from the hospital was there, even some of the nurses who witnessed the murderous showdown. Stay Black was dressed in an all white suit that he said represented his virginity. Yeah right. That was the joke of the reception. I was dressed in white as well. No, I wasn't a virgin, but I was a virgin to my new life in Christ so I rocked with it.

The wedding took place on the beach with all white lawn chairs and a new boob. Actually, my mom ended up buying two new boobs for me so I could double the pleasure for Black when he got a load of them. He could have cared less though because he loved me regardless. The boobs were more for my esteem, and mom didn't mind helping with my self esteem at all.

Faith was my maid of honor and Parri and Tanya were my maids. Black had his homies to line up on his end to make for a perfect union for us. The small crowd was full of familiar people except for one person that caught my eye. There was a woman there in the very back, and once myself and Stay Black kissed, I looked over and she was gone after staying throughout the whole ceremony.

Maybe she was just a passerby who decided to stop in. Either way, as I continued to glance at my loved ones and walk hand in hand again with Black down the aisle, there was a note left taped to the seat where the woman was sitting. I tapped Black for him to slow down and as inconspicuously as I could, yanked it off. It was addressed to us, so why not? From there, I told Black to put it in his pocket until later, and because he was so into the ceremony, he didn't think one thought about it. Just slid it down in there for later.

From there, we ate, danced, took photos and more until it was time to leave. Stay Black actually picked me up and led me away from the crowd into our limo, and we were both full of smiles. He gave me one last kiss for the guests, and we rode off into our new life. Halfway down the road, I remembered the note left on the seat from the unknown guest. Black pulled it out, and the envelope read *To Stay and Jeena Black.* Without hesitation, Black handed it to me, and I proceeded to open it.

It was a card, a white card trimmed in gold with no words on the front, so I flipped it open. The card read...

<u>Congratulations, But This Shit Ain't Over.</u>

My heart sank, and I looked up at Black as he admired me over and over surely wanting the honeymoon to be something special. I decided to fake it, shut the card and grin. I told him it was from an old friend that just stopped in because she had to run and that she wished us bliss. Little did I know, that was the wrong move.

<u>Until Next Time...Pray For Me.</u>

THE END

Read **Ain't Quite What I Thought! 2**
next! Get the synopsis below!

Jeena Delilah Ray is finally MARRIED, but there's more to being the new Mrs. Black than what she bargained for! If nearly being butchered last year wasn't enough, Jeena bites off more than she can chew when she fails to warn her new husband, Stay Black, of the impending danger ahead when they return from their honeymoon. On top of that, she ends up pulled into something more life threatening during the time she finds out that her family life is about to change for good!

Will the new Mrs. Black be able to survive a second dose of broken chips falling into her life, or will those broken chips end up taking her life in Ain't Quite What I Thought 2!

Akirim Press Books

Books by Mirika Mayo Cornelius

Secret

Colored Lily: Poppa Took My Innocence

Paton

Ain't Quite What I Thought!

Ain't Quite What I Thought! 2

Inside the Gates of Doons

Murders at Gabriel's Trails: The Complete 5 Part Series
with bonus Sins of Bain

Sunny Sides of My Shade

First Degree Sins

Cold Blooded Goons

Most Wanted Felon

I Thought I Was Alone

Books by Rod Cornelius

Ugly

Diggin' Gold

The Trusted

Single Again

Ghetto Eyes

The Best Kept Secrets

Books by Cyan Deane

Execution's Karma

Dead Man's Mayhem